To Pet
Best W...
great ...
John Paton

JUST ADD WATER

by

John Paton

Visit us online at www.authorsonline.co.uk

An Authors OnLine Book

ISBN 978-0-755204-16-8

Authors OnLine Ltd
19 The Cinques
Gamlingay, Sandy
Bedfordshire SG19 3NU
England

This book is also available in e-book format, details of which are available at www.authorsonline.co.uk

"For Sandra, my wife, who always
said I had a novel in me."

"…there is nothing – absolutely nothing – half so much worth
doing as simply messing around in boats."
Kenneth Graham *"Wind in the willows"*

CHAPTER 1

"What the hell was that for?" I spluttered, wiping my face with the back of my hand.

Being kissed full on the mouth by a somewhat unprepossessing, male, 16-stone, middle-aged pharmacist was to my way of thinking, unwelcome.

"I thought you looked like you needed cheering up," was Frazer's explanation, "You, my friend, have been a grade-A misery these last few weeks, really you have."

Now I had to agree that I had been less than ebullient recently. I had given some thought to the possibility that the odd passionate embrace might help to raise the old spirits, but Frazer, while being a very dear friend, had not even made the short-list of candidates for that fantasy.

"If you want to cheer me up, you bugger, stop pissing about and buy me a pint." I put down the spoke-shave with which I had been attempting to add a degree of aesthetic curve to a hopelessly knotted lump of oak.

"You'll never finish that sodding boat, you know."

"Thanks, Frazer, I just needed that! I thought you were supposed to be cheering me up!"

The club was as busy as usual. This meant Frazer, me, Eric the barman and the bloke who was always there and knew everyone's name but was so boring that no-one spoke to him enough to find out who he was. He, of course, mysteriously knew everyone's name and hailed us over his half of cider.

"'lo Frazer, 'lo Tom."

"Oh, 'lo, er......"

"What you need is a complete change of scenery, mate. You've got yourself into a rut. Jack in all this crap and bugger off somewhere hot, like you keep promising." Frazer was full of great ideas.

"Are you trying to tell me to go to hell in your usual oblique way or just trying to depress me even more? It's not that easy, you know."

I sipped my pint reflectively while Frazer shambled off to the cigarette machine. He was right, of course.

"You're not getting any younger, you know."

"Jesus!"

"Well, you're not. At least you're still fit enough to do all the daft things you rattle on about. Hang about much longer and bits'll start dropping off."

"Bits only drop off through lack of use and there's only one bit of me in any real danger at the moment."

"If nooky is all you're short of, it's your own fault. There's plenty birds would climb into the sack with you....what about Frieda, she was all over you the other night."

"She was pissed and so was I, and anyway, if Andy found out he'd kill us both....no, I'm off women for the moment."

Frazer replaced his pint on the bar with care.

"Bloody hell, it's worse than I thought."

I had first encountered Frazer in the Far East five years previously. He had been on contract to a Bangkok pharmaceutical company and I was working in my previous incarnation of Marine Engineer. It was years before I found out that he was gay, not because I was thick or unobservant but because he just didn't seem in the least "unusual". My own relatively puritanical Scottish upbringing and subsequent life in Glasgow had not, I would be the first to admit, honed my instincts very sharply in that direction, but really, Frazer was not in the least "poofy". In fact, in many ways he was the exact opposite.

There had been times when the subject of women came up, of course, but I was married and Frazer was a bachelor and so, in the colonial way of things we only mixed socially at rugby club 'do's' and the like. It wasn't until our common interest in sailing found us cooped up together for days on end in a 30ft boat that the subject became unavoidable. His eventual egress from the closet of his sexuality into the utility room of our friendship, two days out from the Azores, came as something of a shock.

As he said at the time, "Look, Tom, I'm not inviting discussion or anything, but I thought it was time you knew, and under the circumstances you can't run away!"

"If anyone else but you had made that announcement in this situation, believe me mate, I'd still have had a bloody good try!"

And that was that. Nothing more was ever said but it was clear that Frazer was much happier, and who was I to object to the odd friendly squeeze in private.

I told Carol eventually....I think I was drunk at the time. Women, of course don't seem in the least bothered by all that stuff; it's funny really how straight blokes seem to be the only people with hang-ups about queers....and only about male ones. All the blokes I know get quite turned on by the idea of two women having it away.

"Two more warm cloudy pints please Eric!" Frazer bellowed along the bar, "Where is that dozy bugger?"

"I bloody heard that! Less of the dozy, if you don't mind. And my beer is not cloudy!" You could get to Eric with the corniest stuff. He wasn't the brightest star in the licensed constellation.

"You should try washing your glasses, then," suggested Frazer, beginning to wish he had never started this exchange, "I can hardly see the beer through it."

"You should try cleaning your own....you could make chips with the grease on these specs!"

"That's honest sweat, mate, not that you would recognise it if you were drowning in it!"

"Christ, Frazer, give it a rest, and your glasses are crappy....what have you been doing for God's sake?"

"Ah, now, I'm getting round to telling you about that. Come on over to the fire away from that nosy bastard behind the bar."

"Less of the nosy, you!" cried Eric, really hurt now. We settled down in two of Eric's 'antique' easy chairs near the fireplace and perched our pints on the edge of the brass-topped table.

"Remember the idea I had years ago for dehydrating alcoholic drinks then dispensing them from a vending machine?"

"Yes, the beer tasted worse than Eric's...!"

"Eric's piss you were going to say....well, anyway, I think I've finally cracked it."

3

"What, mix powder and water and get a pint of draught Theakstons?"

His reply took the form of a deep pull of his pint with raised eyebrows and closed eyes. "And not only that, good buddy, but I don't even have to start with the aforementioned Theaky to get the concentrate!"

"You bugger, you've sold your soul to the Devil again, haven't you. It's the only way you could pull that one off!"

"Simple chemistry mate, simple chemistry."

"I've tasted your simple chemistry before and I swear I never want to repeat the experience again, believe me."

"Oh ye of little faith," cried Frazer, his hand to his brow. Eric looked over from the bar.

"Those glasses all clean now are they, big ears?" shouted Frazer. "Let's get out of here....there's no sodding privacy anywhere these days. C'mon down to my place and I shall give thee a practical demo. Prepare to be gobsmacked!"

CHAPTER 2

Carol was having another one of her off days. These days they seemed to crop up more often than they used to. She couldn't really get to grips with the cause, because when she wasn't having one she felt good and didn't want to think about it, and when she *was* having one it was everyone else's fault and she couldn't do anything about that, now could she?

So the twins had gone into hiding. Actually they were in their room, but since only intrepid explorers and fellow pre-adolescents ever ventured over the threshold, they were pretty safe. The cleaning lady had once dared to 'tidy-up'. Vandalism the twins called it. It had taken her all day. The repercussions had lasted for years.

A heavily armed robot was experiencing some difficulty connecting a kick with what appeared to be a chocolate gargoyle, to the accompaniment of assorted electronic hiccups from the computer and yelps of glee from Tina, her face lit by the glow of the monitor screen.

"Kill the bastard, Zorg, get him in the whatsits! Oh shit, he got me!"

"You're useless at that game," observed Colin, "you always cock it up....here let me have a go."

"Bugger off you! You've had your turn, go and play with your stupid Lego."

"I am not 'playing with Lego'," screamed Colin, "I am designing an articulated lorry. This is Technical Lego actually, and it's a lot more sensible than all that hairdressing you do on that disgusting head thingy."

"I haven't touched that in years....actually I'm going to give it to Oxfam."

"And I suppose they'll send it to Africa....surely they're not that stuck for a laugh!" The badly aimed cassette case bounced away harmlessly into a corner.

"Ha-ha! Couldn't hit the floor with your hat, you couldn't," Colin jeered, "why are girls so hopeless at aiming?"

This time the computer joy-stick found it's mark.

"Ow! Hey you've broken that!"

"No I haven't....look, Zorg can still kick....what was that?"

"What was what?" said Colin, minutely examining the projectile joy-stick.

"I think it was something falling. It was downstairs," said Tina moving towards the door.

"Mum probably threw something....she's having an off day, remember?"

"It's gone awfully quiet now....Colin, do go down and see if she's all right....please!"

"Not on your Nellie....she'll have a fit....no way, Jose."

"Well, I'm going down to see if she's OK. She could be lying there with a heart-attack or something!"

"Don't be stupid....OK, maybe we should have a look!"

Carol had not, in fact, had a heart attack. At least, that had not been the source of the crash. The heavy oak front door falling into the hall had been the source of the crash - the heart attack was almost a close second.

The twins arrived on the scene to find Carol glaring with her mouth open at a very surprised postman who was still holding a bundle of letters at slot height. The door, slot, brass number 8 and lion's head knocker (like the one on Durham Cathedral) lay on the floor between them.

"What in Christ's name did you do that for?" screamed Carol, failing completely to remember that she was dressed only in a pair of black French knickers.

"I...but....fuck me!" stuttered the postman, somewhat taken aback by the sudden appearance of a half-naked housewife. This was the stuff of free pints down the Lion and he intended to imprint every detail on his mind.

"You'll pay for this!" bawled Carol, grabbing for a towel, "I'll sue the Post Office," she raged, "you can't go round pushing people's doors in like that!"

6

"I never touched the bugger, honest!"

"You would say that!"

"Honest!!...I just went to post the letters....there's a council-tax thingy there, by the way....and it sort of fell in."

"The screws are missing," remarked Colin who was carefully examining the collapsed door.

"Don't be ridiculous....how could the....oh, no...he couldn't have!"

Oh, but I had! You see, after Carol and I split up we actually got on much better, so we never really separated, as such. She helped in the boat-yard, I did the odd jobs around her house and everyone was happy. Even Frank, who couldn't tell a left-handed hammer from a banjo, and to whom Carol was now happily married, was happy.

"Think of it this way, Tom," he said at the wedding, "you're not so much losing a wife as gaining a chiropractor!" And the bugger was good, too.

That door had always been a bit sticky, especially in damp weather, so I had taken it off to the yard and planed a bit off the top and brought it back and re-positioned the hinges, and half way through the job my back had gone. Frank, as luck had it, was on hand to give it a good crunch....followed by a medicinal malt or three and one way or another certain things got forgotten. The screws, to be specific. I had subsequently left by the back door....the shortest way to the yard....God knows how Frank got out in the morning, and that stout faithful door had stood it's ground unaided. Postman Pat had proved its ultimate downfall.

"Mr Morton isn't here Mrs Mor....Rogers," Cathy quickly corrected, "I think he went out with his friend, Frazer."

Never to be seen again, thought Carol.

"OK, thanks, Cath....tell him to come over as soon as he gets back, there's some unfinished screwing waiting for him here." Carol hung up with a smile on her lips....Cath was so prim....she probably wet her pants then.

Meanwhile the door lay where it fell. It now bore the tyre tracks of two mountain bikes and an assortment of cat's paw-prints.

"Well, Frazer, you fruity old genius, you've certainly made a breakthrough....oh, yes!"

The one-litre flask had no more than a millimetre or two of brown fluid in the bottom and clear evidence adhering to the sides that something closely resembling bitter beer had recently filled the remainder.

"The secret is a discreet injection of pure ethyl alcohol at the last minute. You can't really dehydrate that, I'm afraid."

"Are you sure that Her Majesty's Customs and Exercise would be terribly happy about people loading bottles of pure red-eye into vending machines?...I mean, they are not well known for their tolerance and understanding."

"Why do you always look for the snags all the time? It's just as well the Wright brothers didn't have you breathing down their necks all the time,....Gatwick would still be a pig-farm....no, that was a bad example, Gatwick still is a pig farm. Anyway, 'course it'll be all right! It also means you can choose to have either alcoholic or non-alcoholic drinks....strange as the second option may sound."

"Well it certainly tastes OK, Frazer, but I can't help thinking that you might need something with a little more eye-appeal than a used coffee and soup machine with all the options scored out and replaced with 'BEER' in magic marker."

"Daft sod....I've got a bloke working on the front panel now. I can do best bitter, lager, and a good imitation of Newky Brown...with or without."

"Alcohol?" I ventured.

"Precisely!"

"A two-pound coin in the slot buys you a pint, eh? Just a minute though, where will you put the machine? I mean it wont go down too well in a pub....people like to have a barman to talk to...OK, OK, forget Eric, he's hardly typical,....but you know what I mean, you can't really put it anywhere kids could get at it."

"The little swine won't break this baby; it's practically bomb-proof. The bloke who got it for me told me about one that was hit by a car. The car was a write-off but the machine still made cups of perfectly good coffee for the driver and his girlfriend until the ambulance arrived....."

"I'm not talking about vandals you silly sod, I'm talking about licensing laws! RU18....remember?"

"Oh shit! I forgot about that....Oh bugger...well, they'll just have to make birth certificates like credit cards and you put them in the slot....yes, that's it! Get your age on the old flexible friend and you don't even need a pound coin....then all we need is a swipe slot and a modem..."

"Frazer, for Christ's sake, you can't market a machine based on a whole new plastic birth-certificate credit card that doesn't even exist. Bloody hell, you'll have to think of some other way to limit who uses it."

"You know, Morton, sometimes you really piss me off, you know that don't you? No wonder Carol left you; you're such a bloody killjoy at times."

"Carol didn't leave me; as you well know, I left her, or rather I didn't....anyway leave her out of this. The fact remains that you have cracked the main problem. I'm sure we can think of some way of marketing it with the aid of another couple of pints..."

"Don't touch that button, Tom!" Frazer grabbed my hand and took my glass away, "Let's have a couple of cans for a change, eh?"

"No way, I like this stuff, it's very more-ish."

"That's the problem Tom, there ain't no more."

"What? You mean you've drunk it all?"

"No, I mean you just did."

"Do you mean to tell me there was only enough to make a litre?"

"Well, yes. But I'll make some more as soon as I can afford more ingredients."

"How much can they cost, for God's sake? Here, I've got a tenner....make gallons!"

"That's the other problem; actually, at the moment it costs about thirty quid to make a couple of pints."

"Frazer," I had spotted another snag, "I hesitate to say this, but I've spotted another snag."

"Economy of scale, Tom, economy of scale....early days, mate, early days."

"Pass me a can professor, you really had me going then. Fifteen quid a pint! Shit, if I'd realised that I'd have sipped it like Y'quem!"

"I'll find a way to do it cheaper, don't worry!" he muttered studying his beer-can as if he might find the formula printed on the side.

"Don't give up your day-job....see you around."

It was with a heavy heart, not to mention an uncomfortably full bladder that I retraced my steps, past the club to the boat-yard. At least there sanity and order reigned.........

"I could have been bloody killed!"

"Carol, please calm down," the phone was beginning to melt in my hand. "You couldn't have been killed. If you had been near enough for the door to hit you it would have been moving relatively slowly. You would have to have been about six inches tall for it to build enough momentum to kill you, and anyway..."

"Don't be a smartarse with me, Tom Morton, you know what I mean. That was an idiotic thing to do."

"Not to do," I corrected.

"All right, not to do!" she screamed, "just you get yourself over here and sort it...NOW! Have you been drinking?"

"Christ, that was good! For someone in a state of near-terminal nervous shock you have uncanny powers of observation. Have you suddenly developed the power to smell booze on my breath down the phone line?"

"Tom, just fix the door, please!"

"Fine, no problem, I'll be right over, all you had to say was please and be calm and..."

"TOM!!"

"OK, OK...." click.

"You should have seen him, Dad, he must have shit his trousers!"

"Tina!"

"Oh, Mum....everyone says that."

"Not in front of me, they don't. And he wasn't the only one!"

"Dad," said Colin," is there any way I can arrange for four-wheel steering without two separate steering racks..."

"Colin, please! Give me a minute..." I was experiencing a little difficulty. "These screws are only going in half-way. Carol, are you sure these are the screws I took out?"

"No, Tom, these are special trick ones I substituted just to see you break your screwdriver trying to put them in....of course they're the ones you took out!"

"Well, I'm buggered if I can get them back in. That's funny..."

"What's funny? Honestly you'd think someone who builds bloody great boats for a living could hang a front door without all this fuss!"

"What's funny is that there are eight holes and only six screws and they look too big.... are you absolutely sure..."

"Tom! I do not keep sets of screws about the place just to confuse you....not that it would be difficult in your present condition....what on earth have you and Frazer been drinking?"

"Dehydrated beer."

"Very funny....ah, Tom?"

"What now?"

"What are these screws in this vase for?"

"Could there perchance be eight of the little swine?"

"One, two, three ...ah, yes actually, but what are they doing there?"

"Screws are like that, they hide in dark places. So where did this six come from?"

"This vase over here," Carol grudgingly conceded.

"That's the wardrobe screw vase! Everyone knows that....bloody hell, no wonder they wouldn't go in!"

"Sorry, I'm sure, I was only trying to be helpful," sniffed Carol, "I wont bother in future!" a huff was definitely on the cards. I could tell because the kids had disappeared again. I silently hung the door with the correct screws and gave it a few experimental slams.

"There you go....it's OK now....hello....it's OK Carol....see you..."

I didn't, for the moment, know why I bothered!

Frazer had been right. Not about the plastic credit card birth certificates but about getting out of here. It seemed that I had all the disadvantages of marriage without any of the perks. Not that I grudged old Frank his nuptials, you understand, but he seemed to be able to waft through life avoiding all the slings, arrows, and fan-distributed waste-matter normally associated with everyone else's outrageous fortune and not by opposing them, either. He just ignored them and they obediently went away. I, on the other hand, tended always to find myself directly in the firing-line. Frank had that mixture of boyish good-looks and hail-fellow-well-met likeability which won him friends of either sex; indeed the female reaction to him varied from, at the least, more than moderate interest to, at best, gibbering incoherence. Cathy, my long-suffering secretary, on first meeting him, had to be prompted to close her mouth, then finally blurted out, "Pleased to Roger you, Mr Meets...." to which Frank gallantly replied, "And delighted to Roger you too, Cathy," with such smooth confidence that she didn't even notice.

You can't help liking a bloke like that.

No, I could never be one of the Franks of this world. I tended to career through bits of my life like a badly driven bobsleigh on a litter-strewn Cresta run. I remember when I first tried skiing. I had borrowed a pair of rather superannuated skis, strapped them to my Doc Martens and started side-stepping up the nearest snow-covered slope to Glasgow, (a wet place called Glenshee, I recall), I had seen someone do this on one of these 'Learn Skiing' programmes on TV. This rather awkward crab-wise ascent continued until such a point as the skis started off down the slope of their own volition, probably out of boredom, taking me with them, of course. Eventually we would all reach the bottom, a tree, another skier or any unavoidable obstacle, (in my case, all of them were unavoidable), when we stopped. The decision then had to be taken as to whether we would crab back up the hill again or give in and go to the pub. I don't recall any of it being remotely enjoyable and there was a great deal of giving up and going to the pub done.

Right now I was on a sideways-up-the-hill phase of my life, vaguely wondering when the uncontrollable descent to disaster would start, and, indeed, where it would end.

I had an uncomfortable feeling that I might not have long to wait. The boat, which Frazer predicted I would never finish, was a Freedom 40 hull, rig and engine called 'Sligo Bay' which I had acquired as settlement of a bad debt. The guy had gone bust before I could finish the fit-out which ultimately would have been a very spacious live-aboard. He simply handed me the papers and walked away. Since then I had worked on her between regular yard work with a general plan to turn her into a sail trader; crew quarters in the stern below a wheel-house, central hold, and workshop up at the sharp end. The unstayed wishbone schooner rig would be a doddle to handle with a small crew and lent itself to a high degree of automatic control. All I had to do was finish her, sell the yard, and disappear over the horizon to the Caribbean, there to tote small cargoes from island to island under perpetually blue skies, in my own time. At least that was the theory. A 40-footer is much bigger than you would think, and the volume of timber, fibreglass, resin and paint it consumed with no apparent change in its appearance was staggering. A tin of undercoat which seemed to fill the back of my little van, visibly shrank to the size of a bean-tin as I lowered it into the hold. Obviously I had to move into a higher gear unless Frazer's prediction was to prove accurate. Maybe when Steve was finished epoxying the harbour launch I could spare him to finish the decking, meanwhile Dr. James's Contessa awaited it's new Yanmar engine and there was that Fisher which lost it's wheel-house coming under the railway bridge on the back of Ron Smith's 'low' loader....silly sod. So there I was, too busy earning a living to make enough money to do what I really wanted to do. Lumbered with an ex-wife who lived with everyone's favourite guy, a homosexual best friend and an ex-girlfriend, (you'll love this), who only broke it off with me when I divorced Carol because she felt sorry for her, for God's sake! Talk about honour among thieves! She and Carol now go out drinking together on Tuesday nights and probably tell one another what a bastard I, and all other men, no doubt, are.

Then, of course, there was Frieda.

I knew she fancied me and I sure as hell fancied her. We flirted and touched and did all the daring things that grown-up people are supposed to be able to do without it really meaning anything and without anyone getting the wrong idea, and that was as far as it got. I really believed that Andy would have gone berserk if he had thought that there was anything even remotely serious going on and he was a big, big bloke. Rumour had it that he was in the SAS until recently and I tended to believe it. If it came to a choice between Andy and a brick shithouse when the bomb went off, I know behind which one I would line up.

And don't even ask about Cathy. First of all, she worked for me and I had one rule....never mess with employees. I had no personal experience to tell me that it was a bad idea but I had seen it cause trouble so often before with others, and anyway I didn't actually fancy Cath. Not that she was a pain or ugly or anything, in fact she was very pretty, but in a fragile, doll-like way. It was utterly impossible to imagine her with her legs locked round a hairy behind, head back, screaming in orgiastic frenzy. Frazer reckoned that if you took off her clothes you would find a 'CINDY' trade-mark on her bum....and that she never, never farted....ever. She was, however, the most loyal, hard working and uncritical secretary I had ever had and I intended to keep her.

13

CHAPTER 3

"Here's a man that might be able to help you!"

The harbourmaster was in one of his expansive moods as I walked into the Port Office. The loud remark was obviously aimed in my direction so I tried to look interested. I was still feeling generally fed-up and to crown it all I had the distinct sensation that I was about to have a pretty good-going cold....you know the feeling when your aim through doorways is poor, even sober, and the back of your throat feels like you've been snorting powdered glass.

"Tom here has a boat that might suit you....gent's looking for small shallow-draught cargo vessel, Tom, like an old Clyde puffer....nothing like that around these days I reckon, but I thought that there yacht of yours might be just the thing."

Arthur had always been a bit disparaging of my aspirations in the cargo carrying department ever since I had told him about my idea in the club one night over too many pints. He was now, in his heavy-handed way trying to take the piss. I decided to play it dead-pan.

The 'gent' was very obviously from out of town. He was one of those short men that people used to call 'dapper'. He was wearing a suit of the type I always imagined was Pierre Cardin but was probably nothing of the sort. I couldn't read the label still attached to the jacket cuff. His flowery tie matched his hanky. The after-shave he had apparently spilled on himself succeeded in penetrating my cold and I started to sneeze uncontrollably. The harbourmaster, now warming to his subject and ignoring my noisy distress, continued to elaborate on the virtues of my yacht which was by now growing in his rhetoric to the proportions of the 'Cutty Sark'.

"Arthur...please!" I gasped, dragging him aside, "Sligo's not in commission yet....you know that." He would have the gent signing a contract if I didn't intervene quick.

"Yes, but you keep telling me how she's nearly there, Tom. Good boat like that shouldn't be lying about. Get her out earning a living. I'm sure you could use the money!"

"To be honest, Arthur, I never really thought about using her in British waters....it was more of a tropical paradise thing, but now you come to mention it, there's no reason why I shouldn't use her here."

Our man was pretending to be engrossed in the large-scale chart of the estuary tacked up on the office wall.

"The harbourmaster seems to think that you and I could do business. Want to talk about it?" I ventured.

"OK squire, Marine Hotel, tonight, eight o'clock in the 'Bosun's Locker'." And off he wafted leaving Arthur and me staring at one another like a couple of wallies.

"I don't trust him," said Arthur.

"Oh thanks very much, Mr Harbourmaster, sir, you bloody started this, don't forget. I thought you knew him."

"Never seen him before in my life, poncy little git. Smelled like a poof if you ask me." Growled Arthur.

"You can't always tell 'em by the smell, Arthur. He certainly believed in splashing it on, though."

"What are you doing here anyway?" Demanded Arthur, "you usually avoid this place like the plague in case I ask for harbour dues or something."

"Arthur, that is a calumny which I shall treat with the contempt it richly deserves. Actually I came to tell you that your launch is ready and we put it back on the spare mooring, but now that I'm going into the cargo business I'm going to need that mooring back soon aren't I?"

"And you'll be able to pay all your back dues out of all that lovely lolly you're going to earn too!" beamed Arthur.

"Let's not count our chickens, mate. We'll see what 'Mr After-Shave 1970' has to say tonight. He's probably after something much bigger than I can provide. I'll let you know, though."

It had been misty and cold earlier, but as I strolled back to the yard the sun broke through and you could tell that it was going to be one of these beautiful early spring days which Lord Alfred said make young men's minds lightly turn to thoughts of love....or that some other guy said young girls had been thinking about all winter. The harbour breeze was holding its breath and the normally choppy water looked like it had cling-film stretched over it. All the boats nudged their moorings and were pointing in different directions. Even the gulls seemed to be paddling carefully to avoid making too many ripples. One of the big Westerlies had unrolled his genoa for inspection and it hung like a huge translucent banner, barely moving. A lone windsurfer stood forlornly waiting for a stray gust to bring him ashore, the reflection of his sail in the glassy water turning him into a huge high-tech butterfly. My spirits rose. Even my cold seemed to be better.

I found myself mentally listing all that I would need to do to finish 'Sligo Bay', or at least to make her seaworthy with some basic creature comforts. To my surprise, the more I thought about it the less I could think of to do. Most of the accommodation was complete, the engine had been in for some time. The hold needed planking up and covers made, but the masts, which didn't have any standing rigging, were complete and ready to step. Why hadn't I figured this out already? I realised that the nearer I had got to completing the boat the slower I had been going. A cold shiver ran down my spine. I was nearly ready to move on. I was running out of excuses. Did I really want to do all these things I had promised myself? It was time to ask myself a few searching questions. I was not sure if I wanted to know the answers. I was aware of blood surging in my ears....excitement, or fear?

Perhaps if this cargo job, whatever it was, came off and Sligo was just what these people were after, it would be a way of breaking me in gently, so to speak. I could get a taste of working sail without travelling thousands of miles to find out I hated it. As I turned into the yard lane I saw her....she was difficult to miss, towering over the modest slip, her dark blue bow pointing sea-ward. She seemed to be grinning at me.

"Go on with you, you windy bugger," she was saying, "stop pissing about and get me into the water. I'll show you what we can do together."

Then I saw Frieda standing just beyond Sligo. She was wearing a pair of sprayed-on cut-offs and a short tee-shirt....definitely just a tee-shirt, and she was smiling at me with a smile that seemed to echo what Sligo had just nearly said.

"Hell," I thought, "spring must really be in the air."

"I've been waiting here for you for absolutely ages." she mock-scolded me, "How dare you go for a walk when I decide I want to talk to you."

"Sorry Frieda, the old crystal ball must need a decoke or something. Fancy a cuppa?"

"OK. Let's have it out here though, I want to sit in the sun."

I filled two mugs with coffee in the office, trying to avoid Cathy who I felt sure would have something vitally important and long-winded to tell me, but she wasn't anywhere to be seen. The answering machine was on so I figured she had gone out on an errand.

When I got back Frieda was sitting on an old railway sleeper with her back against the boat-shed.

"D'you think anyone can see us here?" she asked looking about.

"Why?" I asked trying to control a tremor that seemed to have crept into my voice.

"Well, I just thought I could take off this tee-shirt and get a bit of sun on the old boobs. They've been shut away all winter and they're all pale....look!"

She lifted the front of her shirt to reveal two long-standing objects of my desire in all their admittedly milky-white splendour.

"Frieda, please put them away. The one person who can see you from here is in no fit condition to stand the strain."

"That's not very nice," she pouted, "saying it's a strain to look at me." I was becoming uncomfortable about the way this conversation was developing.

"I'm saying that it's a strain to stop myself from staring at you with my mouth open and with dribble running down my chin!"

She smiled slyly and deliberately and entirely unnecessarily slowly, smoothed her tee-shirt over her chest....that hurt too....

"Can I tell you what I wanted to talk to you about?"

"Of course....you know I'm always happy to see you, Frieda. It's just that the way you come on gives a man ideas he shouldn't have about his friend's wife."

"Sorry Tom, I'll try to behave in future."

"All right then." I was taking this news worse than I felt I should be, "what's the problem?"

"No problem. I want to buy a boat, and I want you to teach me to, you know, drive it."

"Frieda, you hate boats. You get seasick in the yacht chandlers. You needed about ten Stugeron washed down, if I remember correctly, by three or four stiff gins just to go on the Isle-of-Wight ferry!"

"That is a gross exaggeration, Tom, and you know it. I've decided to make an effort and learn to sail. It looks such great fun. I always feel so left out when everyone else does it. Please find me a boat and teach me, Tom." She had my hand now and was looking pleadingly into my eyes. This was murder! I really couldn't stand much more of this close-quarters stuff.

"What about Andy?" I suddenly realised her husband might have an opinion about all this new-found saltiness. "He's not really into sailing, being a power-boat man. He's not going to take too kindly to me dragging you off sailing every other day."

"Don't worry about Andy, Tom. He agrees that I should learn to sail. Reckons it'll keep me out of mischief maybe. I could always ask someone else, of course, if you're too busy...."

"No! No...OK, let's look at a few boats." I declared, getting to my feet too quickly....I sat down again, dizzy.

"Oh, Tom, are you all right?" she had her arm around me now.

"I'm all right....just a bit of a cold....stood up too quick....I'm fine, really." I got up more slowly this time and led the way to the boat storage yard.

"Not all the boats here are for sale, obviously, but we can have a look and decide what size you need and take it from there."

I showed her a Wanderer dinghy....she didn't want one like that, too near the water she said. She pointed to a dazzlingly-painted X-boat racer balanced like a ballerina on her knife-like keel within its spidery cradle.

"That's a nice one!"

I shuddered....she got the message. A rather nice Folkboat I had been keeping an eye on was dismissed as 'too old-fashioned'.

Then we spotted the little Cornish Shrimper.

"That's pretty?" she ventured.

Now the Shrimper is a pretty boat and this one had just been re-painted and re-varnished for the season and was, as it happened, for sale. I thought about her suitability for a beginner and for the life of me I couldn't think of any major problems. She was gaff-rigged, but not like the old gaffers which were built for men of steel and needed a couple of trained gorillas just to raise the mainsail. Definitely not for beginners. She had a lifting centre-plate....nice for getting in close to shore and settling on a mud berth, but also very forgiving of the odd tidal calculation cock-up. This boat, I knew, also had a nice new inboard engine. I had fitted it myself this winter. She wasn't going to be cheap, but Frieda wasn't stuck for a few bob so I suggested a closer look. She was on her road trailer so we clambered aboard fairly easily.

"Well, there's plenty of room in this one," declared Frieda looking round the roomy cockpit, "and plenty of sunbathing space over there," she added surveying the foredeck. She grabbed the tiller and started pumping it up and down.

"That bit steers it, Frieda, go easy, it's not the village pump. We could look below if it's unlocked." I suggested.

"Below what?"

"Deck....below deck, you know, downstairs."

"Do you mean that this little boat has a downstairs?"

"Of course it has, what did you think was in all that space at the front?"

"I don't know, really, wood, I suppose." It crossed my mind she was having me on, but it wasn't Frieda's style. These lessons were going to have to go way back to basics and I mean Archimedes. I removed the washboards which were unlocked as I suspected they would be and we clambered into the tiny cabin.

"Gosh, I'd no idea all this would be in here," she said, fiddling with the cooker and looking under the cushions, "there's sleeping bags and everything in here."

"What do you think of her?"

"Oh, Tom, she's lovely, I suppose the beds are quite comfy?"

I had been trying to avoid the subject of the 'beds' but realised that a demonstration was now inevitable.

"You can have two single berths, they're called berths, Frieda, or one big double when you put this fill-in bit in place."

"Oooh...." she was getting really interested now, "Let's see how much room there is." It seemed unnecessarily stuffy under the circumstances to refuse her invitation. The berth was pretty snug and close contact was unavoidable. One little friendly peck wouldn't hurt, I reasoned, so I kissed her. It was one of my many miscalculations. I am a weak man and when a girl I fancy comes on that strong I'm a goner. We were all over one another in about three seconds flat. She had all the buttons of my shirt undone and was taking it off over my head when a hazy vision of Andy working out in the gym crossed my mind. I pulled away as gently as I could and retrieved my shirt.

"Look, Frieda," I gasped, "you're lovely, you're sexy and nothing in the entire universe right now would give me greater pleasure than to do beautiful things to your body, but I've grown very attached to my boyish good looks. I'd hate to have Andy re-arrange them."

Frieda smiled. "Andy knows I fancy you," she said.

"Oh my God, I'm dead."

"No you're not, silly, he likes you."

"He likes Good Old Tom The Boatyard Man, Frieda, not Tom Who Is Screwing His Wife! If he found us here together like this he'd use you to kill me with."

"Tom, he won't, you don't know Andy. When I say he likes you, I mean he approves of you, you know, for me."

"Just a minute, Frieda, are you saying that Andy doesn't mind you and me....."

"He suggested it."

"Bloody hell, but why?"

"Tom, Andy's gay."

"What?! Andy?? Gay???" my voice was almost ultrasonic by now and my credibility gap had opened to Grand Canyon proportions. "I don't believe you."

"Why should I bother to make it up?" I toyed with the idea of feeling hurt by that remark, but let it pass. "Do you remember when we moved here?" she asked.

"Well, yes, it was just after Frazer moved into the old gate-house. I remember he threw a party for you because he felt sorry for you in that awful flat."

"We followed Frazer from Cambridge, Tom, so that Andy and he could be together."

"Are you saying that Andy and Frazer are....?" Frieda was nodding furiously,"...well bugger me!"

"With pleasure," she grinned and started in on my buttons again.

"Wait a minute, Frieda, please, I have another question."

"Only one more then," she said, putting on a sulk.

"Where do you fit in to all of this, I mean it's a bit odd, you must admit."

"Not really, Andy is my brother." she said.

"WHAT???"

"Tom, you are becoming strident, you know." I was becoming hysterical, to be honest.

"What the hell next?" I croaked.

"That's about it really," she said pulling her tee-shirt over her head. The sight of her breasts once more revealed had a strangely calming effect and I gathered my wits into a loose heap.

"Christ, you're lovely," I blurted. Very little else coherent was said for some considerable time.

"Well," I finally surfaced, "do you want this boat or what?"

"Bugger the boat," she said to the headlining as she struggled into her shorts, "you didn't really believe all that, did you?"

"Madam," I sat up indignant, "do you mean I've gone to all this trouble to demonstrate the outstanding features of this vessel when all the time you were only after my body?"

"Of course. You said it yourself, I hate boats. In fact, can we get out now; I'm beginning to feel a little queasy."

"Perhaps you should put the rest of your clothes on first. We're not moored off a desert island, remember."

"Prude!"

"Well I only wish one thing," I said, struggling into my clothes.

"What's that?"

"That you conned me into a bigger boat, I'm covered in bumps and bruises." She threw a shoe at me.

"We shall continue the sailing instruction ashore, very shortly," she promised, "Andy is off to Saudi for three weeks on business."

"I did not, for one moment imagine it would be for pleasure. I just can't get used to the idea that you and Andy are brother and sister. We all thought you were married."

"Yes, that's how it worked out. We didn't set out to deceive anyone, everyone just assumed we were. Same names of course helped, in fact, the first time someone referred to me as Mrs Prentice (I do believe it was you, Tom), we went along with it for a laugh. Then afterwards we realised that there were situations where it could be quite useful, so we decided to keep up the pretence."

"You certainly had us all fooled, and that bit about Andy....! I thought that I was the only one around here who knew that Frazer was gay and all the time he and Andy...I knew he spent some time round at your house but I just assumed he was doing the lonely bachelor act. Now I come to think of it, he was on about you fancying me just the other day. Are all of you in on this little conspiracy to pair us off?"

"Oh, Tom, it wasn't a conspiracy, although I have talked to Frazer about you. He was saying that you were a bit down in the dumps these days. He felt you were sort of cutting yourself off socially since the divorce and needed cheering up."

"I hate to sound ungrateful, Frieda, but a chap likes to think that a girl goes to bed with him because she lusts after him, not because she feels sorry for him, for fuck's sake."

"You men! You're always after a standing bloody ovation or grovelling adoration. Why can't you accept an act of true friendship at face value and leave all the mushy stuff to the readership of 'Hello' and the like." I was having difficulty believing my ears. I had never heard any woman talk like this before, much less Frieda.

"Of course I like you, Tom, I like you a lot. There's a limit to what even I am prepared to do for charity if that's any sop to your pride. Do I see you tonight or not?"

"Ehh....yes, yes! Of course....I'll be in the Bosun's Locker in the Marine after eight."

"OK, see you there." She kissed me lightly on the lips and strode off.

I was still standing on the same spot some five minutes later when I became aware of Cath's voice beside me.

"....you all right, Tom, you look a bit shaken."

"Ah, yes, I'm fine Cath, just got up...ah...a bit too fast, that is, got a bit of a cold."

"Got up too fast?" she was puzzled.

"Yes, and grew up too slow." I mused.

"Sorry?"

"Never mind Cath, everything OK?"

"Yes. I just went to the printers and when I got back there were a few messages on the machine. I've been looking for you everywhere; I knew you were back because I found your coffee mug out in the yard. Where have you been?"

"Oh, just showing someone the finer points of the Cornish Shrimper. Anything important on the machine?"

"Well, the harbourmaster rang to say that he had found out who the, er, 'poof' was. He's a Mr Damien Coombs, from London. That's what he said, Tom. Oh, yes and Frazer rang."

"Yes?"

"He didn't actually leave a message as such."

"What do you mean 'as such'?"

"Well what he said was 'And this is Frazer's flipping answering machine asking if there are any human beings left alive on this planet,' and then he made a funny noise and hung up, only he didn't say 'flipping'. You're not allowed to use language like that over the phone, are you, Tom?"

"I think you're thinking of the VHF radio, Cath, but I will tell him you were offended...what kind of funny noise did he make?" Cath puckered her mouth preparatory to blowing a decorous raspberry.

"No, don't bother, I think I can guess." I stifled a guffaw at the thought of poor old Cath faithfully transcribing Frazer's outburst. He hated answering machines to the depths of his soul and always left rude messages. That one was mild by his standards. It was obviously toned down for Cath's benefit. The boy was getting soft.

"Do you need me any more this morning, Tom, only I would like to get some shopping done for Mum during lunchtime? All the typing and stuff is up to date."

"Of course, Cath, off you go." I wandered back to the office and sat down behind my desk. What a bloody morning! I looked out of the window. Three feet away was the wall of the boat shed next door. I always felt cheated by that wall. The view out of my window should be a vista of the estuary from which I could draw inspiration and learn deep truths about the meaning of life and other such tosh. What do I get? A square yard of black corrugated iron with BUM painted in the bottom left-hand corner. Not very inspiring. I once set out to go round there and paint out the offending graffiti but found such an impenetrable jungle of brambles, thistles and small poisonous plants that I gave up. I'm convinced that there's a whole undiscovered eco-system between these two sheds that would keep David Attenborough in programmes for years. Come to think of it, I'd probably be sued by the Nature Conservancy people if I so much as took a pair of scissors to it. I couldn't stop thinking about Frieda and what she told me. She couldn't have made it all up, could she? And yet I had heard her say things today which I'd never have dreamed she would even think. I dialled Frazer's number. He would tell me the truth if anyone would.

"Yes, who is this?"

"It's me, Frazer, Tom, have you got a minute?"

"I wanted to have a word with you. I phoned but only got that God-forsaken machine. Where the hell have you been?"

"Christ, it's worse than being married sometimes around here. I was, ah, otherwise occupied, and stop leaving rude messages on my machine, it upsets Cath."

"Balls! She loves it. Makes her day. Goes home and tells her mum about all the decadent friends you have."

"If only she knew half of it!"

"OK, I'll apologise," said Frazer sounding almost serious. "Listen, Tom, did you know Andy has gone off to Saudi Arabia for a week or two?"

"Yes, ah, Frieda did mention it to me. We had a bit of a chat this morning, actually."

"Oh....what else did she tell you?"

"She did mention something about you and Andy...."

"OK, Tom, say no more old fruit, not over the public telegraph, anyway. Come round to the Gate-house and have a bite of lunch with me. There's something I have to ask your advice about."

The thick plottens, I thought to myself. I re-set the answering machine and locked up. I had a feeling it was going to be a long lunch hour.

"It's all sort of come to a head in the last few weeks, really," said Frazer staring gloomily into his half-eaten pasty. "I was quite content to maintain the status-quo, so to speak. I mean, it wasn't perfect, by any means, but I'm not big into taking stances and all that crap. I'm really happy here, Tom. I've got loads of good mates who take me at face value and don't give me any hassle, but only because they don't know about my sexual preferences. Crazy, isn't it? I know I'm being hypocritical by pandering to their hypocrisy, but, fuck-it, Tom, it's so comfortable!"

"Who am I to comment?" I was stuck for words, frankly. Agony Aunt was not a role I was used to.

"I know, Tom, you're different, somehow, from the others, you seem to take people as you find them. Anyway, now Andy wants to 'come out' for fuck's sake. He's been reading some book or other which says that you should be truthful and open and it rattles on about fulfilment and all that shit. I just can't face all that at my age. So, anyway, we decided that Andy's trip abroad would be a good chance to look at our relationship in a cool and logical way. I mean, Tom, with all this AIDS thing going on, guys like us are not exactly flavour of the month. We're not all promiscuous, you know."

"Well, I know that now, Frazer. I must admit, though, that before I knew you, my conception of what constituted a homosexual was coloured by the behaviour of your more outrageous brethren who seem to populate the arts and media. Perhaps if more people like you and Andy did 'come out' people would be a little less afraid to accept you." I was amazed that I was expressing a point of view of which I wasn't aware until that moment.

"I can't help being reminded of something that happened to me in London. I was in Harrods, doing some gift shopping, I think it was for Carol's birthday. There was a big rumpus behind me and I turned round to see two Arabs, a man and a woman, in full Arab gear, you know, nighties, veils, dish-cloths, the lot, being hustled off by police for shop-lifting. There was this guy beside me, obviously of Middle-Eastern origin, but in a suit. 'You know,' he said to me, 'it's cunts like that who give us Arabs a bad name.'" Frazer burst out laughing.

"Tom, you bastard, I love you. I can never be serious in your company for long. By the way, have you screwed Frieda yet?"

"That, my dear Frazer is a secret between me and the other party involved, but you might as well know now as later. Yes I have. Or rather, more truthfully, it was more of a vice versa situation really."

"Come on a bit strong, did she? She said it was going to be shit or bust with you. I told you she fancied you, didn't I?"

"What you didn't tell me was that Andy was a paper tiger, as they say in China."

"Hmm....damn clever these Chinese. I wonder if Chairman Mao would have had an answer to my present dilemma?"

"He'd have you shot as a filthy subversive more than likely."

"Yes, we don't know how lucky we are, really, do we?"

"Frazer, I have to confess to an unworthy thought which I'm sure has no foundation in fact."

"Spit it out and meet your punishment like a man!"

"Well, it did occur to me that all this about you and Andy

coming out and Frieda coming on strong with me could be, in some way, connected."

"Meaning?"

"Well, it would be terribly convenient if Frieda and I teamed up together to let you and Andy become an item, so to speak. I am not in the mood for a meaningful relationship right now, thanks very much, all the same. You'll have to work out the practicalities without my assistance, I'm afraid."

Frazer silently contemplated the scenery beyond the window.

"Well, I would be lying if I said the subject had not been touched on," he admitted with an uncharacteristic weariness in his voice," but by Andy, Tom, not by me. And Frieda wasn't in on that conversation. No, I think that part really was a coincidence of timing. She really has had her eye on you for quite a while," he drained his can, "I must stop drinking this stuff. British cat's piss is bad enough but God only knows what kangaroo's piss does to your insides."

"I'm meeting her tonight for a drink. Would you like me to take along a tape-recorder or will a written transcript of the proceedings be sufficient? Oh, that reminds me. What do you know about local regulations governing carriage of sea cargo?"

"You going into business here, then?"

"Well, I might be. I'm meeting some bloke in the Marine tonight who is looking for a small freighter for something. I've no idea if it's a goer but I thought it would be worth a listen."

"Good on yer, Cap'n," said Frazer, "ye'll be needin' a first mate then, oi reck'n. Where do oi put me mark? Aharrrr!" Frazer had mentally acquired a wooden leg and invisible parrot and was leering at me grotesquely across the room.

"Look, me hearty, don't book your amputation just yet, we don't even have a ship."

"Tom, that bloody boat is going to bugger off by itself one of these days. You and the boys could have it ready for the sea in about two weeks if you set your minds to it!"

"Nearer two and a half weeks. I worked it out."

"Well then, what are you waiting for? Even if this thing tonight is a load of balls you could still find plenty of work. Get your certificates and papers and start hauling cargo!"

"Give me another beer, quick, you're beginning to sound sensible. Who would run the yard while I'm away on the high seas, for God's sake?"

"The same bloody people who run it when you're here, of course. You don't imagine for one minute that you are in the least bit indispensable, do you?"

"Thank-you for your vote of confidence, Mr Chairman, pass the cyanide capsule, if you please."

"No, but really, Tom, that place could run itself for weeks on end. Most of your punters are regular as a bran-fed robot and your boys have been with the yard longer than you have. Anyway, we all know that it's Cathy who runs that show really, so you've no excuse."

I had the distinct impression that the old finger of fate was limbering up for a bit of wall-writing I was by no means sure I was ready to read. I had a feeling in my bones that my meeting with Mr Coombs might be fateful. Little did I realise quite how fateful it would turn out to be.

CHAPTER 4

The Marine Hotel had seen better days. It always reminded me of a badly iced wedding cake. The cemented facade had been patched and painted so often that it was unlikely that there was any of the original exterior left. The result was a kind of free-hand drawing of a hotel with decorations suggested here and there and corners rounded on one aspect but squared off on another. As you went through the front door you expected to be carried back to the twenties with its Lloyd-loom chairs, potted palms and chenille drapes but you weren't. The time-machine only made it to late-utility fifties where pale blue fake leather (worn smooth) and wood-effect wall panels were the prevailing decor.

Its one redeeming feature was a huge bay window which framed a relatively uninterrupted view of the estuary and the Channel beyond. Uninterrupted, that is but for the fact that it was neatly bisected by a telephone pole which still carried the scars inflicted by the previous landlord, who, one night in a drunken rage tried to chop it down with a fire axe and nearly succeeded in severing his foot at the ankle. British Telecom had been deaf to further requests for its removal after that. The bay window formed one wall of the Bosun's Locker, a room which was heavily embellished with items nautical as interpreted by mail-order catalogue. The bar consisted of three huge barrels supporting a copper-covered counter to which was attached a modest selection of pumps dispensing ales local and foreign.

I passed through the crumbling portico and headed for the Bosun's Locker. I was, to be frank, rather more enthusiastic about spending the evening with Frieda than talking business with Coombs. I didn't expect that anything would come of it anyway, business with Coombs, that is (I had high hopes of considerable business with Frieda) so I was keen to get it over and done with.

"What do you mean you don't have any Tequila?" Coombs was bawling as I entered, "what kind of bar runs out of Tequila, for Christ's sake?"

"We aint run out on't mister, we never 'eard on't, and mind your langwidge, if you please, there's ladies present."

"Ladies?...Ladies?? There's not another bloody soul in the whole sodding hotel! What have you got, then?"

"We got bitter and Foster's and whisky and...look, mister, I can't stand here and recite the whole bar to you, I'm a busy man, you know."

"I'd hate to see you with time on your hands! Give me a pint of Foster's then."

"Straight or handle?"

"I DO NOT GIVE A SHIT, THANK-YOU," enunciated Coombs.

"Only asking, no need to be like that. Some clients are quite partic'lar about their receptacle, you know."

"As long as it's clean and I can drink out of it I don't care if it's shaped like the Taj Ma-fucking-hal!! Could we please get on, I'm gasping!" The barman poured the pint into a straight glass with FOSTER'S printed on the side.

"Why all that palaver about receptacles when you've even got a special glass made for the bloody stuff, Jesus!" The barman ignored this latest outburst.

"That will be two pounds fifty, please."

"Up to date with the prices, I notice," remarked Coombs as he turned to find a table. I had been behind him during this exchange, trying to attract his attention, so I narrowly missed collecting his hard-won pint down my shirt.

"Evening Mr Coombs." Coombs looked as if he had been struck.

"How did you find out my name?" he demanded.

"The harbourmaster told me, why, is there a problem?" He seemed highly agitated and started to look about in a hunted sort of way.

"How did *he* find out my name?"

"Buggered if I know. Someone must have told him, that is your name, is it?"

"Oh....yes....of course!" a broad smile struggled on to his face

29

and reluctantly settled down looking like it wasn't planning to stay for long. "Just call me Damien, Mr ahh..." a carefully manicured paw was thrust in my direction.

"Morton, just call me Tom." I shook the hand and had an uncomfortable moment or two trying to resist the urge to wipe my hand on my trousers. This was a very nervous guy.

"Well, Tom, thanks for coming along. I'm sorry I was a bit off-hand earlier but that harbourmaster was getting right on my threepennies. Nosy git."

"He can be a bit direct at times," I agreed, "I'm just going to get a drink, you all right just now? Can I get one in for you?"

"No, no, it's on me tonight, Tom. Tom Cruise over there knows what I'm drinking. You get what you want on my tab. I'm staying here for a few days, God help me."

I wandered over to the bar while Damien found a table.

"Friend of yours, Mr Morton?" asked old Reg, who had been behind that bar since the place was built, it seemed.

"Not really, Reg, business acquaintance you might say, hardly know him. Pint of Fosters please."

"Nasty piece of work, if you ask me," confided Reg, pouring the beer, "filthy tongue in his head. I had to remind him there were ladies present." I looked around hopefully, the place was still as quiet as a Russian supermarket," this being the lounge bar and all," continued Reg.

"From London, I gather," I explained. Reg nodded sagely as if all was now clear.

"Thought so," he said ringing £4.60 up on the till. I pretended not to notice and carried my pint back to the table Coombs had settled on.

"So, ah, Damien, what's the deal you have in mind?"

"I gather you have a smallish cargo vessel with off-shore capability," said Damien.

"It's not quite ready to put to sea, but, yes, I own a forty-foot sailing trader. She can't carry anything very heavy, about five tonnes, I suppose, her hold is about fifty cubic metres."

"I want you to ship some beer for me, from southern Ireland. It's rather special beer, you know how the kids are with unusual labels, and not a hell of a lot at a time, you could call it a pilot study, you know, just to see if they like it. All you have to do is pick it up at the Irish end and drop it off at Avonmouth....easy!"

"Look, Damien, wouldn't it be a lot easier just to get a normal carrier to do the job, I mean, one truck could easily take anything 'Sligo Bay' could carry."

"We've tried that already and it spoiled the beer," explained Damien," it's the vibration from the road, or something. By the time it travels from the south to the nearest port then across on the ferry then by road again to London, it's knackered. No, this way we get a relatively smooth sea crossing and then a relatively short road journey to London. They can bring it to the boat at the other end on a horse-drawn dray; the brewery is only five miles from the coast. Anyway, we intend to make a big thing of the traditional bit, you know, horse and cart, sailing boat now, pity it has to be a lorry on the last leg, a horse and cart would be a bit slow."

"I doubt if they would be too keen to let you take it down the M4," it all seemed a bit unlikely, but I was being carried along by the silliness of the idea. "How much would we need to carry on each trip to make it worth-while, financially I mean?"

"Don't worry too much about the economics of it, as I said, it's a bit of a pilot study so we're not looking to make too much at first. I reckon about four hundred cases per trip will do nicely." I was furiously calculating on the edge of my beer mat.

"I reckon that a case of bottled beer weighs about ten kilos, so we're talking about four tonnes. That shouldn't be a problem. What I'm worrying about is the bit about a relatively smooth crossing. That bit of sea can be bloody bumpy, and it'll take at least forty-eight hours to get back."

"This beer doesn't seem to get sea-sick," said Damien, "it's the vibration from the road that seems to do it in, as I said. So can you do it or not?"

"Well, yes, I suppose I can, really." What was I saying?

"Right, when can you go and how much do you want?" asked Damien drinking up.

"Eh....I....bloody hell, I don't know, I could be ready to sail in about three weeks. I'll need a crew of two, provisions, diesel...." I was struggling with figures I was pulling from the air and about which I knew nothing. "It'll cost at least a couple of grand, I think."

"Ok, squire, I'll contact you in a couple of weeks to finalise the arrangements. You can let me know if you need any more money. Two grand doesn't sound like enough to me." And off he went once more leaving me feeling like it all hadn't happened.

31

"Why are you standing up all by yourself in the middle of an empty bar, Tom?" asked a voice at my elbow, "you really are behaving a bit strangely lately, you know, Tom?...TOM!"

"Frieda! Hi!..What are you doing here?"

"Tom Morton, do you mean to say that you don't even remember that you came here to meet me tonight? I think I'll go home and knit."

"Sorry, Frieda, of course I remember, it's just that I've had the most extraordinary conversation which momentarily blew my mind. It's happening rather a lot lately. Sit down while I get you a drink and I'll tell you all about it. G'n'T?"

Frieda listened politely while I outlined Damien Coombs' proposition. She didn't seem in the least amazed.

"So what's the problem? Go for it, it's bound to be good practice and you obviously aren't going to lose out of it. He seems very generous, your Mr Coombs."

"That's one of the things that's worrying me actually. He seems too generous for a wheeler-dealer which he obviously is."

"What would you do if you had nothing to worry about, Tom. Now, are you going to take me home and fuck me senseless or are you going to feed me first?"

"Jesus, Frieda, you don't beat about the bush, do you? Actually I am a bit peckish and I've always worked best on a full stomach. Where would you like to eat?"

"If it's going to be hard work maybe we should find a transport cafe."

"I was trying to be funny. Do you fancy the new bistro beside the old harbour? I've heard it's very good."

"If they serve oysters it will be perfect."

CHAPTER 5

"Has anyone seen fucking Morton anywhere?" I could hear Frazer yelling to the yard in general over the roar of the compressor. He seemed bemused by the unprecedented amount of activity. Two of the lads were slopping generous amounts of anti-fouling on to the bottom of 'Sligo Bay' while another was standing scratching his head over the unfamiliar rig of the Freedom now laid out on the slip having just retrieved it from the boat-shed.

"Where the hell is Tom?" Frazer asked the rigger.

"Over in the shed, I think," replied the rigger without looking up, "oh, and Frazer, if you find him, tell him that I'm fucked if I can figure out this rig. Looks more like the makings of two sodding great windsurfers than a proper boat."

"Over here, Frazer!" I shouted from the shed where I was pulling acres of white sail out of two large sail-bags. "Here's where we discover we have a full set of sails for a gaff-cutter instead of a Freedom schooner. I've never bothered to check these sails until now, I hope to Christ they're all OK."

"How many should you have, anyway?" asked Frazer casting around for more bags.

"Only the two, as it happens, and sodding big ones. They look as if they should be OK. I'm a bit reluctant to spread them out here to check, though, this place is a shit heap."

"Want me to give it a hoover out, dear?" asked Frazer, "you boys really must try to be a bit tidier, you know."

"Fuck off Frazer. Here, make yourself useful and help me lug this lot out to the slip."

"Oh, yes, your man out there seems to be struggling a bit with the finer points of the bits you plan to hang this lot out on. He asked me to tell you."

"I heard him," I snorted, "fuckwit!"

"Am I to assume from all this unseemly activity, the like of which I have not witnessed since the night Bill Webb's Rottweiler had a fit in the snug of the King's Arms, that we have a voyage in the pipeline?"

"Oh, yes, I haven't told you about last night, have I?" I dropped my end of the sail-bag, making Frazer fall over his end.

"Bugger it, Tom," grumbled Frazer from the comfort of the bag which he was now moulding into an approximation of a settee, "why should I want to hear the sordid details of your sweaty thrashings with a certain member of the opposite gender who shall remain nameless...."

"For Christ's sake Frazer, shut up, I don't want the whole fucking yard to know about me and you-know-who, not yet anyway, and that's not what I was talking about."

I quickly outlined Damien Coombs' proposition to Frazer who had now stretched out comfortably on the sail-bag with his hands behind his head and his eyes closed.

"Sounds too good to be true, me old mate," he sighed, "a couple of trips over to the old Emerald Isle to pick up a take-away sounds pretty close to heaven to me. What's the snag?"

"That's just it," I said, "there doesn't seem to be one, not that I can put my finger on, at any rate, except that the whole idea seems a bit far-fetched."

"Hmm, I know what you mean, but I've heard of even dafter things being done which turned into gold-mines for someone. What about these Teenage Mutant Ninja Turtle things the kids all used to be daft about."

"What about them, for Christ's sake?"

"Well, I heard that the guy who invented them did it for a laugh, you know, to see if he could come up with something really stupid, I mean, mutant turtles who practise martial arts, live in a sewer, eat pizza and are named after Italian Renaissance painters takes a bit of twisted thinking."

"What the hell are you raving on about?"

"Turtles! Surely even you have heard about them, Jesus, Tom, sometimes I think you go about with your head up your arse."

"This may come as a big shock to you, Frazer, but I haven't read a comic since Alf Tupper was a lad, and pardon me for tugging on the straps of your strait-jacket, but what the holy hell has all this got to do with shipping beer from Ireland?"

"Just that the guy has made a fortune from a crazy idea, basically, and you might be in line to do likewise."

I was beginning to regard Frazer with deep suspicion. The thought of spending days cooped up with him when he was obviously becoming prematurely senile was beginning to lose its appeal.

"Look, Tom, just forget I ever mentioned it, OK? Are we going to put these sails aboard or what?"

"No, just put them over there with the rest of the rig for now. We'll load them with the rest of the stuff once she's in the water. I've ordered the crane for tomorrow. It'll be easier to do the stuff that still needs doing at the dockside. So, are you coming or what?" I had decided to give him the benefit of the doubt this time.

"Try stopping me! I wouldn't miss this for all the rope in Manila," said Frazer, "and, anyway you can't be trusted without a responsible adult. Who else is coming?"

"I thought of asking Cathy's young brother, George, along. He's done a bit of cruising in the Channel and he's a good steady lad. Does what he's told, if you can get past the Walkman headphones, that is."

"Plays a mean game of cricket too, I hear. Didn't he have a trial for the county last year?"

"I think I remember Cathy saying something about that. I'm not really interested in cricket, I'm afraid."

"Don't worry, Tom, your secret's safe with me. Do you think three's enough?"

"Three's plenty. The rig's a piece of cake to handle; we've got the wind-vane and the autohelm as a back-up. There's bugger-all to do. Anyway, I've only finished three bunks so far."

"So when do we leave?"

"Soon as we're ready, basically. Shouldn't take more than a couple of weeks. We can have a quick shake-down, say to Dartmouth and back, then we stock-up and off."

"What about all the bumf? Is that not going to take forever?"

"Don't think so. I spoke to Arthur this morning and he's going to help all he can with his various contacts. We need to organise a full survey for the insurers and the Ministry, Arthur assures me that it's all straightforward."

"I'll believe it when I see it in triplicate. Arthur just wants you off his back for a few weeks, I suspect, he's not given to bursts of helpfulness isn't Arthur. I suppose a cup of coffee is out of the question?"

"Yes, come on, it is about that time, I could do with a cuppa myself."

I could see Cathy sitting at her desk as we came into the office from the boat-shed.

"Everything all right, Cath?" I shouted through the partition. She didn't seem to have heard me. I stuck my head round the door.

"OK, Cath? Any major disasters?" still no response. I went into her office and stood in front of her desk.

"Cath? Hello, it's me your adored boss. Earth to Cath!" She was alive because I saw her blink. She was staring at a large brown envelope on the desk in front of her as if it had just introduced itself personally and asked for a date Friday night. Slowly her eyes rose to meet mine.

"Two thousand pounds in twenties," she said.

"Beg pardon?"

"Two thousand pounds in twenties," she repeated, "I counted them."

"Where did it come from?" I asked. I half expected her to tell me the fairies brought it.

"A man came in and put the envelope on the desk. 'I'm Coombs' he said, 'This is for your governor, two grand as agreed, count it.' I asked if he wanted a receipt and he said he trusted me and went out."

"I'll look after that for the moment," said Frazer reaching past me and picking up the envelope, "two strong black coffees if you please, Cath," he ordered, "we'll take care of this."

"What do you mean 'we'? That's my money, I think. You heard what she said. It was Coombs and he said it was for the gov'nor, and that, unless I'm very much mistaken, is me!"

"Shut up, Tom," said Frazer, "go on, then Cath, we're gasping!"

We went into my office and closed the door.

"Curiouser and curiouser," said Frazer, taking the money out of the envelope. There were lots of twenties indeed, and all second-hand, by the looks of them.

"Our man seems very keen to do business," said Frazer.

"I don't like the look of this," I admitted, "I mean, legitimate business people don't pay in advance in used twenties."

"Tom, very few legitimate business people pay at all unless you practically sue them, much less in advance. However, this does not mean that Mr Coombs is bent, necessarily, but it would pay to tread very warily from now on in. I suggest that you put this cash, as it is, in the safe and resist the temptation to dip into it for the time being. A safe deposit box at the bank might be even better."

"Do you think the money might be 'hot'?" I ventured.

"Dear me, Tom, you've been watching 'The Bill' again. No, not really, but let's just play this super-safe."

"So what now?" I asked.

"We wait," said Frazer mysteriously, "continue with the preparations. Coombs will come to you; it seems to be the way he wants to play it. All you have to do is make sure everything you do is above board. Check all the paperwork he gives you and you can't go wrong. He could simply be a slightly eccentric businessman."

"Slightly? I don't know, Frazer. Maybe we should go to the police. What if he's a con-man or something?"

"If he's a con-man he's not a very bloody good one, dishing out bundles of cash. Anyway, what would you say to the police? 'Look here officer, this man has just given me money to do a job for him, do you think he might be bent?' they'd have a good chuckle over their Horlicks at that one!"

"You're right, I worry too much. Where's Cath with that coffee?"

Cath appeared with two large well-worn mugs and set them down heavily on the edge of my desk.

"Now that's what I call a cup of coffee," Frazer enthused, "thanks Cath, you saved my life!"

"As it is or with central heating?" I asked, finding the rum bottle in the drawer.

"Purely medicinal, of course," said Frazer, holding out his mug. I slopped a good measure into each mug.

"Cheers," said Frazer, and he slurped noisily, "I do believe I can feel e'en now, the strength flooding back into me old veins!"

We sipped reflectively for a few moments. I signed a couple of letters Cath had left and flicked through some paint brochures which had just come in.

"I wonder how Andy's getting on out there among the Arabs?"

"Hmm..." Frazer stared into his mug for several seconds, "I just

37

hope he knows what he's doing. It's been decidedly dodgy out there these days. You know that he's involved with the military, don't you?"

"I knew that he used to be in the forces, but I thought he was in computers these days."

"Soldier's computers, to be precise, target acquisition and all that stuff. Seems wars are won or lost by computer programmers these days."

"I hope to hell they're better than the ones that work in my bank. They'd have the guns pointing at one another."

"Yes, well, Andy's the man who makes sure the guns are pointing in the right direction at the right time. The Saudis are spending an awful lot of Riyals on that kind of stuff just now."

"So he's still a soldier?"

"Not in the strictest sense, but he is paid by the MOD."

"But he was a soldier before?"

"Officer in the Parachute Regiment. A brave lad with gongs to prove it.....but enough about our Mr Prentice, I came here to talk to you about my little project."

"What project? Oh, you mean the dehydrated beer?"

"Yes I've managed to get the cost down by changing a few ingredients, and the flavour is still pretty good, but I'm running out of room in my kitchen. I really need a bit more space to work. I was wondering if you could spare a corner of the boat-shed for a few months?"

"Yes, sure there's plenty of room, certainly, but it's not very clean, and we use some pretty awful smelling solvents and resins in here."

"Oh, that's no problem; I'll make a polythene tent to work in. Most of the process is closed anyway."

"OK, you can use the space the sails and stuff for Sligo was in, and that will give you a window as well."

"Great! What's the rental?"

"Bugger off, you can pay me in ale."

"I think rent might be cheaper!" Frazer headed for the door, dodging a volley of small chandlery I was throwing at him.

There was no doubt about it; life was taking some strange turns these days. Someone once told me that the pivotal events in one's life are governed by a seven year cycle, and, so far there did seem to be a discernible pattern. I don't, to be honest, remember anything very momentous happening when I was seven, but I do remember I earned my first real wage when I was fourteen, planting potatoes on a local farm. At twenty-one I left college, having got a degree of sorts, and went out into the big, bad world to earn a living. I made my first major career shift from industrial engineering to marine research, (there's a story in itself), at twenty-eight, and at thirty-five I went abroad. In three days it would be my forty-second birthday. There had to be something in the theory, if, of course you could disregard the inconvenient facts like my near-death from peritonitis at nineteen, my marriage at twenty-six, first becoming a father at thirty and getting divorced at forty. Obviously the cycle was career oriented and not emotional. Except that I bought the yard only three years ago. Oh, fuck it, I'll be reading my stars in the Daily Mail next. I had to admit, though, I was really excited at the prospect of some real sailing, and being paid for it!

CHAPTER 6

"I do wish you'd given me a bit more warning, Tom," said Carol. "I've never launched a ship before, my hair's a mess and these jeans are ancient. This is just typical of you!"

"Look, all you have to do is say 'I name this ship Sligo Bay, may God bless her and all who sail in her' and bash that bottle off her bow when I say so. We're not launching the QE3, you know."

"Well, all right then. I just hope you've not forgotten any important screws or anything. I'd hate for the thing to fall on me!"

I would treat that remark with the contempt it richly deserved.

It had, prior to that conversation, been a long day and I had to confess I was getting a bit tetchy. I had asked Mike Strong ('....the STRONG men will lift it!' I hated that ad.) to bring his mobile crane round for three o'clock and by half-past he still hadn't turned up. I was on the phone to his wife,"....can't understand it, he left half an hour ago...." when Frazer walked in and asked who was performing the ceremony.

"What ceremony?"

"The launching ceremony, you know; name the ship, bless the crew, write off a perfectly good bottle of bubbly, etcetera?"

"Oh, bloody hell, Frazer, I forgot all about that! I suppose we have to do it?"

"Well, I, for one would be less than willing to take to the high seas in an un-blessed vessel," announced Frazer, "I mean, there's no telling what misfortunes may befall her and her unfortunate crew!"

"But the crane's about to pitch up any minute. We'll never get a launching party together now!"

"Well, it just so happens that I, in my infinite wisdom, foresaw

40

this omission and stowed a half-case of the aforementioned fizzy stuff in the boot of my car."

"You're a genius, Frazer. You don't happen to have Victoria Beckham in there too, by any chance? I like her; she'd be great at launching."

"Not quite, Tom, but I do happen to know that Carol, Frank and the kids are headed in this direction. I gather someone told them that something special was about to happen in this vicinity. Something they wouldn't want to miss."

"Carol? Yes, she would love to do the honours, wouldn't she? Do you think she will though? I mean I'm not exactly flavour of the month with Carol just now. She still hasn't got over that business with the front door."

"Oh, I think she'll do it all right, Tom, if you ask her nicely, very few women can resist a compliment like being asked to launch a ship. All the same, I would stand well back when she swings that bottle if I were you!"

A loud roar announced the arrival of the mobile crane. This was quite a machine and Mike was having difficulty fitting it between the gateposts at the yard entrance.

"Hey, Tom!" he shouted cheerfully, "you couldn't move these sodding gate-posts a bit, could you; I don't want to scratch me paintwork!"

"I wouldn't worry about it mate," shouted Frazer, "I think you can forget winning any concours d'elegance prizes with that brute, anyway, you could build flats in the room you've got either side, c'mon, steady as you go!"

"The crane eased forward. There was just enough room, and with me at one side and Frazer at the other, the monster was eased through the gap.

"Told you," said Frazer, "A piece of p...." and at that point three telephone wires descended upon his head.

"What the fuck!"

"Who forgot about the phone lines above the gate, then?" I quipped vaguely wondering who had been cut off.

"Oh, I'm sorry, Tom," said Mike, surveying the damage, "I'm forever doing that. It's the big jib on this thing. It's higher than you think and you can't see anything overhead for it. Never mind, I'll fix them later, done it hundreds of times."

"Hundreds?"

"Shut up Frazer," I said as Mike blithely clambered back into the driving cab, "if he says he can fix them, he can fix them. British Telecom will probably charge the earth, never mind the telling-off we'll have to stand and take."

"If I park her on the quay-side over there, I'll be able to do it in a single lift," yelled Mike, "can you clear all the crap that's in the way?" He was referring to Sligo's rig, but I let it pass. Jason, Mike's son had materialised from the crane cab and was starting to take an interest in the proceedings.

"You got a lifting frame, then?" he asked rather unenthusiastically. His hands were deep in his overall pockets and it seemed he intended to take no more than a technical interest.

"Stop fiddling with your balls, Jason, and go and get some timber to put under them jacks!" bawled Mike, "lazy little sod," he added as an aside. Jason slouched off in the direction of the boat-shed looking very odd since he seemed to be unable to operate with his hands at his side. He tried folding his arms then he sort of flapped them to the side and finally settled on clasping them behind his back.

"Silly sod," muttered Mike, "taught him all I know and still he knows fuck-all. Where's the launching party?"

"Don't you start," I said, "I believe the Royal Family are on their way now. Couldn't get Paris Hilton, I'm afraid."

"Tesco's got Sally Gunnell," Jason offered, "and she came in a vintage car!"

"Vintage cars have that effect on some women," grinned Frazer. Sometimes he could be so coarse.

"I thought I told you to go for bits of wood!" said Mike to Jason who seemed to have reappeared as if by magic.

"Couldn't find any," mumbled Jason.

"Couldn't find any?" Mike yelled, "Couldn't bloody well find any?? There's a cubic foot of it between your bloody ears, for a start! You couldn't find your arse with both hands, you thick bugger. There's bloody tons of it lying about this yard, look at it! Half a bloody rain forest over there!" He nodded in the direction of a stack of iroko I had been carefully seasoning.

"I'd rather you didn't use that wood, if you don't mind. There are some cut-up railway sleepers in front of the shed you can use. There's a wheelbarrow over there, too." Jason looked blank.

"To bring the sleepers back in," I prompted, "they're heavy."

"Oh! Yeah, OK, then," and off he slouched, nearly putting his hands in his pockets again.

"God forgive me, Tom, one day I'm going to strangle that boy. He inherits it from his big sister, I reckon!"

"There's an interesting bit of genealogy," muttered Frazer.

"Yes, she's thick and lazy too," continued Mike, oblivious to Frazer's sarcasm, "works down the Co-op at the cold meat counter. Says she enjoys a challenge. Can't see it myself."

"It's all these salamis," said Frazer, "easy to see how a young girl could be over-stimulated."

"For God's sake Frazer," I hissed, digging him in the ribs. He kept a poker face.

"No, she don't like any of that Eye-talian stuff," Mike rumbled on, "prefers a good old English black pudding. Mind you, so does her mother." This finally got to Frazer who turned away, his heaving shoulders causing Mike to look concerned.

"You all right, Frazer?" Frazer nodded frantically and pretended to be taking grit out of his eye.

"Let's get the crane in position, Mike," I suggested, trying to steer Mike away from the subject of sausages. Frazer composed his face into a bland mask and tried to look interested. We walked over to the crane.

"Quite likes the odd faggot, too," offered Mike and Frazer folded. I kept walking with Mike who was looking back at Frazer, now on his knees, heaving helplessly.

"Funny chap," observed Mike and climbed into the cab. The roar of the engine forestalled any attempt on my part to answer.

You could see that Mike had done this sort of thing a few times. As Snoopy once said, it's the difference between the true professional and the merely enthusiastic amateur. In a matter of minutes the crane was positioned, jacks chocked with sleepers, slings slung and padded and the big lifting frame hooked on to the massive hook. With only a little adjustment of the position of the slings, the hull was inched clear of the chocks. She hung there, swinging almost imperceptibly. Jason casually nudged her steady.

"Ready when you are!" yelled Mike.

Frank's timing was as impeccable as ever, and Carol's enquiry as to the identity of the launch-person and discovery that she was that person prompted the earlier-mentioned exchange.

"No, really, Tom, you must let me go home and put on a dress and do my hair. I refuse to launch a ship looking like a scare-crow."

"I bet Helen of Troy didn't say that when she launched her thousand," offered Frank.

"I fucking bet she did," said Frazer less than sotto voce.

"Look, please Carol, it's not that big a deal. We can't keep the crane hanging around any longer. Just do it as you are, please, for me," Frazer was mock-vomiting in the background much to Carol's annoyance.

"All right, Tom, but if he makes one remark out of place, so help me I'll hit him with the bottle."

"My lips are sealed," said Frazer, surrendering.

"Right, what do I say again?"

"InamethisshipSligoBaymayGodblessherandallwhosailinher!!!"

"Is that all?"

"That's all."

"Seems a bit abrupt, you know, lacking in ceremony."

"Please, Carol, that's all you've got to say, then you bash the bottle off the sharp bit."

"I know what bit to hit, thank-you."

"OK, then, go ahead!" and we all stood back expectantly.

"I name this ship," Carol enunciated, in a very passable 'My husband and I' voice. "What's she called again, Tom?" she hissed.

"Sligo Bay!" I hissed back.

"Sligo Bay! May God bless her..." maybe it was nearer Princess Anne, but it was getting to Frazer. He snorted."...and all who sail in her, stop laughing Frazer! Tom, he's laughing!"

"Never mind, Carol, the bottle, hit the bow, hard!"

She wasn't captain of the hockey first eleven for nothing. The bottle exploded in a million wet, fizzy fragments. There was a loud cheer from the assembled crowd and Carol promptly burst into tears. Her sobbing was drowned by the roar of the crane engine as Sligo Bay slowly rose from her cradle and swung out over the harbour.

There is a heart-stopping moment every time you put a boat into the water just before she reaches her marks. This is the moment when you wonder if you remembered to close the sea-cocks, or maybe you forgot the depth-sounder transducer. Visions of water welling up into your fresh, clean bilges flood your imagination, then mercifully the slings go slack and she's afloat, just as she should be, bobbing gently and comfortably with an almost audible sigh of relief. You leap aboard and scramble below ripping up floor-boards, but nine times out of ten all is dry and drama-free. This time was no different, except that there was a lot more bilge to check and, of course, I had forgotten my torch, but my routine check procedure had been thorough. There's always that little thorn of doubt, though.

"Can we come aboard, Dad?" called Tina.

"Yes, of course, all of you, bring the rest of the bubbly, Frazer, it's party time!"

We were well on our way to finishing the third bottle when Mike appeared at the quayside.

"I'll be off then, Tom," he shouted, "I've sorted these phone lines and put the wood and lifting frame over by the shed!"

"Oh, Mike, I forgot all about you! Come aboard and have a drink with us. You did a great job, really you did!"

"Nah, thanks all the same, Tom, this big bastard is hard enough to drive sober, and champagne affects me something rotten!"

"OK, Mike," I fished a tenner out of my jeans, "here's something for the lad. Drop your account off at the office next time you're passing."

"Thanks, Tom, Jason will appreciate that, see you."

There was no doubt about it; a boat always feels happier in the water. Carol always used to complain that she felt unsafe at the Boat-Show clambering about these boats just parked there, and I knew what she meant. No matter how big a boat is, there's always a bit of movement as you make your way about her which tells you she's in the water and sort-of relaxed. On the ground she feels, somehow, tense, nervous maybe. It's also strange to see a boat down in the water after months of getting used to her towering above you.

Colin and Tina had clambered into the quarter-berth and were playing happily with the various toys children of that age always seem to have secreted about them. Frank was having a meaningful dialogue with Frazer about the Middle-East crisis or something equally depressing and Carol was having a good look round. Could I detect a wistful look in her eye? I knew she enjoyed sailing, particularly in good weather. She knew her way about a boat and was still a very useful pair of hands around the yard in the summer when things got hectic. We'd had some great times together cruising the Channel and out to the Scillies, I wondered if she still had at least a few fond memories....

"Does the stove work, Tom? I'm gasping for a cup of coffee."

"Yes, it should do, Carol, but we've no supplies aboard. Tell you what, I'll get some bits and pieces from the office and we'll have an inaugural brew-up. How many mugs do we need?"

"Only four, but Tom, can you find some Cokes or something for the kids?"

"OK, I'll be right back. Don't go away!"

I sprinted back to the office and found a box. I was collecting kettle (filled), mugs, coffee, milk (powdered), sugar, Cokes and anything else I could think of that might be useful, when Sam Wells from the yard next door walked in with a cordless phone in his hand.

"It's for you!" He said, obviously harassed.

"How do you mean, Sam, that's your phone, isn't it?"

Sam thrust the phone into my hand and sat down.

"Just take the call, Tom, and get rid of the annoying bugger on the other end. I've got work to do and he won't stop ringing up insisting on speaking to you. I keep giving him your number but he keeps calling back here. I think he's a bit cracked if you ask me!" I took the phone and put it to my ear like it might bite me.

"Hello? Tom Morton speaking, who is this?"

"Thank Christ, you at last!" bawled Damien Coombs down the line. "I thought I was never going to persuade that cretin to get you to the phone. I kept phoning this number and the idiot kept saying I had the wrong number and giving me the same number to call back. I think he's a bit of a looney if you ask me."

"Sorry, Damien, there does seem to be a bit of a mix-up, ah, what did you want to talk to me about?"

"I've got some bumf for you to sign. Can I come round some time when you're going to be there?"

"Yes, sure, give it about an hour, I'll be here all afternoon but I'm a bit tied up right now."

"An hour from now will suit me fine, see you then. And get rid of that storeman or whatever he is, he's not doing your business a bit of good." He hung up.

"Yes, fine, 'bye then...." I said lamely into the dead instrument.

I handed it back to Sam with a weak smile.

"Thanks, Sam, says he's sorry he bothered you, don't know what happened there...." Sam grabbed the instrument from me.

"Don't mention it, Tom; I just hope he doesn't make a habit of it!" The phone warbled in his hand and he put it down on the desk and backed away from it like it had suddenly become red hot.

"You answer it, Tom,," he said. I picked it up and pressed the 'talk' button.

"Hello?"

"Oh, hi, Tom, I'm glad I got you in," it was Frieda and she didn't seem to be the least bit surprised to find me at Sam's number.

"I wondered if you'd like to take me out tonight, there's a band I like playing at the George in Kingsbridge."

"Yes, um, great, Frieda, yes I'd like that, ah Frieda, why did you think you would find me at this number?" there was a pregnant silence from the other end.

"You know, Tom, you are behaving very strangely these days. Why shouldn't I find you at this number? You work there, for one thing. Pick me up at eight, OK?" And she hung up. Once more I found myself looking blankly at Sam's phone wondering what the hell was happening. Sam snatched his phone from me and stormed out, muttering to himself about people with funny friends. I was just leaving with the box of goodies when the phone rang. I struggled with the box back into the office and grabbed the phone.

"Yes?"

"Three Quattro Staggiones and a garlic bread for Bartlett, I'll collect them in half an hour, OK?"

"No, not really, I think you might have the wrong number. This is Morton's boatyard."

"Oh.....sorry mate, cheers." I hung up. Something strange was going on and I was beginning to suspect what it might be. The phone rang again as I guessed it might.

"Three Quattro Stag...."

"Hold it a minute," I interrupted, "you've got the boatyard again. What number exactly did you dial?"

"788923. It's in the book, under Tino's Pizzeria. It must be right because I use it quite a lot. Mind you I don't always get the Quattro Staggioni...."

"Will you please stop going on about Quattro Staggioni for a minute. Tino's is further down the road. I think I know what's gone wrong. Try dialling..." I quickly looked up Sam's number,"...787554, that should get you Tino's."

"Nah, you can't fool me, mate, that's Sam's number. I should know, I'm phoning from there. Here, this isn't one of them wind-up programmes on the tele is it?"

How could I explain to this chap that a crane had brought down the phone lines and Mike Strong had connected them wrong?

"Look, try it, I promise it'll work. There's a problem with the lines. Should be sorted out soon."

"OK, I'll try it," he sounded unconvinced, "cheers anyway."

I waited for a minute to make sure the pizza addict had got the message and took the phone off the hook. I collected the box once more from the desk and headed back to the boat.

"Thank goodness, Tom, we all thought you had got lost. We're gasping here!"

"Never occurred to anyone to come and give me a hand, I don't suppose?"

"Oh dear me no, Tom," said Frazer, "we were very busy putting the world to rights, weren't we Frank?"

"Too right, mate," said Frank, "dangerous to interrupt an intellectual discussion in full flow."

"Intellectual my foot," snorted Carol, "the champagne is doing all the talking from where I'm standing."

"Listen, Carol, I'm going to have to leave you to make the coffee and go and get British Telecom to come over." I explained about the phone mix-up as briefly as possible.

"Better hurry before Tino twigs what's going on or he'll be phoning his mama in Milan on Sam's bill."

"Oh, shit! I never thought of that. I was only thinking of people phoning us. We'll all be ringing on one another's bills."

I ran back to the office. Getting through to the telephone engineers was easy. Explaining to them what the problem was, was not. They finally agreed to sort it out right away.

"And can we take the telling off as read?" I humbly requested.

"Sorry?"

"When your man comes to fix the lines, can we assume I'm suitably sorry and not lay on the row too thick, please, I feel stupid enough as it is."

"Oh, I see, no we won't be over there for quite a while anyway. We'll just switch you over at the exchange for now and fix the lines later. Who do I send the bill to?"

"Better make it to me, Tom Morton, Morton's boatyard," I hadn't the heart to send it to Mike, "I didn't realise you could do that, you know, with the lines."

"Oh yes, dead easy. People often want to move house but keep the same number. As long as it's the same exchange it can be done. We could hardly be expected to start moving wires all over the place, would be like a cat's cradle eventually."

"Yes, I suppose it would," why was I being so thick?

"'Bye then. Try not to use your phone for the next ten minutes or so, you might get cut off."

I wandered back to the others at the boat hoping there hadn't been too much mayhem at Sam's and Tino's. There was a lot to be said for cellphones.

"One cup of coffee coming up, you look like you could use it, too!" Frazer handed me 'my' mug, "get it all sorted out, then?"

"Yes, I just hope they connect them up the right way. Do it all at the exchange, apparently."

"Wonders of modern science, mate, you've got to hand it to them. Would never have happened with the old PO Phones. We'd have had to fill out an accident report form in triplicate and still wait for six weeks for an inspector to come, then another four for the engineer who wouldn't have the bit he needed, so he would have to go to Swindon or some damn place, by pony, and then...."

"Frazer, for goodness sake!" yelled Carol.

"Yeah, give us a break, Frazer," I pleaded.

"You young people nowadays just take the wonders of New Labour for granted," went on Frazer, "why, when I were a lad...."

He was finally silenced by a substantial and spontaneous bombardment of paint-rags, books, garbage and small off-cuts of mahogany. The children looked on in wonder. They were used to, and ignored, our silly discussions but a bit of adult bad behaviour was always worth a watch.

"Can we throw something at Frazer too, Dad?" asked Colin.

"Well, only something you can safely lift. Don't want you hurting yourself!"

"Do you mind?" protested Frazer, "it's bad enough that you try and inflict GBH on my good person without leading minors astray as well. Could we call a truce on the basis that ice-creams are on me?"

"Oh, yes! Yes! Please, Frazer, yummy, yummy, yummy," chorused the children and Carol.

"Wonderful with the kids, he is," said Frank, putting on a mumsy voice, "don't know what we'd do without him."

"But we'd like to find out!" everyone joined in.

"To the ice-cream shop!" yelled Frazer and led the charge on the quay, "last there's smelly!"

"Frazer, really," Carol giggled.

As the mob thundered out of the yard it parted either side of a somewhat bemused Damien Coombs. I sheepishly separated from the pack.

"Hello, Damien, just going for some ice-cream. Want some?"

"No, ta, Tom, not right now," he said watching the others disappearing down the street, "could we just get this lot signed so that I can get back to the land of sane people."

"Tell you what, Damien," I said, remembering what Frazer had said about checking everything out, "why don't you just leave them all with me and I'll fill in all the details and signatures and I'll drop them off at your hotel tomorrow?"

"OK, then, but don't take too long. I meant what I said about getting out of here. They're all bloody barmy, the locals. I don't know how you stand it. You seem quite sensible, by comparison that is."

"Thank-you." Was this a compliment?

"See you soon, then," and off he hurried.

As I strolled back to the office I suddenly remembered that I had a date with Frieda that night. A smile spread across my face. I realised that I was feeling happier than I had felt for some considerable time. The only cloud on the horizon was that I was damned if I could remember what time I was to pick her up.

"What's the name of this band, again?" I asked as we drove towards Kingsbridge.

"The Tin Men," said Frieda, "they're from Truro. Play jazz mostly with a bit of new stuff thrown in. I think you'll like them, Tom."

"I'm sure I will. It seems like ages since I've heard any decent live music. All the pubs seem to have these days is some guy with a guitar and a box of tricks that sounds like a robot's idea of the London Philharmonic. I always get the impression that the poor singer is being dragged through the song against his will. Doesn't make for easy listening."

"I know what you mean. I sometimes wonder why the act bothers to turn up at all. He could just send along a recording of his set and let the landlord play it over the P.A. with maybe a big photograph of the singer standing up at the end of the bar."

"Yes, it seems to be impossible to deviate from the pre-set programme, and you can forget requests!"

We sat quietly as a twisty and rather attractive bit of road was reeled in towards us. The sun was low and shone through the trees with that mellow warm light you only get in the evening. People were out walking dogs and we had to slow down occasionally for groups riding ponies. There was no rush and you usually got a nice smile from the girl riders if you gave them plenty of room. I had a thing about jodhpur-clad bums in any case...

"Tom! There's a car coming the other way!"

I pulled back in sharply.

"Your courtesy is all very commendable, Tom, dear, but I'd rather not spend the rest of my life in a wheelchair with dribble running down my chin. I don't think the driver of that Jag was terribly impressed, either. I think he was indicating that you should look twice in future."

"If he can't take a joke to hell with him," I tried to look cool but I was furious at my carelessness. I tried hard not to wipe the beads of sweat that had formed on my upper lip.

"A little bird told me there was a bit of a ceremony at your yard this afternoon."

"Oh, that. Yes, I'm sorry, Frieda, I should have invited you. It wasn't meant to be anything special, in fact I forgot all about the formal side of it. If it hadn't been for Frazer there wouldn't have been a ceremony at all."

"It's all right, Tom, don't panic. I don't mind. In fact Frazer had mentioned it to me before and suggested I turn up at the crucial moment to do the honours, but I declined. I felt you weren't quite ready for that."

"So Carol was Frazer's second choice," I mused, "I hope she never finds that out!"

"Don't worry, I won't tell her, anyway, I'd have missed the boat with the bottle or thrown it across the harbour or something inauspicious. Carol has a stronger right arm than I have."

"Carol has a stronger right arm than lots of people, believe me! That's why I hope she never finds out she was first substitute."

51

"Oh, my poor Tom, did the nasty Carol beat you?" Frieda was taking the piss in a very physical way and the car was finding its own way down the road.

"Give over, Frieda; my driving's bad enough without sabotage from you."

"You're definitely going to do this, then?"

"What, the Ireland trip? Yes, I think so. It's all going to plan. Coombs brought the papers round today. I'll go over them with Arthur, the harbourmaster, tomorrow to see if there's anything dubious looking. The boat will be ready to test some time next week with luck."

Frieda said nothing and looked out of the side window.

"Frieda? You all right?"

"Yes, Tom," she said looking back at me with her special smile, "I shall miss you."

"Listen, Frieda, I won't be gone for long, you know. Ireland isn't that far."

"That's not what I was thinking about, Tom. I reckon that this is only the start of something much bigger. You know, the trial run for the real thing?"

"Well, you could be right, but let's not worry about that yet. I mean, I might finish up hating commercial sailing and decide to stay here. I do like it here, you know. I'm not going to rush into anything. There's many a slip...." who was I trying to convince?

"Of course you're right, Tom, I'm being silly, there's a parking space up there on the right...."

I liked the George. It was a pub you could feel comfy in. I don't mean it had soft chairs (although it had) but the locals weren't too local, the youngsters not too young, and the landlord always seemed to be there behind the bar, where he should be. There's something about a good steady landlord that makes a pub. He could even be a bit of a sod, as long as you could depend on him being there and not an assortment of assistant managers who don't know whether you're a regular, a tourist or an escapee from the local loony bin. "Evening, sir," they'd say to a punter, "you here on holiday?" "No lad," he'd reply, "I've lived next door for t'last sixty years, is it Fred's night off again?" "Who's Fred?" "The landlord!" "Never met him, the assistant manager hired me by phone...." Ridiculous. No, the George wasn't like that. The landlord was there, behind the bar as we walked in. He nodded to me (I was hardly a regular but had been there often enough to be recognised) and beamed, somewhat familiarly I thought, at Frieda.

"Friend of yours?" I asked.

"Not really," said Frieda, "I do come here quite a lot to listen to the music though."

"With Andy?" who was I worrying about?

"No, with Frazer, actually." I didn't know what the landlord would be thinking but he'd be wrong on several counts.

We found a table not too near where the band were setting up their gear. There wasn't terribly much of it; a good sign, I reckoned, a couple of small amps, a drum kit with no more than two or three drums, a small keyboard, and the rest consisted of instruments in cases which looked like they had been used to ward off small-arms fire. The Tin Men were a strange assortment of people. One of them was very obviously a woman, for a start, most attractive. I assumed that she was a guest singer until she hoisted a very shiny alto sax out of it's case and blew the most complicated warming-up riff I'd ever heard. This was beginning to look like it could be fun. The drummer looked like my bank-manager, and so, now I could see him, did the keyboard player.

"Brothers?" I asked Frieda, nodding in their direction.

"Father and son, I believe, although you wouldn't think so to look at them. The sax player is the daughter...."

"And, don't tell me, the trumpet player is her mum in drag," I quipped. Frieda ignored my witty remark.

"Aren't you going to get me a drink? This is a pub, you know. They might sling us out if we only sit here and listen to the music. The poor man has a living to make...."

"OK, OK, I get the message, G'n'T as usual?"

"No thanks, I'll have a pint of Murdstones thanks."

I slunk to the bar somewhat perplexed. This was another side of Frieda I had never suspected. A real ale freak, yet! Frazer's influence obviously, but Murdstones! Not everyone's tipple. It was the kind of beer out of which serious amnesia cases are born. I once got up one morning after having drunk three pints, honest officer, only three pints, and found my trousers in the garden. And it wasn't even the ones I had been wearing! I was still wearing them. Frazer knows something about it but the swine refuses to say any more than "It was a stupid game anyway." Bastard.

"A pint of Murdstones and a half of low-alcohol lager, please."

"Got her well trained, then?" said the barman, nodding in Frieda's direction.

"Pardon?"

"Got her to drive so you can have a real drink, eh?" he persisted.

"I'm driving tonight, actually," I said, not enjoying the way this conversation was heading.

"Christ, mate, are you sure that's wise? I mean this stuff is a bit strong. Your original electric soup if you get my drift."

"The Murdstone's is for the lady, actually," I said trying to get away.

"Waayy-haayy!" said the barman, and winked an exaggerated wink. The sound of the band striking up loudly suddenly broke the thread and allowed me to retreat in confusion to our table.

"What were you and the barman talking about?" asked Frieda.

"He was wishing me a pleasant evening."

"That's what I like about this place," said Frieda, "they take an interest in you, find time to chat, nice that."

"Lovely," I agreed, glaring at the barman who kept looking over and raising his eyebrows. If it was my local I'd have a word with the landlord about that barman. I decided to ignore him. This band was good. They had opened with a very good arrangement of a Dankworth number I can never remember the name of, and then slid into a nice easy 'Honeysuckle Rose'. I never know whether to clap at the end of a number when I'm listening to music in a pub. Sometimes you clap wildly and not only do all the punters look at you like you had just stood up on the table and farted, but the band smile in an embarrassed sort of way like they had been playing, hoping no-one had noticed, and now that you, you fool, have clapped, the cat's out of the bag and they'll have to acknowledge the audience, who really wanted to be left alone anyway. Or alternatively, usually when you are sat right at the front and the band play a stonker of an opening number, you gauge the silence, lift your pint respectfully to your lips and find your hair being parted from behind by an ovation that Pavarotti only dreams about. The band notices, of course, and hates you for the rest of the night. No amount of sycophantic applause will mollify them, especially the drummer, and your best course of action is to leave during the second number.

This was a music pub, though, and polite ripples were the order of the day. I was fascinated by Frieda. She was really into this band. During numbers she would lean forward, her eyes wide, like a kid at a toy-shop window, tapping her nails on her glass, or maybe at a quiet bit lean back with her eyes shut, sort of letting it wash over her. Fortunately she drank her pint slowly, (or unfortunately, from the barman's point of view, on two counts), and I only had to sneak back to the bar a couple of times for a refill of L.A.

"I'm starving!" she announced as we left the pub, "I fancy an Indian."

"Have you told him, or are you keeping it a secret?" Well, it was the best I could do. She humoured me with a giggle.

"They do a nice Tandoori Tikka at the Rajah, it's just down the street."

We bought our curry and drove it home to Frieda's house. I'd never eaten Tandoori chicken tikka in bed, stark naked, with a girl who would easily spoil Madonna's evening, but I entered into the spirit of the thing that night. It's amazing where all that red sauce can get to, and when you haven't got a napkin handy......

"What on earth are you doing, Tom?" Frieda demanded from the cooker where she was preparing the first cooked breakfast I had had in years - cooked by someone else, that is.

"Licking tikka sauce off my knee, I must have missed it in the shower. Gets everywhere, doesn't it?"

"Hmm..." she blew me a kiss. What a girl! There she was, starkers except for a pinny, a perfect example of what is often described as an 'hourglass figure' and she was, at least for the moment, all mine. I tried to remember why I wanted to disappear over the oceans. It wasn't even as if I could take her with me. She really was a terrible sailor, I had as much chance of persuading Frieda to come with me across the Atlantic in a sailing boat as I had of winning the lottery, and I don't do the lottery.

"One coronary for M'sieur," she announced as she plonked the plate of bacon, eggs, sausages, tomato and fried bread down in front of me with a flourish.

"Ah, so that's what you're up to! Wangling your way into my good books and thence my last will and testament only to finish me off with a surfeit of saturated fat. Why, you hussy, you're only after my money, and all the time I thought it was my sparkling intellect and manly body you craved."

"Damn! Found me out. Oh well, there's nothing for it, I'll just have to do the honourable thing and end it all. Move over and pass the ketchup." Her plateful looked bigger than mine.

"You certainly believe in letting the punishment fit the crime."

"Shagging gives me an appetite," she said through a mouthful of bacon, "and besides, I've got a busy day in front of me!"

"Oh? What are you up to then?"

"I'm coming to help you at the yard. I'm going to help you get your boat ready."

I choked on a piece of bread.

"Are you sure that's wise?" I croaked, eyes streaming, "She is actually afloat, remember, she might move if another boat goes past."

"Don't you want me to help, Tom? I mean, if you think I'll only be in the way...."

"Frieda, look, I'm sorry, I would love you to help. God knows I need all the help I can muster. I was only concerned that you might feel, you know, a bit...." I mimed throwing up.

"I've decided it's all in my mind, Tom. I'm determined to beat this once and for all. I'd even like to come for a sail with you. Maybe not to Ireland, but just a short sail to, well, get my sea-legs."

I chewed carefully to avoid a further choking fit and tried to digest what I had just heard. Frieda sailing? Maybe I should check behind the door for a telegram from the Lottery people after all when I get home. I have to say at this point, that in my opinion, and that of most sailors I know and respect, being seasick is most definitely not all in the mind. The mind is the last place it reaches after rampaging through the entire body and then only to leave the message that death would possibly be preferable to further attempts to impersonate a human being. Seasickness is sneaky, too. It creeps up on you when you're least expecting it. I don't mean when you're walking down the street, or having a bath (thank God), no, it will hit you when you're just about to plot the last fix you could get before the visibility shuts down for the day, and you find yourself showing your bum to the helmsman, while feeding your dinner to the fishes, trying to remember the bearing of the Portland light and at the same time keeping the hand-bearing compass on it's lanyard out of the stream of vomit. Oh, yes, all in the mind. Bloody hell, Nelson got seasick, we are continually reminded, with monotonous regularity. I bet the ship's surgeon didn't tell him to pull himself together. He'd have found himself on sick-bag collecting duties before he could have said 'Kiss me Hardy'. The funny thing is, though, that all sailing nuts I know who get seasick are just as keen on sailing in all weathers as the nuts who keep their cookies firmly ensconced. Most non-sailors don't understand this. Mind you, I'm not saying that I understand it, sitting here at home in front of a word-processor, but when I'm at the helm of a well-found yacht, broad-reaching towards a favourite anchorage, be the weather fair or foul, the handicap of a chance attack of mal-de-mer is as far away from my mind as the outcome of the next episode of Eastenders. No, people are either sailing nuts or not, and either prone to seasickness or not, and the two need not necessarily go together conveniently. And you can take all the sea-sick pills you like or strap on all the fancy wrist-strap gizmos in the chandler's, but as the man said, when it strikes bad, the only cure is the shade of an oak tree. I think I'll get off this subject now, if you don't mind, I'm feeling a little odd.

"You're dreaming again, Tom!"

"Sorry, I was miles away. Are you serious about helping me with the boat? I can actually think of a dozen jobs you could do."

"Sure I'm serious, c'mon, clothes on, Captain, and point me at whatever bilge you want scuppered. Or maybe you have a mainbrace to slice?"

"Splice. The expression is 'Splice the Mainbrace', dates back to the square riggers, and I think we did that last night!"

"Did we? I didn't realise they had so much fun in these days."

I dressed reluctantly. There really was a lot to do in a short time. Willing hands to do some painting and varnishing freed more expert hands for rigging and wiring.

"You go on, Tom, I'll be there shortly. I'll just wash up and find some old clothes."

I went to where my car was parked, behind Frieda's house. It was quite convenient where she lived, out in the wilds in a fashionably converted barn. No-one ever passed, so no-one would have noticed that I spent the night with Frieda. I could do without local gossip about me and Andy's 'wife'. Anyone who noticed that my car wasn't outside my house would just think it had broken down again, but they wouldn't connect me with Frieda.

I drove straight to the yard and parked the car on the Quay next to Sligo Bay. She would soon be ready for the off, but would I?

CHAPTER 7

I was beginning to panic. The chart had to be here somewhere, my God, I must have used it recently to get us this far, why the hell wasn't it here now? And where did all these other charts come from? Sumatra?? What the hell was I doing with a chart of Sumatra? And all these others, there must have been a pile a foot thick, and not one of them showing anywhere within a thousand miles of the south coast of Ireland. I looked around the floor to see if it had slid off the chart table. I had to admit, this Indian rug was very nice. I couldn't remember putting it there, must have been Frazer, nice touch. There was a lot more room below deck than I expected, too, you could have lost a couple of lifeboats down there. I decided to go on deck to see if I could figure out where we were going. We should never have agreed to take all that deck cargo. I mean, the wire cages full of chickens were OK but the Land Rover? Hardly left room for the piano, and whose idea was that? I hardly needed to ask.

"We're going to have to tack soon Tom," said Frazer, "the wind's heading us, I can't hold her on this course."

"OK, then, ready when you are," I agreed.

"We can't until we move the deck cargo. It's getting in the way of the sails."

"I bloody knew we shouldn't have taken on so much. How are we going to move that lot?"

"Don't worry, Tom, the crew have done it loads of times."

And sure enough, dozens of little Chinese crewmen were at that very moment manhandling all the junk on deck round the front of the masts letting Sligo pass through the wind.

"Where the hell did they come from?" I asked.

"Came with the boat as far as I can tell," said Frazer, "they're no trouble and they work really hard...EASY WITH THAT PIANO!!...nearly had that over the side, then."

I had to admit, it was a lovely day for a sail. Not a cloud in the sky, a nice steady breeze driving us through a remarkably smooth sea, and, now that I noticed, tending to blow the hem of Frazer's flowered dress well above his knees.

"I wish you wouldn't wear that, Frazer," I remarked.

"Why not? No-one else will see me, I thought you were broad-minded about these things, Tom," and he started to sob quietly to himself. God, I felt embarrassed! How could I have been so insensitive? After all, I must have looked slightly ridiculous in this 'Treasure Island' get-up I appeared to be wearing although, I had to admit, this velvet coat was very warm, but the three-cornered hat kept blowing off.

"Pull over into this service area, Frazer, we can ask someone where we are...." wait a minute; this is silly, service area? Better answer the phone, it's been ringing for ages....my face hurts, and I can't move my arm. I prized my face off the desk blotter and fumbled the phone off the hook.

"Hmphimmm...?" I attempted.

"Hello, who is this? Is that you Tom? Are you all right?" Frieda sounded concerned.

"Oh, hi, Frieda, yes, it's me, you woke me up."

"Woke you up? It's three in the afternoon, Tom, and you are supposed to be at work. You need to get more sleep, at night, my lad!"

"Hmm, that would mean we would have to go to bed at six-thirty and we would miss Eastenders."

"Damn! I never thought of that. Oh well, you'll just have to get a comfier desk. Listen, Tom, the reason I phoned. It's Andy, he's coming back early. He'll be home tomorrow about dinner-time."

My blood ran momentarily sub-zero. Was this a problem? Had she been lying all along about being Andy's sister and was now going to reveal all in a fit of remorse and throw me on his mercy? Was I about to become 75 kilos of dog-meat? Was I a man or a mouse? Could I get Sligo across the Atlantic before tomorrow dinnertime? Does a heart rate of 250 beats per minute necessarily mean a man of my age is about to have a heart attack?

".....thought it would be nice if you and Frazer came round for dinner so that we could celebrate coming out of our various closets." I was going to live after all! At that moment I would have agreed to root canal surgery without benefit of as much as a whiff of Eric's bar towel.

"Oh, yes, oh my goodness, yes, that would be wonderful, oh, gosh! Yes, I would really like that..."

"All right, Tom, don't over-do it, it's only dinner. I thought we could do sukiyaki, it's Andy's favourite. Could you be a dear and pick up a couple of bottles of saki? I think they have it in Tesco's."

"Sure, no problem, and I'll bring the rest of the celebratory Champers, I think there's a bottle or two left."

"I was going to ask Frazer to bring those actually, they are his after all."

"WERE his, any booze left on my boat becomes my property...law of the sea is that, and speaking of Frazer, are you sure he wants to de-closet himself? The last time we talked about it he didn't seem too keen on the idea."

"Well it's make-your-mind-up time for Frazer, I'm afraid. Andy agreed to me seeing you before he left, and I'm buggered if I'm going to continue for very much longer skulking around the place with you just to protect Frazer's sensitivities. It's time he faced up to the world and stopped pretending to everyone that he's some sort of misogynist."

"I have a horrible feeling this isn't going to work, Frieda. I mean, Frazer's just the sort of bloke who will say 'bugger the lot of you, I'm off' and we'd never see him again."

"Oh, I don't think so, Tom, Frazer's too well established here to throw it all away. Andy will talk him round, just you wait and see."

"Well, bugger Frieda and her match-making! That's it, I'm out of here!" roared Frazer. Perhaps I should have been a little more circumspect in bringing up the subject, and intended purpose of, tomorrow's little soiree. Calling it a wife-swapping evening was, on reflection, a little insensitive.

"I'm sorry, Frazer, honest I was only joking. I thought you of all people would see the humour of the situation. Please, mate, we're buddies. We can joke about these things surely?"

"I don't find it in the least fucking funny, Tom. I told Andy that I didn't want to 'come out' like I was some fucking spring flower. I'm just not an evangelical gay. I don't even like the use of the word 'gay', for fucks sake!"

"OK, Frazer, I get the picture, calm down. Let's go along to Andy's tomorrow anyway and see if we can work this out. Frieda is obviously not prepared to carry on with their little charade for much longer. Maybe we can figure something out involving the job with Sligo, just don't go swinging your handbag around, someone we both love could get hurt."

"Yeah, yeah, Tom....you're right, of course....we can't go on like this for ever. Its time I grew up and found out just how difficult it is to be a middle-aged, balding queer in twenty first century Cornwall."

"If you can find twenty first century Cornwall, that is."

"Christ, you're right; they'll hang me as a witch!"

"I bet you most of them won't even notice. I mean, you're not obliged to wear a badge or anything."

"Well, they haven't noticed up to now, but they just might if I announced it loudly in the pub."

Frazer had been setting up his new beer-making plant in the screened-off corner of the boat-shed when I had accosted him and made him blow his cool so noisily.

"Getting anywhere with this?" I asked, to change the subject.

"Yes, I've got most of the problems licked except this alcohol business. I'm still convinced the answer lies in getting alcohol in dry powdered form. There's a process where you can encapsulate liquids in very thin-walled micro-spheres which makes it behave like a powder, but I think it's rather complicated and expensive, and the coating, of course, has to dissolve in water but not in alcohol. Tricky one, that."

"Jesus, and you accuse me of dreaming up problems!"

"These are not problems, Tom. We scientists look on them as opportunities."

"Well, let's see how you deal with the opportunities at tomorrow night's little get-together."

Frazer cuffed my head and made my ears ring.

"That's for being a smartass, and nobody loves a smartass, now do they?" Sometimes I wished he was a little bit less butch, I really did.

CHAPTER 8

"Here Frazer, catch!" I shouted, aiming a case of lager at the lad, who was at that moment striking a suitably salty pose on the deck of 'Sligo Bay'.

"Ah, to be sure, Cap'n, you're a gentleman to the core. I always say a well lubricated crew is a happy.... Jesus Christ, Tom, what is this addiction you have for Aussie beer? What's wrong with the good old English brew as drunk in vast quantities by our forefathers? It's not as if it was unavailable at the usual outlets in handy and hygienic containers, drinking public, for the delectation of. Have you bought shares in the company, or what?"

"When you're quite finished venting your spleen over MY refreshments, you'll find that there is a vast store of your favourite ale under the cabin sole. And before you head off looking for it would you mind helping me aboard with the rest of this stuff?"

"God, Tom, you really do know how to make a guy feel small. All right, treat me like your slave, I can take it, but my spirit is proud, and just remember, maybe generations from now, one of my descendants will be ordering your descendants about, and I shall laugh, LAUGH, DO YOU HEAR?"

"What are you drivelling on about, Frazer? You're about as likely to have descendants as Michelangelo's David. Let's get this boat under way before the estuary freezes over."

Within minutes Sligo's big diesel was punching us out and over the bar at the mouth of the river. I turned her into the wind and soon the sails were running to the tops of the two reassuringly stout, but still, to my traditional eyes, worryingly unstayed masts. We intended to sail to Dartmouth and back by whatever route the wind suggested when we got out to sea. It was a perfect cruising day;

clear sky, smooth sea, a modest sea breeze, our cups were running over. Would that it could ever be thus.

Now, you can call me a sentimental old romantic if you will, and I'm sure many a nautical scribe before me has already covered this ground, but I always feel that the moment you switch off the engine and harden in the sheets, when the boat surges forward under the power of wind alone, is undiluted magic. The fact that the wind so often is blowing *precisely from* the direction of your intended destination is decidedly un-magic not to say a pain in the rudder, but this is, after all, what makes us yachtsmen rather than just sailors. It is astonishing how many otherwise erudite people believe that sailing boats trundle about the oceans with the wind permanently rammed up their arses. Nothing could be further from the truth! The kind of yachts you are used to seeing about the place these days look that way precisely because they are designed to sail 'close to the wind', that is to say into or against it. Some even go best that way and are raced over vast distances of open, evil ocean by people known in sailing circles as 'nutters'. But I digress, and as the old saying goes, close is good but you get no cigar. What you get is wet, cold and knocked about. I can sympathise with those, who, in the good old days considered it to be ungentlemanly to sail too close to windward.

Another common misapprehension most people have concerns the speed of sailing boats. They are by any standard, very slow. A small boy on a bicycle could beat the socks off the average 40-footer, so you tend to take ages to cover fairly modest distances. But as the man said, it matters not how long the journey takes, but the manner in which it is executed.... or something like that. Basically, if you're in a hurry, don't go by sailing boat.

"Christ, Frazer, she isn't half hoovering along!" I was having the time of my life, and Sligo was obviously enjoying herself too.

"Whassat?" Frazer was fiddling around the chart table.

"I said she's going really well."

"Considering," said Frazer.

"Considering what?"

"Considering we're sailing north on the M5 out of Exeter. I must say the traffic is a lot lighter than I remember it was the last time I was there. Could be the wet road that's doing it."

"Is that Decca still acting up?" I groaned.

"Well either that or the tide didn't half come in last night. I thought you got it fixed after you took it out of the old Nicholson?"

"I thought I did too. Try hitting it." A loud crash was heard from the cabin. "Fuck me, Frazer, not that bloody hard, bloody hell!"

"Sorry, I dropped the Reid's into the cutlery drawer. Have you seen the corkscrew?"

"What in God's name are you going to do?"

"Open a bottle of Tesco's best Bulgarian Cabernet Sauvignon, what did you think I was going to do?"

"I thought you were trying to fix the Decca. Why did you have the Reids?" this was getting silly.

"I was going to......"

"....hit the Decca with it. Why did I ask?"

"Yes why did you ask if you already knew? It was your idea anyway." Frazer was deeply offended. "I suppose a new GPS will be a better bet really. I just like that old Decca somehow."

"What have we got to eat with that wine? I'm getting decidedly peckish."

"We have ze long French bread, we have ze Camembert, ze saucisson, and, joy upon joy, two dead tortoises."

"Look, Cathy means well Frazer. She thinks we don't eat properly and her pasties are quite nice."

"Thinks we don't eat properly? What does she imagine we do? Stuff it in our ears?"

"You know what I mean. How about heating the pasties up? I quite fancy one actually."

"Suit yourself skipper, I'll stick to the Froggie picnic food thanks."

"Couldn't do this driving down the M5." I remarked, sipping my wine, nibbling my pasty, steadying the wheel with my hip.

"True, true," agreed Frazer, "you'd never get your arse to the wheel of the Transit for a start!"

Dartmouth was as busy as ever and having fought our way through the weekend traffic and avoided being run down by the harbour ferry we found all the bases at the town pontoon well and truly loaded. We decided not to stop and headed back out to the Channel.

"But I wanted an ice-cream!" protested Frazer.

"Shut up and practice your bowline."

The wind had started to freshen from the southwest and there were angry looking clouds forming on the horizon so we started up the big Perkins diesel and motor-sailed her back home.

"I don't know about you, Tom, but I thought that was a most satisfactory day's sailing," announced Frazer over a pint in the Yacht Club later that evening.

Indeed I had to agree with his assessment. It had been a most agreeable day's sail, with no major hitches and relatively few minor ones, Sligo had romped through her first sea trial with style. True, I would have to admit defeat with the ageing Decca and get something a bit more reliable, and probably a radar set while I was about it, but in general all the bells and whistles worked and any string-pulling was rewarded with the expected results.

"Seems to me suspiciously like she's ready," I admitted. I'll get in touch with Coombs in the morning. No point in delaying any further."

"You're the boss," said Frazer," I can get some time off more or less any time so you're stuck with me whether you like it or not."

"I've got young George teed up as well. He's really keen. I reckon that he'll be a really useful pair of hands."

"Well that's it then. We're in business. Let's celebrate with another pint!"

"Not so fast my friend," I had been rather dreading this moment, "I take it that you have forgotten that we are invited to dine chez Frieda and Andy tonight?"

"Oh, bugger, no I hadn't, but I'd hoped you had. Do we really have to go?"

"No, Frazer, we don't!" I was becoming exasperated with Frazer's petulance in this business, "but I'm bloody going. Anyway, I've bought two bottles of saki to go with the sukiyaki and it's also my birthday dinner, if you want to sulk like a menstrual schoolgirl and stay away that's fine with me!"

"Sorry! Sorry, Tom. I'll be there. I know when I'm beaten. Just keep me away from the sauce, I'm likely to get totally blitzed and say the wrong thing."

"I reckon it's up to Andy to do the running tonight. Frieda and I are more or less sorted out and it's him who wants to change your status. Oh, by the way, do you mind if I bring along the rest of the bubbly you bought for the launching?"

"There's some left?"

"A couple of bottles I think. I stuck them in the bilge."

"No, I don't mind," Frazer was sounding gloomier by the minute. This was going to be a fun evening. Spot of food-poisoning would round it off nicely.

"OK, we're due there in half an hour. Don't be late. And Frazer?"

"What?"

"Shave!"

"Yes, mother."

"So there I was, lashed to the wheel, fighting her every inch of the way out through the pounding surf, the wind howling in the rigging...."

"Frazer, there was hardly a breath!" he seemed to be in a better mood now that we had got to Frieda's so I didn't want to be too heavy on the criticism.

"Hardly a breath? Listen to him, Frieda, there speaks a true sailor, snatches his frail craft from the very jaws of death and destruction, yea, from the wrath of mother nature at her most wrathful and shrugs it off with a snap of his fingers! He was just the same when we had to operate on his gangrenous foot without so much as a bullet to bite on....."

"What?! Tom, he is joking...." Frieda was looking a bit green.

"Of course he is, Frieda, I bit down on the very bullet we took out of my foot only a week previously."

"Stop it you two!" Andy was giggling in his 'wine-cellar', a cupboard under the stair, "I nearly dropped the Burgundy, I've been looking forward to this Hermitage for years."

"OK," said Frazer, "come on Frieda, I'm sure there are a few things you need my help with in the kitchen."

Andy emerged with the wine and four good roomy glasses.

"We'll let that little beauty breathe for a minute or two, you'll like this one, Tom, I've been saving it for a special occasion."

I let that remark pass for the moment.

"How was Saudi?" I asked.

"Bloody, as usual," said Andy going over to the hi-fi with a determination that should have told me to drop the subject, "what kind of music do you fancy?"

"Oh, I don't mind, nothing too heavy."

"OK, how about some George Benson, he's Frieda's favourite."

"Fine. So...what did you get up to out there?"

"Oh, this and that, you know."

"No, I don't know, actually, but if you want me to mind my own bloody business I won't be in the least offended, really, I'll sob a bit for a while, maybe toy with my dinner, but I'll understand."

"Oh, bugger it, Tom, I'm sorry, it's just habit. As you probably know, I've got military connections still and almost everything I do has some level of classification so it's easier not to discuss it at all. You're privileged. Most people get my standard cover story which consists of a long rambling, and very boring description of research into hydroponic crop cultivation. Very few people ask for further details, I assure you."

"I'm sorry, too, Andy, I wasn't prying, just putting off discussing what we all know this evening is about."

"What, your birthday? Why, are you some special age or something?"

"No, not particularly, I don't mean that." Andy was looking blank and I was beginning to feel foolish. Surely she wouldn't have arranged this evening with all its planned revelations without Andy's agreement. What if...! No, I'd more or less reassured myself on that score, and Frazer had corroborated the story too.

"Ah... Frieda was talking to me the other day about learning to sail, actually," I said, changing tack," she seems quite keen."

"Yes? I thought she hated boats. Just takes Frazer to do one of his Captain Ahab impressions and she needs a Kwell. Are you sure?"

What was going on? I tried something different.

"Frazer was saying to me how you and he were finding a lot in common these days, common interests...." Andy was looking puzzled again. What in God's name was going wrong? Could this be the ultimate wind-up? If it was, I was really up shit creek, cuckolding Andy and suggesting he was having a homosexual relationship could, as the Government warning would say, endanger my health.

"What's been happening while I've been away, for goodness sake? I must say, you're all behaving a bit oddly. Is there something you should be telling me, Tom?"

"....." my voice fired a blank as I heard a stifled guffaw from behind me. I spun round to find Frazer and Frieda in stitches, holding one another up. The penny dropped.

"You bastards! I was just about shitting myself there!" I checked Andy, just to be sure, and he was grinning broadly, "I really thought my moment had come! Bloody hell, don't ever do that to me again." I collapsed into an armchair, "I need a fucking drink!"

"Champers do?" asked Frazer, popping a cork extravagantly and spraying the entire room.

"Steady, Frazer, you're not Lewis Hamilton, for goodness sake, don't waste the wine!" Andy was following the jet with his glass.

"Shit! I really had picked out a window, then. I reckoned I was leaving."

"Sorry, Tom, it wasn't planned, if that makes it any easier for you. We couldn't resist it."

"Well, Frieda, you'll just have to make it up to me somehow. I'm sure you'll think of something."

"I'm not sure I like you speaking to my wife in that way, Tom Morton," said Andy.

"Cut it out Andy, my bloody heart has had enough for one night. How do you feel about me talking that way to your sister?"

"I suppose I should be equally outraged, but she's a big girl now, I'm sure she'll deal with you herself as she sees fit. Fuck me, if she hadn't finally nailed you this week, I reckon I'd have had to take her to the vet to get sorted. She's been driving me nuts! Now how's the food? I'm starving!"

"The starter is on the table, gentlemen."

"What are we waiting for, then," said Andy leading the way.

The table was set out Japanese-Style complete with chop-sticks, bowls, and little earthenware flasks of warm saki. Andy plonked his bottle of Hermitage down in the middle of it all.

"Andrew!" scolded Frieda, "we're having saki! It's Japanese food tonight!"

"Andrew??" Frazer and I mouthed at one another.

"Listen, Frieda, you drink what you want to, but I'm having this Hermitage before it dies on us. It'll go well with the dried beef starter, anyway."

During this exchange, Frazer and I had our Burgundy glasses held out towards the bottle Andy was brandishing, huffing Frieda even more.

"Come on, Frieda," I said, "we'll demolish this bottle before we start the sukiyaki. Let's drink a toast."

Frieda filled her glass.

"To us! Whoever we are!" I proposed.

"To us!" they chorused. Several more toasts followed starting with 'Sligo Bay' and followed by progressively more silly ones throughout the starter including Morecambe Bay (Frazer), Stugeron (Frieda) and Osama bin Laden's Piles (Andy). The evening was shaping up well.

68

As the meal progressed, however, it became increasingly obvious that Frazer's sudden buoyancy had been born of a determination to avoid the intended topic of the evening at all costs. He took the proceedings by the scruff of the neck and verbally frog-marched us all through a riot of anecdotes, dirty jokes and non-stop Frazerisms until it became hazardous even to try to place food into one's mouth for fear of losing it to the four corners of the room or choking. Soon, however the others realised what he was up to and his efforts, while doubling and re-doubling, fell on increasingly stony ground. Midnight came and went.

"Charades!" cried Frazer, "we haven't played charades for ages! I'll go first!"

"For God's sake, Frazer, we give in," said Andy, "no-one wants to play fucking charades."

"Trivial Pursuit?"

"No!"

"Monopoly, then!"

"No, Frazer, nothing! We don't want to play anything, thank you. I know that you've been furiously avoiding the subject all evening, but we must decide on some course of action for all of us and we must decide soon!" Andy had finally silenced Frazer by the simple expedient of pinning him to the settee by the shoulders and talking to him from a distance of less than a millimetre. Frieda and I watched with interest.

"Ohhh! You can be so masterful sometimes Andrew!" lisped Frazer. He wasn't smiling. The fun was over. Andy turned on his heel and left the room with a muttered curse.

"Go after him, Frazer, he's really upset," said Frieda.

"No, Frieda, we're both too pissed for a serious discussion. Tomorrow, I promise we'll sort it out tomorrow."

"Are you sure he'll want to talk to you tomorrow, Frazer?" I asked, "he seems pretty pissed off with you."

"Don't be daft, Tom, we've had worse fall-outs than this and survived intact. He'll be fine."

"Well I'm so fucking relieved to hear that, Frazer!" Frieda spat, "you've no idea how deliriously happy that makes me! God forbid that there should be any trouble between you and precious Andy. Well I'm sick to death bending over backwards to protect the finer feelings of a couple of pathetic old closet queers. I went to a lot of trouble over this evening. I really thought you two would come to your senses and make a decision. Obviously I was wrong. Well bugger the both of you, and I won't ask you to pardon that expression. Tom, is there a spare bed or a couch at your house I can have tonight? I've had it with this set-up!"

"Yes, sure, Frieda, but aren't you over-reacting a little? I mean we've all had rather a lot to drink. I'm sure Frazer means it when he says he'll sort it out tomorrow."

"Sure he does. Just like he always means it when he says he'll sort it out tomorrow. Tomorrow never comes. Tom, you haven't lived with this for years! The two of them have promised to sort themselves out over and over again and each time they let me down at the last minute. Well, this time Andy Prentice's wife is leaving him. She's had enough! The strain of covering up her husband's homosexuality has finally become too much. And don't worry, Tom, I'm not palming myself off on you, I just want somewhere to stay the night. I'll look for a flat in the morning."

"Jesus!" said Frazer. He had sat quietly, looking suitably sheepish throughout Frieda's peroration. He now stood up rather shakily. "I'll go and find Andy. I think tomorrow just arrived," and he slunk out of the room. Frieda collapsed into my arms like a rag-doll.

"Take me home, Tom, and fuck my brains out!"

"Get your bag. I assume it's packed?"

"What do you think?"

"Poor Frazer," I conceded, "he never stood a chance."

CHAPTER 9

If the man who now stood before me had not just announced very loudly that he was Dawson from HM Revenue and Customs I would probably have guessed it in two. My first guess would have been hit man for the Social Services Department. Mr Dawson was a grey man who had a vaguely constabulary look about him which told me immediately that he hadn't come to swap sailing anecdotes.

He also appeared to be suffering from acute indigestion.

"I'd like to speak to Mr Thomas Morton. "He demanded between suppressed burps. He was clutching his stomach with one hand and steadying himself on a chair-back with the other.

"You're speaking to him....are you all right? Would you like a Setlers or something?"

"Yes please, if you have one, I've just had the most disgusting pie and pint at that so-called yacht club down the road. I think it's time we got the weights and measures boys to pay that bloody barman a visit. I'm sure he's putting something in the beer....not water, mind you, that would improve it."

"Yes, well, Eric's beer has always been like that I'm afraid. I'd worry more about the contents of the pie, if I were you."

"Are you serious?" burped Dawson. He looked stricken.

"No, only joking, he gets them from the supermarket, anyway, what can I do for you?" I decided to steer the conversation away from Mr Dawson's digestion.

"Eh? Oh yes. I understand that you are the owner of a small cargo vessel called..." he consulted a grossly over-loaded Filofax, "....Sponge Bag?"

"Sligo Bay, actually," I corrected as dryly as I dared, "she's a sail-trader, registered in Plymouth. What about her?"

John Paton

"Sligo Bay," he mouthed, scoring out heavily in his book, "bloody dyslexic secretary. Sponge Bag! Thought it was a funny name at the time. Mind you I've heard dafter ones. I saw a yacht the other day which appeared to be called 'Magical Mr Mestopheles' for God's sake! Imagine yelling that lot over the VHF in an emergency. Bloody boat would have fish measuring it for curtains before you got half way through." He looked at me blankly, obviously waiting for some sort of reaction. I beamed back expectantly. "What was I saying a minute ago?" he demanded.

"My boat, Sligo Bay."

"Oh yes. The small cargo vessel. I gather you have been hired to ship a small quantity of beer from Eire to UK for a company called..." another quick look at the Filofax, "...Bandark International?"

"Yes, I think that's what they're called. It's all kosher, I checked. All the bumf is as clean as a Blue Peter script."

"Oh, yes, that's all fine. We're not worried about the beer anyway. It's the boxes the bottles will be packed in that interest us."

"The boxes?" Surely there wasn't a new rule about importing illicit cardboard from abroad or some such nonsense. I was puzzled.

"Special heavy-duty, tri-wall pack compartmentalised cases, made in the USA to be precise," he recited.

"I don't doubt it for one minute," I said, "but surely you can use whatever boxes you like, within reason?"

"Normally, yes," he replied trying hard to look enigmatic, "but in this case bottles are not all that these boxes will contain."

"I'm sorry, you've lost me. What else would you want to put in a beer crate?"

"Designer drugs. In the cardboard. A new one to us but we reckon a street value of a couple of grand in every box. Bloody sight more than the beer's worth."

"Bloody hell!" I was stunned, "but how did you find out? Have they done this before?"

"As far as we know they've done it a couple of times. Always a small cargo vessel, off the beaten track, like. Stumbled on it purely by accident. One of the boys is a bit of a CAMRA nut, you know the game, spends his week-ends travelling to Wanking-on-the-Tit to sample the latest offering from the Humpover brewery. Usually called 'Old Indigestible' or some bloody thing, then comes back quoting specific bloody gravities and ph values, never mind what the muck tastes like or how many pints you can down before becoming terminally ratted. Boring little git really. Not as bad as Smithy, though. He's a bloody train spotter! Now that's boring, particularly nowadays with all these bloody diesels and electric trains. In my young day there were still big bloody steam..." I was trying to look interested, but an unguarded glance at my wrist-watch caught Dawson's attention. He stopped in mid-flood. "..what was I talking about?"

"I think it was something to do with discovering the drugs," I offered. I realised I was locked into this conversation now and decided to abandon the plans I had to do some paperwork in the relative peace of my office. It was Sunday morning, after all.

"Drugs? Oh yes, the beer. Anyway, Charlie decided he had to taste this new beer, Bantry Bitter they were calling it, so he shot off to look for someone selling it. Well, as it turned out he was buggered if he could find it anywhere. So we decided to look a bit closer, on the quiet, like, and discovered that the stuff was going into a warehouse in Bristol and wasn't coming out. Not in bottles anyhow. Bloody drains smelt great, though! And the bottle-banks for miles around were really busy." Dawson was warming to his subject and had, somewhat high-handedly I thought, pulled up a coil of rope for a foot-rest.

"Coffee?" I offered.

"Love one! Milk, two sugars. So then some bright spark noticed that while they seemed to be junking the bottles and the beer, no-one had ever seen an empty box. And that led to the question of why they weren't using crates like everyone else? Well, finally we got lucky and found a bit of box caught up on the fork-lift they were using. We passed it to the lab boys and they came up with the aforementioned dizzy-dust."

"Dizzy-dust?"

"Well, we call it that. Actually it's a new one on us. Lab boys say it has an effect similar to alcohol when you dissolve it in drinks but much stronger and with no hangover. A teaspoonful in a gallon of water gives a drink more potent than neat scotch but it's completely tasteless."

"Don't see the point, myself."

"Yes, well, neither do I actually, but it's what the kids seem to want, these days."

It was beginning to dawn on me that a certain friend of mine might be quite excited by the information I was being made privy to. The kettle boiled and I made a couple of mugs of coffee.

"So I take it that you want me to help you to bring these felons to book?"

"That was the general idea." His smile became ingratiating to the point of nausea.

"Not on your life. If you think that I'm going to get mixed up with drug-traffickers and their like you must have a screw loose. These guys don't just nick your pocket-money when you upset them, you know. I've watched Miami Vice."

The smile fell off his face and slid to the floor.

"OK, squire, I will start by appealing to your sense of public duty. You must realise the misery and hardship these people cause. They prey on impressionable youngsters who should be spending their hard-earned cash on excisable liquor and getting ratted in the traditional manner. I will continue by assuring you that there will be no danger to your good self or crew. One of our best under-cover agents will accompany you every inch of the way. He will, incidentally be armed."

"Reassuring, but the answer is still no."

"In addition I must point out that those contributing to the apprehension of the suppliers are in line for a reward of no less than ten thousand pounds."

"That's playing dirty."

"It's a dirty game. Are you in or out?"

"Do I get to meet the body-guard before I give my final answer?"

"You have already met him."

"I have? Who?"

"Me."

"Oh."

"Well?"

"I'll think about it."

"Oh, thank you for your resounding vote of fucking confidence, I must say! Listen, mate, I'm not the turkey that you obviously think I am. I've seen a lot of action in my time!" From a safe distance, no doubt, I thought.

"With respect, you're not exactly Mel Gibson. You look a bit out of shape to me."

"Is that so? Care to try your hand at a bit of unarmed combat?

You're looking at a man who competes in the London Marathon every year! When did you last run more than twenty miles?"

"OK, OK, I believe you; I still want to think about it though. I have to consult my crew. They'll be involved in it too, you know. I can't go making decisions like that on their behalf, now can I?"

"No, I suppose that's true enough. But you tell them that they'll be quite safe. They have the word of....ah, my word on that!"

"Yes...by the way, what is your first name? I can't go on calling you Mr Dawson if you're coming on a sea voyage with us; I mean you'll have to seem like one of the crew."

"It's Leslie, actually," he grudgingly offered.

"Leslie? Les?? Les Dawson?! You're kidding!"

"Look it's not my fault! Presumably he wasn't famous when my parents Christened me. There must be plenty of Les Dawsons in the world."

"Yes, I'm sorry, I wasn't really taking the piss; it's just that you're about as unlike the late great Les Dawson as you could possibly be. Do you prefer Les or Leslie?"

"I prefer Les, actually. Leslie's a bit poncy and that's worse than being called Les Dawson."

"Yes, I see what you mean, although I don't think this particular crew will mind too much one way or the other."

"Oh? Why?"

"Never mind, silly remark, really."

"OK, sorry I was a bit shirty; it's just that I get fed up with all the remarks sometimes."

"No problem. Sorry I was rude. Tell you what, give me a couple of days to talk it over with the others and we'll give you an answer. Let's meet here on Tuesday night at eight. If we decide to go for it we'll all be here."

"Fair enough, Tom, Tuesday at eight it is, and he turned to leave. He paused as he opened the door, "Oh, by the way, Tom, I assume I need hardly remind you that this conversation must not be repeated to anyone except those who will actually be involved. I'd hate to blow the operation at this stage," his voice held a menacing edge I had failed to notice before. Perhaps Mr Dawson was right. Maybe he wasn't the turkey I had made up my mind he was.

"So there you have it," I said, "please don't feel in any way embarrassed about withdrawing your offer to crew for me. The whole thing sounds a bit bloody dangerous to me, despite what Dawson says. If I go it'll be to collect the reward money and run."

I had just given Frazer a full resume of my earlier conversation with Dawson. I had found him in his little plastic tent at the back of the boat-shed working on his apparatus. I was anticipating a swift and blunt refusal.

"Not go? Are you kidding? I wouldn't miss this for all the cakes in Pontefract! This is more like it, mate! A bit of real excitement for a change. And that stuff they're smuggling! It's exactly what I'm after! Eu-bloody-reka!!"

"I thought you'd have kicked it into touch! You're not normally so keen to help the law with its enquiries."

"No, well not normally, but this is different, isn't it? I mean, this is adventure on the high seas! This is 'Mission Impossible'...'You have one day to decide whether to accept this mission, this tape will self-destruct in ten seconds...' whooosh!" and a box of filter-papers self-destructed all over the floor.

"Look, Frazer, I don't think you quite realise the gravity of the situation. This guy Dawson carries a gun, loaded, I'm sure with real bullets. The baddies are real baddies who have done this before and are probably quite good at smelling rats and disposing of them."

"Don't be so melodramatic, Tom. You've been watching too much Miami Vice. I bet you a pound to a pinch of shit that the minute they twig that they've been rumbled they'll vanish like Aberdonians on flag-day. These people only mix it if they're cornered, and I can give you my solemn word, I ain't gonna corner 'em."

"Yes, I suppose you're right. We can't take young George, though."

"Oh, Christ no! That's for sure. Poor kid's going to be really disappointed. He was really looking forward to this trip. He's been boasting about it to all his mates ever since you asked him. I don't fancy being the one to break the news to him. I suspect he'll ask to have his legs broken to avoid losing his 'cred'. What are you going to use as an excuse? You can't tell him about the drugs and Dawson, can you?"

"We could just slip out of harbour at night without him and when we got back we could say that we thought he was on board asleep and didn't realise we had left him behind until we were well off-shore and it was too late to turn back?"

"And he'd believe that?"

"No, I don't suppose he would, really. I suppose we could say that this guy Dawson from the brewer's insists on coming to supervise the loading. There are only three bunks, after all."

"It'll have to do, although knowing George he'll offer to stand continuous watch or sleep on deck or something."

"Well, we can spin some cock-and-bull story about DoT approval of crew numbers, or maybe..... Oh, fuck it Frazer, he can't come!"

"I know, I know, I'm not arguing, I'm just saying I don't fancy being the one to tell him, that's all."

"Yes, Frazer, you've made your point! I'll tell him! The buck stops here!"

"You're the skipper, Tom."

"Yes, I'm the skipper, and just you remember you said that when I ask you politely to unblock the Lavac!"

"There's no need to pull rank on me, Tom. We've sailed together often enough to know the score."

"Oh, sure! I suppose laying odds with the rest of the crew on our landfall being in the right country is showing respect to the skipper?"

"Oh, don't dredge that one up again, Tom, it was a joke..."

"I saw you take the money, Frazer! It's very embarrassing to have your crew pass money surreptitiously to your first mate while sniggering behind your back. I'll never be able to show my face in that bar again."

"Don't be so sensitive, Tom. Anyway, you got the right country, didn't you? And all these little Spanish harbours look the same during the day..."

"OK, OK, drop the subject! I'm sorry I started it! So you're coming along then?"

"You'd have to fight me off with a mop, mate!" said Frazer, still chuckling at the memory of my discomfiture at landing in Spain on my first sail as skipper....two hundred miles away from where I was sure I was. I even (God, will I ever live it down) argued with the harbourmaster about where we were! Well, at least we hit Spain. Another fifty miles further west and we wouldn't have stopped until we hit Africa! No, I would have realised, wouldn't I? Well, wouldn't I?? Oh thank you very much! Whose side are you on anyway?

"What about Coombs?"

"What about him?"

"Well," said Frazer, "do we assume that he's a baddie and watch what we say to him like a hawk, or do we assume he is merely an innocent shipping agent...."

"...and still watch what we say to him like a hawk. It doesn't matter what side he's on, Frazer. Dawson said tell no-one except those going along. And that includes girlfriends, boyfriends, lovers and ex-wives, I assume."

"You don't need to knock it home with a lump-hammer, Tom, my lips are sealed. Mind you, I can't help thinking that Andy'd be no great handicap if he came along."

"Forget it Frazer, the last thing we need is you and Andy doing your George and Mildred act in the middle of all this mess. I don't think Dawson would see the joke."

"Yes, well, maybe you're right. Anyway Andy doesn't know a mainsheet from a wet noodle. He'd be useful in a ruck, but he'd be strictly deck cargo the rest of the time."

"Give the Chinamen something to do, at least," I mused.

"Eh? What Chinamen?"

"Oh, nothing, just a dream I had."

Frazer gave me a pitying look.

"About Chinamen?"

"Well, it was actually about this trip, but there were Chinamen in it, and...."

"No more, please Tom. I'm sure Freud would find this fascinating, but I could live without these insights into your tortured psyche. I'll never forget the night you woke me, and everyone else in St Peter Port Harbour screaming 'Aargh! Not the bran flakes! Please not the bran flakes!!' I had to practically smother you with a pillow to shut you up. The people in the next boat didn't half give us some funny looks next morning."

"Yes I remember that. Don't know what that was all about. I just have very vivid dreams. I can't help it. At least I don't sleep-walk. That could be a bit dodgy on a boat."

"I once met a yachtsman who did," said Frazer, "had to sleep wearing a life-jacket always. Tried sleeping in a harness but nearly strangled himself one night."

"Bloody hell, did he ever actually go over the side in his sleep?"

"Only once. Landed in the next boat's tender. Put his foot through the bottom and sank it. Broke his ankle too. They had a hell of a time getting him out of the water with his foot caught in the dinghy. They finally had to call out the inshore lifeboat and they tied flotation bags to the whole mess and towed him to the slip where they could cut him free and get him to a hospital. Poor bastard was half-dead of shock and exposure by the time they got him there. Swears to this day he can't remember a thing about it."

"Don't suppose he was too keen to go sailing again after that."

"That's the funny thing. He's as keen as ever, but he never sleepwalks now. Cured him completely that did. Skippers one of these sail-training ships now. Nice bloke."

"I'm afraid something like that would put me off a bit. Anyway, you're still on for the trip, then? We've to confirm with Dawson on Tuesday night."

"Yeah! Sure. Count me in skipper. I've promised myself this sail. I'm not going to let some drug-pushers do me out of it. Fancy a pint?"

"Er..." I eyed Frazer's gurgling equipment with some trepidation.

"Not this stuff you silly sod, it's not ready yet. No I mean at the club. Should still be open." Frazer took off his lab-coat and hung it on a nail.

"I think your stuff half-made might taste better than the stuff at the club. Let's go to the 'Nelson' and we can get something to eat as well. I'm starving."

CHAPTER 10

"He'll be terribly disappointed, Tom. I'll tell him tonight, but I do feel it would be better if you told him yourself. I'm not sure I could explain it as well as you." Cathy had listened patiently to my long-winded explanation of why George could no longer come with us to Ireland. It wasn't that she didn't believe me; Cath believed every word most people told her, but even she was having difficulty with the flimsiness of the various excuses I was cobbling together.

"I know what you are saying, Cath, but Frazer felt that he might accept it better coming from you. I mean, if I told him he would start trying to persuade me to change my mind and you know what a softy I am, and there's no way we can take him along this time, believe me Cath, just no way."

Cath looked dubious. Even she could see that I was chickening out of facing George. What are secretaries for after all? I had a lot to do and Cath would see George tonight at home. I was sure he wouldn't have time to trail all the way down here so that I could tell him myself. No, I wasn't chickening out, I was delegating.

"Hi, Mr Morton, how do you like my new set of oilies? I just got them today. They'll be ideal for the trip, won't they?"

Cath left the office quietly as George pirouetted in front of my desk in a brand new set of obviously expensive oilskins. What the hell was he doing here today? He should have been at school, or something, shouldn't he? I'd need to tell him myself now. Oh, God, look at him, he was doing up the storm cuffs and pulling up the hood.

"Bit, ah, overdressed for the weather, eh George? Ha, ha..." I wasn't making a very good start.

"Yes, well, I'm only wearing them to let you see them, you

know, to make sure they'll do. Cath gave me the money, Mr Morton, and I got them at the chandler's this morning. What do you think, then?" He was beginning to go very red in the face and his feet were beginning to slide off his flip-flops.

"Absolutely perfect, George, really! Wish I had a set as good as these myself. You look after them, now, and they'll last you a long time," especially if you never get to use them in anger, I thought to myself, ruefully, "now take them off, son, before you die of heat exhaustion. I've got something to talk to you about."

George fought his way out of the oilies and pulled up a chair in front of my desk. Why on earth did he have to lean forward all wide-eyed and alert like that? This would be much easier if he would be laid-back, bored and cool like any normal teenager. Had the lad no pride?

"Is it about the trip, Mr Morton?" he asked, brightly.

"Yes, actually, George, it's about the trip. I'm afraid I've got some bad news for you. It won't be possible for you to, ah, on this particular occasion, ah, as they say, come. Actually. Sorry." I smiled weakly. George deflated like a punctured Lilo. He blinked once and looked out of the window.

"Oh."

"Look, I'm really sorry, George. It's out of my hands. DoT regulations and insurance conditions and stuff, you do understand, don't you?"

"Yup," he gathered up his new oilies in a loose bundle and headed for the door.

"Look, George, I promise you can come on the next trip, really. You're not upset are you?"

"No, it's OK, really. I'll see you then Mr Morton, 'bye."

I could hear Cath calling after him as he went out but with no success. Now I was for it. Not that Cath would dream of saying anything to me in any way critical, but I would get the 'treatment'. Oh, well, it would all come out in the wash eventually. The sooner this shambles was over and done with the better. Cath brought in my morning coffee. Yes, the treatment had started. At least an inch of freeboard in my second favourite mug (the one with the chip right in the noshing zone), and slightly too much sugar.

"Thanks, Cath."

Typetty, typetty, typetty. Oh well...

John Paton

Frieda was no more understanding when I told her about the change of crew that evening over dinner.

"I'm not surprised the poor lad was disappointed. Getting him all tweaked up, encouraging him to buy new kit and everything and then letting him down at the last minute like that."

"Look, I didn't encourage him to buy new kit. Cathy gave him the money. I thought he would maybe borrow a set of oilies or something. Last time he came out in a boat with me he was wearing a pair of fishing waders and a Barbour jacket."

"Yes, and knowing you and your cronies, he got a rough ride because of it."

"Certainly not. Anyway he has to learn to take a bit of friendly banter now and then. My only complaint was about the mud still sticking to the waders. Made a bit of a mess of the cockpit they did."

"Well I still don't see why he can't go with you. There's plenty of room in the cabin. He doesn't need a proper bunk."

"Look, Frieda, if I tell you something about this trip will you promise faithfully not to repeat it to a living soul until I get back?"

"Tom, you don't need to be so serious, who would I tell?"

"Promise!"

"All right, all right, I promise. What's the big secret?"

"We are involved with the customs people trying to catch drug smugglers."

She gave me a 'Frieda' look.

"Oh, come on, Tom, you don't really expect me to believe a story like that, do you? You don't need to make up silly excuses for me. I don't care whether you take George or not, I just thought it was a bit of a shame, that's all. Drug smugglers, indeed!"

"It's true! Les Dawson was in my office yesterday and he asked me to help in the investigation."

"Les Dawson was in your office?" She had been about to top up my wine glass but she quite deliberately stopped and corked the bottle.

"That's the customs man's name, really, Les Dawson. I thought it was funny too. He says he's fed up with people laughing at him but it's better than being gay."

"Tom, if you'll pardon my saying so, you're not making a lot of sense. Since when was Les Dawson ever gay?"

"He wasn't. I didn't say he was...did I?"

82

"I think you'd better start again from the beginning. I feel like I walked in half way through the movie."

"OK, but can I have some more wine, please?"

She poured me some wine and I told her the whole story. She was very quiet when I finished and sipped her wine, looking at me over the edge of her glass in a very serious non-Frieda sort of way. There was a long pause before she spoke again.

"Oh, fuck me. Of course you must go, Tom, and I see now why George can't. If there is one form of low-life I honestly believe should be eradicated it's drug-dealers. I'm terrified and I wish to God it wasn't you and Frazer who got involved but choice doesn't come into it in this case. If I was religious I'd pray for you."

"I must say, I'm slightly surprised by your reaction, Frieda. I honestly thought you'd have a fit and beg me not to go. I wasn't expecting a blessing."

"My heart is screaming for you not to go, Tom, believe me, but I have good reason to want these people removed from the face of the earth."

"I hardly dare ask what that reason might be."

"Well, since it's swearing to secrecy time, it can be your turn now." She slid back the sleeve of her jumper and held the inside of her forearm very close to my face.

"What?" I was beginning to shake inside. What was she telling me? What had I to look at? I looked into her eyes where tears were now welling.

"D-do you see these marks on my arms? Look, fuck it, Tom, if you have never seen them before, and I have no reason to believe you have, you are looking at old needle tracks. Veins damaged by having stuff injected into them that never should have been injected into them," there was a cold rage in her voice I had never heard in anyone's voice before. The tears were now coursing down her face. I couldn't see anything. My own eyes were full. My brain raged at what she was telling me. I never knew a drug-addict before. Stinking junkies! Deserved all they got, didn't they! Not the sort of people I would get involved with.

"Aren't you going to ask me how? Why?" I wanted to but I couldn't speak. I shook my head in misery. "No, I don't blame you. Don't want to know anyway. Not a funny story. Important thing is I survived with the help of some very special people. And before you ask, I'm not HIV positive, so you're all right." I looked up to protest at this remark, but still could not find my voice. If a drug-dealer had walked into the room at that point I swear I would have torn him limb from limb with my bare hands. I stood up and went to her. We clung together for an age. I felt totally wrung out. I also realised I loved this girl with a passion I had never realised was possible. A cold fury grew inside me. I would make sure this trip was a success if it killed me. I had a mission. I was a crusader.

"One day you can tell me all about it, my darling," I said when my voice finally returned, "but not tonight."

"No, Tom, not tonight," she agreed.

I went straight to the office from Frieda's on Tuesday morning. My head was still swimming from the effects of the emotional energy that had been flying around the night before. So many pages of the well-thumbed rule-book of my life had been torn out and tossed away in the last few weeks with whole new chapters added that I felt positively disoriented in the most familiar surroundings. I know I got through that day, Cathy was still distinctly cool, I do remember that, but I worked mechanically, my mind re-running the events of last night and coming up with all the un-asked questions it had dared not even contemplate then. How had it all happened? When? Where? How did she kick it? Why had I not noticed her arms before? Who were the special people who helped her? Who was this girl I knew as Frieda Prentice?

"Mind if I come in, Tom?" Frazer's cheery face appeared round the door.

"No, of course not, come in Frazer, I'll get Cathy to rustle up some coffee. Cathy!"

"I think she's probably gone home, Tom, I'll get it, shall I?"

"Gone home? I knew she wasn't talking to me but I didn't realise she'd buggered off without a by-your-leave." This wasn't like Cathy at all, I thought.

"Well, it is seven o'clock, Tom, you can't expect her to work the hours you put in, mate. She does have her mum to look after."

"Seven o'clock? You're kidding!" I checked my watch. He was right. I had worked right through the day without a break. What was happening to me? My stomach at least should have protested at the usual three-hour intervals. Had I eaten? I honestly couldn't remember. "What are you doing here, anyway?"

"I came for our meeting with Dawson at eight. Thought it might be a good idea to come a little bit early to talk over any last minute points."

"Oh, yes, Dawson's coming for an answer tonight, isn't he?"

"You're still in favour of going through with it then?"

"You bet your arse I am, mate. It's time ordinary people like you and me made an effort to put these filthy bastards behind bars where they belong."

Frazer paused mid-pour of the kettle.

"Wow! Bit strong coming from you, Tom. I thought you were in it for the reward money."

"Not me mate. That can go to charity, for all I care. You're looking at a very committed guy, for a change."

"Ah, Tom, may I ask what brought about this miraculous transformation? You haven't been following signposts which say 'Damascus 10 kilometres' by any chance?"

"Damascus? No, er, I was thinking about all the poor sods who have been victims of these drug-dealers and just felt it was time I made, you know, an effort."

"Oh dear.... You, ah, didn't, by any chance, mention to a certain mutual female friend that you were involved with illegal substances, maybe, in the heat of the moment, perhaps?"

"No! Of course not! It's a secret. What do you mean?"

"Oh, nothing. I just felt that an incautious remark on the subject of drugs to a certain person we both love dearly may have precipitated a reaction not entirely to be expected."

Frazer put the kettle down carefully and gave me a knowing stare.

"You're talking about Frieda, aren't you?"

"I might be."

"And drugs."

"Could be."

"She said it was a secret, Frazer."

"Better not mention it then, eh?"

"No, best not. You know all about it, though, don't you?"

"Yes, Tom, and I suspect you don't, so I'll let Frieda give you the whole story or not in her own good time. OK?"

"Yes, but Frazer....." he held his hands up as if in surrender and finished making the coffee. I realised that this line of conversation had come to an end. As he rightly said, Frieda would no doubt tell me what she wanted me to know when she was ready. All I needed to know was that she was all right now. I had an answer to one of my questions, though. One of her 'special people' was busy making coffee for us both.

Dawson was five minutes late and rather out of breath.

"Sorry chaps...got held up...oh, let me catch my breath."

"OK, Les, pull up a seat, no hurry. This is Frazer, he'll be the third crew member," Frazer offered a paw.

"Oh, right, pleased to meet you Frazer," Dawson shook hands warmly," I take it that you've decided to help us, from what you just said?"

"Absolutely, Les, you are definitely on, all systems go etcetera. Let's go out there and get the bastards."

"Excuse me, Tom, I appreciate your enthusiasm and all that, bit of a change from Sunday, I must say, but you won't be doing any bastard-getting on this trip if I can help it. Your job will be boat-sailing and Les-disguising, as a yachtsman, that is, not an easy task, I'll grant you. This isn't going to be a commando raid, just a nice, clean, successful investigation...I hope. What brought on the sudden enthusiasm, may I ask?"

"Tom's been shown the light, ah, Les. May I call you Les?" Frazer was being polite. Not a pretty sight.

"Yes, Les is fine, Frazer, I assume you are quite happy about what we're trying to do?"

"Dead keen, mate, you might say I've got a vested interest in this."

"Oh, involved with the drug problem are you?"

"I, ah, have been, yes, years ago, but that's not what I meant. It's the beer I'm interested in really."

"I wouldn't get too worked up about it mate. You won't be getting as much as a sniff of it, not that it's any great shakes anyway as far as I can gather. No, all we do this trip is go over there and collect the stuff, I'll do a bit of snooping of course, bring it back and follow it all the way. We want to get as many of the gang as possible, from the bottom to the top, and it has to be done all of a sudden, like, without them twigging we're on to them. It's like a cancer. You've got to get it all or the little bit that's left will grow again and we're back where we started. So no bloody heroics whatever happens, got it?"

"Yessir!" Frazer saluted smartly. Les grinned and shook his head wearily.

"Sorry, lecture over lads. OK, when do we sail?"

"Any time you're ready, really. Coombs says they can have a shipment ready at a few days notice."

"Oh, yes, by the way, what's this Coombs look like, then?" asked Les.

"Small build, shifty looking, black hair, wears flash suits."

"Bit poofy looking?"

"Er, you might say so," Frazer smirked out the window.

"That's Jim Briggs; we are most definitely on the right track. That's why I was late. I clocked Briggs in the Marine Hotel...what a dump that is! He was having some sort of argument with the barman about not having Tequila or some such nonsense. I tried to see what he was up to because he's a known dealer in London. I didn't think he was connected with this lot. Anyway, by the time I found out he was staying there it was eight o'clock so I had to leg it over here quick."

"You ran from the Marine to here in five minutes? Christ you are fit."

"Yes, well, as I said, don't be fooled by appearances. It can be quite an asset in my line of work to look a bit of a prat."

"I thought it was a condition of employment," remarked Frazer.

"Watch it sweetheart, you're hardly one to make cracks about false impressions."

"Wh.....!?" Frazer's jaw hit the floor.

"Don't worry, your dark secret's safe with me, oh, and HM R&C Investigations Department of course."

"Bugger me!" said Frazer.

"Yes, well," said Les showing a restraint I didn't believe possible, "we like to know as much as possible about those with whom we are dealing."

"But you didn't know I was coming until just now," stuttered Frazer," and how the hell did you find out about my, ah, preferences anyway."

"You are involved with a senior member of Her Majesty's armed forces. We don't make judgements, we keep records."

"Well fuck me pink!" Frazer was very pale.

"And we had a good idea who the other crew member would be after a few local enquiries, OK?"

"Someone has had a bug in your closet, eh Frazer?"

"And how! I'm totally flabbergasted by God!"

"Let's not dwell on it too much, eh?" said Les. "Now, can we decide on a sailing date, please?"

"Yes, of course, I've looked at a few dates over the next couple of weeks," I dug my notebook out of my desk, "we've to pick up the stuff from Crookhaven. The contact is a man called Brendan McCauley. Now I reckon I want to be closing the Irish coast before dawn to pick up the Old Head Light then we can make landfall in daylight. Don't want to go into the wrong harbour." I glanced towards Frazer but, bless him, his expression of rapt attention never wavered. "We need to allow about 36 hours for the passage so we need to leave at about four in the afternoon, and that means we have to go Sunday or Monday at the soonest to get favourable tides both ends." I sat back to await the admiring applause.

"Fine, Sunday it is, then," said Les getting up.

"OK, see you then," said Frazer, also getting up and showing him to the door.

"Wait a minute, you two! I worked bloody hard on these figures. Don't I at least get the odd 'well done Tom' for my pains?"

"We know you're wonderful, Tom, why should you need our admiration?" Frazer's sense of humour was peeping through the clouds of his earlier discomfiture.

"Wait for me, then, and we'll go for a pint to seal the deal."

"OK! The club, the Nelson or the Marine?"

"To the Nelson!" we chorused.

CHAPTER 11

"Well, that lot should keep us going nicely until we get to Ireland," said Frazer, eyeing the mound of food on the saloon table from the comfort of his berth. He popped open a can of lager and took a swig, "who baked the cake?"

"It was Cath's mum, actually," I admitted, "Cath must have forgiven me slightly for disappointing young George. She dumped it on my desk this morning and muttered something about it being full of stuff that was good for a long, cold voyage."

"Are you sure she didn't mean stuff like knitted balaclavas, woollen socks and hot-water bottles?" Frazer had sampled Cath's wrath before.

"No, it's kosher enough, makes a mean cake does Cath's mum. You could keep an Everest expedition going on one of Cath's mum's cakes. We'll have a bit with our coffee once we've stowed the rest of the grub. Come on you lazy bugger, give me a hand."

Frazer struggled out of his bunk and started poking tins into the galley locker.

"Where's double-oh-bloody-seven, anyway? He's going to miss the boat if he doesn't get his act together."

"I don't know. He said he'd be here at three. What time is it now?"

"Well that brass monstrosity over the chart table says that it's quarter to ten, but I suspect that it's a bit off the mark. I make it three-fifteen."

"Oh, wind the stupid thing up, Frazer and set it roughly for now. We'll pick up a time signal off the radio later."

"Wind it up? I thought it was a battery one. I haven't seen a windey-up clock for years! Where did you get it?" He lifted it down and started examining it minutely.

"I can't remember. It's been kicking around the stores for years. Cath polished it up recently and I thought it would look nice over the chart table next to the barometer."

"Which is where?"

"In the locker, I haven't screwed it up yet, but the screws are there somewhere. I'll probably get round to doing it over the next few days."

A hefty thud above our heads interrupted the conversation.

"Hello! Is anyone home? Tom?"

I stuck my head out of the companionway in time to see a case of export Gordon's being swung aboard to join the case of Grouse already looking very much at home on the side-deck.

"Compliments of HM Revenue and Customs," shouted Dawson, "I've got some beer here as well if you would care to give me a hand and he indicated half-a-dozen or so packs of cans on the dock-side."

"This is very generous, I must say, but it's a bit much for three blokes to guzzle in the short time available, even taking Frazer's capacity into account."

"Think of it as a gift to the boat, Tom," said Les, "also you'll be amazed at the co-operation and information available from a normally reticent native once a bottle is placed in his horny hand."

"Never mind the natives, mate, place a bottle or two in my horny hand and I'm yours for life, or until the bottle's empty, whichever comes soonest. Welcome aboard! By the way, you did bring some kit as well as booze, did you? I mean, that blazer's very fetching, but you might feel a bit draughty round the cloisters between here and the Fastnet rock."

"Yes, my kit's in the car. I got a nice new set of oilskins off a youngster I met in town. Never been worn, he said, bargain at fifty quid, I thought."

"Wasn't called George, was he?" I ventured, wincing.

"Yes, he was, now you mention it. How did you know? Here he's not bent is he? I can't afford to be caught wearing stolen property."

"No, Les, he's not bent. A little bruised perhaps, in the street-cred department, but I'm sure your fifty quid has gone a long way to heal any wounds."

"Real or imagined by you, Tom," said Frazer, "well, we may not have the original crew, but we appear to have the original oilskins."

"George was to be the third crew-member," I explained to a puzzled Les. I glared at Frazer.

"Oh, that could explain why his girlfriend said 'Never mind George, you're heaps better looking than that old wanker' and gave him a big kiss. I had to agree with her mind you, but I couldn't see the connection at the time."

"I didn't know George had a girlfriend!" Frazer chuckled, "at least not one who dishes out public smackers and uses words like 'wanker'. Don't kids grow up fast these days?" And he disappeared forward shaking his head.

"OK, Les, get your kit aboard and we'll hit the Channel. Taken a Stugeron or anything? I do recommend it; it can be pretty bumpy out there."

"It can be pretty bumpy in here too!" bawled Frazer from the head compartment.

"What, in the bog?" Les enquired.

"No, I mean inshore. Last time out I was tossing my cookies two minutes after we crossed the bar."

"I don't for one minute suppose it was anything to do with the surfeit of pints the night before, or the cooked brekky that morning?"

"'Course not, Tom. Well, not entirely anyway, no. Mate, I'd take the pills if I were you," he advised Les as he emerged from the head clutching a battered paperback, "I've been looking for this everywhere, Tom. Just realised I must have left it here on our little shake-down trip."

"What is it, Frazer?" I asked, my curiosity overcoming my trepidation. What on earth would Frazer read, over and over by the look of the book?

"Nothing special," he muttered and tucked it into the waistband of his trousers.

"Come on Frazer, no secrets, own up!" I made a lunge for the book.

"Bugger off, Tom, you'll tear it," Frazer yelled batting my hands away, but catching his arse a direct hit on the corner of the saloon table. "Owww! Shit!!"

The action of enthusiastically rubbing the injured zone dislodged the book which fell with a thud to the floor. Les swooped.

"Winnie The Pooh!? Winnie The Jolly Fucking Pooh?!" Les held the book between forefinger and thumb as if it was contaminated with some dreadful tropical disease. Frazer snatched it back.

"What's so shameful about reading Winnie the Pooh in the heads?" I enquired. Les was now regarding us both in turn with increasing unease.

"Perhaps I misjudged you two gentlemen," he said," but I could have sworn that you were both, at least, over voting age. I also thought that Winnie the Pooh was a children's book, or did I miss a lot of fine points when I was in primary school?"

Frazer shot me a poisonous glance.

"Look," he offered wearily," I just find it a refreshing read in this age of turgid literature full of heavy messages and moral pontificating."

"Yes," I added," for instance, you can describe almost everyone you know in terms of one of Milne's characters. Frazer, for instance, is very much like Pooh," I glanced at him. He seemed to be looking for something to eat. "And I'm a bit like Piglet, I suppose. Hey, Frazer, who do you think Les could be?"

"Eeyore," said Frazer, "Definitely Eeyore."

"Typical!" said Les.

"See!" we chorused, "you have read it!"

"Well, I did years ago, but it's still a kid's book, isn't it?"

"Nonsense!" said Frazer, much cheered, "pass me one of those beers."

I fired up the diesel and it rumbled amiably below us.

"Cast off the lines, Frazer, we can finish stowing the food on the way out. No point in hanging about any longer."

Many words have been, and I am sure, will be written about the sea passage between Land's End and the Fastnet Rock off the coast of Southern Ireland. This is not a sailing manual and I am no Adlard Coles so those among you who are yachtsmen will excuse me if I refrain from reproducing the text of my log. Suffice to say we made good time without too many navigational errors and picked up the loom of the Fastnet light more or less where we expected it to be, and, if anything, slightly sooner than expected.

Ever since the disastrous Fastnet race of 1979 when so many

lives were needlessly lost, this stretch of sea has had a bit of a bad name. But as was proven by the experts at the time, while the weather was horrendous, most of the losses could have been avoided. These, it was shown, were due mainly to the balls-out nature of the race and the cutting of corners in the seaworthiness department of the yachts in the interests of speed. Many lessons were said to have been learned but, really, they were lessons any experienced cruising yachtsman already knew, as indeed I am sure did the racers. But racing is racing and you go on the gun and if making your boat lighter than the other man's will make it go faster, then you make it lighter and take your chances with the weather.

Some would argue that these chances are worth taking, as would those among us who race motorcycles, jump out of aircraft or climb high, cold mountains. I, personally, do not hold such views and seek fulfilment at a more sedate pace, but I do feel uncomfortable about imposing limits on those who seek the meaning of their own life in such excesses. I know, I know, we must think of the lives endangered in the course of dangerous and heroic rescues, but I've never yet met a member of any rescue organisation on land or sea who said he'd rather do something else, thank you, or that such dangerous activities should be banned. No, rather he talks of education, training, improving reliability of equipment, in other words ways of allowing the activities to continue.

So what happens? Sure, safety at the levels of the time is improved, one result of which is to allow the participants to move onward to greater challenges and find other ways to get into trouble. There will always be people who have to risk life and limb to feel truly alive. I, thank God, am not one of these people. I need no more than a good hangover to remind me of my fragile mortality.

What I think I am really trying to say here is that the nautical by-way which forms an invisible boundary between St Georges Channel and the Mighty Atlantic is no more or less than a rather open piece of ocean subject, as all others, to the vagaries of wind and tide. If you wish to race up it without even being allowed to choose your moment, you are taking as big a chance as the man who thrashes his Honda 750 around that beautiful and normally safe road on the Isle of Man on a rainy day. Excessive, yes, but you might otherwise just be saving yourself to die a slow death from cancer at 80. No one I know gets too excited at that prospect.

God this is morbid. Longish sea passages do this to me. I get all introspective and philosophical. It is a cold fish indeed who can stare at the Milky Way of a clear night watch and not wonder what the bloody hell we are doing here. Here we are, for instance, chasing people who make vast amounts of money by selling toxic chemicals to other people who become dependant on these chemicals and ruin their lives, and often the lives of others around them. In human terms a disaster, a waste.

But think in geological terms. Then think in astronomical terms. No wonder religion was invented. It must have come in really handy around the time people started to dare think beyond their basic urges. Someone once wrote that there were three levels of civilisation which could be defined in terms of hunger. The first was HOW can we eat; the second WHAT shall we eat; the third WHERE shall we eat. I would like to propose a fourth level; WHY should we eat. Regressive, maybe, but perhaps if we all gave more thought to the WHYs of life we might make wiser decisions about the HOWs the WHATs and the WHEREs. Come to think of it, that's what religion is all about, isn't it? Well, isn't it??

The bright flash from the north-west jolts me from my deliberations.

"One hundred and one, one hundred and two, one hundred and three, one hundred and four, one hundred and five, (flash) right on cue, that's the Fastnet, OK."

I fished out the hand-bearing compass and took a quick bearing. I transferred it to the chart and stepped off a rough dipping distance for the light. Not far off track at all. It's always nice when even the simplest bit of dead-reckoning works out. I altered course a few degrees towards north to bring us a bit closer in to the rock. There would be some dawn light in the east sky soon, and a sight of land in a couple of hours. Time to wake Frazer for his watch. I put the kettle on.

CHAPTER 12

I woke to the smell of bacon frying. I looked round to see Frazer braced in the galley, prodding at a well-filled frying pan. The morning sun shone in through the galley port-hole, lighting his sparse and unruly hair like a halo.

"Wh'timesit?"

"Oh, my!" Frazer exclaimed, "welcome to the land of the living, Mr Van Winkle, I must say. Might have guessed that the aroma of an imminent bacon sarnie would have worked better than a kiss from Prince Charming!"

I focussed on the clock to find that it was nearly nine.

"Jesus, Frazer, you should have woken me ages ago! Where are we?"

"Fear not, skipper, all is as it should be. If you stick your head out you will see the entrance to Crookhaven Harbour a handful of miles dead ahead," and he nodded in the general direction.

I tumbled out of my bunk and climbed the companionway steps into the cool morning breeze to find Les at the wheel, grinning all over his face.

"'Morning, Tom. This is the life, eh?"

"'Morning, Les. Certainly is, mate, is she holding her course OK?"

"Like a dream, Tom, like a dream. Never would have guessed this could be so much fun, you know. I think I'm hooked!"

I smiled to myself and wondered if he would be singing the same tune if the sun wasn't shining and he was collecting a gallon of salty water down his neck every couple of minutes. I looked forward. Well, what certainly looked like a promisingly large chunk of Ireland filled most of the horizon, and, yes, there was what could well be the inlet to the harbour.

John Paton

A bacon sandwich weighing about half-a-pound ascended from below in Frazer's fist.

"Get yourself outside of that lot skipper," he yelled, "I reckon we've got about half-an-hour before we have to change course for the entrance."

"Cheers, Frazer, any chance of a cup of coffee to wash it down with?"

"Coming up, skip. Reinforced or as it comes?"

"What do you think?"

A generous tot of rum always makes a cup of otherwise disgusting instant coffee into a drink fit for a king. It's just about the only alcohol I can stomach early in the morning. I never was one for the buck's fizz champagne breakfasts or even the hair of the dog. I tried hard with the slivovitz with breakfast in Yugoslavia, and was even talked into whisky and porridge in Skye, but I suspect I was being conned, the porridge was salty and made the whisky taste horrible.

An over-full morning bladder drove such musings from my mind so I found a safe corner for my breakfast and went to the lee rail.

"You got any of your boys looking out for us out here, Les?" I shouted. A large, official-looking cutter was bearing down on us fast, and my morning constitutional was being scrutinised by several pairs of binoculars on its bridge. "Nosey buggers, you'd think that out here at least you could have a quiet pee without an audience, for God's sake!"

"I'm not expecting company, Tom, maybe it's just a routine check."

"Pass me the Q-flag Frazer, we should have hoisted it ages ago. Maybe that will satisfy them."

I ran the yellow 'free-pratique' flag up to the mast-head and watched for a reaction. The bows of the on-coming cutter dropped as he slowed his headlong progress, but he continued towards us. I could see one of her crew making his way forward with a loud-hailer.

"Hello! Sligo Bay! Please switch on your radio and go to working channel 25!" he yelled.

I was sure the VHF was on. I remembered seeing the channel number light as I passed the chart table. I dived below to check. It was on but the volume had been turned all the way down.

"What the hell is the point in having the radio on if the volume's off?" I demanded.

"Sorry, Tom, I did that," admitted Frazer," I thought you needed the sleep, and any traffic there was was a bunch of Irish fishermen gossiping about who they had screwed last night."

I cranked up the volume and punched up 25 on the channel selector.

"..go Bay, this is Crookhaven Harbourmaster, respond please!"

"Crookhaven Harbourmaster, this is Sligo Bay receiving over," I responded with as casual a voice as I could muster.

"Thank Christ for that, Sligo Bay. B'Jasus we all thought you were going to be up our arse before you noticed we were here. It's a fucking big place, Ireland. Makes a hell of a bump when you hit it."

"Sorry Harbourmaster, technical hitch, got it sorted now," I shot Frazer a lethal glare.

"Glad to hear it. B'God, the only reason we knew there was anyone alive on there was the smell of bacon frying."

We looked at one another...no he couldn't have. He was guessing....surely? We waited for another burst of Irish sarcasm.

"Sligo Bay, are you still there? Over." I was relieved to hear he was using a more conventional radio procedure at last.

"Still here, Harbourmaster. Over."

"Right, then, I've got a message for you from the brewery. He says to go straight to the fishing jetty, near the dock crane, you can't miss it and tie up there. He says he'll meet you in O'Sullivans. He'll have a pint waiting for you, and a lovely pint it will be too begod. How many aboard? Over."

I had certainly never got the drinks in over the VHF before, and who was 'he'?

"Three bodies here, thanks, harbourmaster, and, ah, who is 'he' we've to meet? Over."

"Ask for Brendan, if he doesn't spot you first. Oh and drop your papers in when you have a minute, will you? I'll probably see you in the pub first, though. Out."

I was beginning to like the sound of Crookhaven.

Now, I'm sure that all of you who have ever been invited to tie up at a fishing jetty in any part of the world, will know exactly what we found when we got there. Yes, I can see you all nodding your heads sagely. There was the dock crane, we couldn't miss it really, towering over the dock-side positively 'conspic', as it says on the charts. Clearly visible it was, among the jumble of trawl derricks, deck-houses, radio aerials, radar scanners, and all the other things you would expect to find attached to the tops of several ranks of fishing boats.

"It's full up!" said Les in dismay. "We'll have to go somewhere else."

"Don't be daft," chided Frazer, who had suspected something like this would happen, "we just tie up to one of the fishing boats."

"But they're all dirty and rusty," Les grimaced. He had fallen in love with Sligo Bay, and was clearly worried about her nice shiny paint job.

"Don't worry, Les, I'll pick a clean one for you. Fenders out! Port side! Millions of them, please!" I ordered, coasting Sligo in gently to give Frazer time to show Les how to tie the fenders to the guard-rails and how to handle the mooring warps. I enjoyed watching this little lesson. Frazer should have been a school-teacher. He really had a way with words when it came to explaining tricky points.

"Fuckin 'ell, Les, are you deaf as well as stupid? Look you silly bugger, over the top and through the bloody loop! NO!! Over... Oh shit, here give me it... DON'T PUT IT THERE!! God give me strength..! WE HAVEN'T GOT ALL FUCKING DAY!!!"

Les, all credit to him, absorbed this torrent of abuse stoically and did his best to salvage some shreds of useful advice from among it. Soon both men were poised amidships with a coil of warp ready to leap lightly aboard the lucky trawler I had selected to be our berth-mate. As we closed on its rusty topsides a head appeared from the deck-house.

"Fock off!" it snarled, "we don't want you lot outsoide of us, go on, fock off somewheres else!"

"What?" Frazer was for once stuck for words. I shrugged and opened the throttle a touch to take us back out into the harbour. We could find a friendlier boat, I was sure, no point in getting our knickers in a twist.

Les, however, whether it was because he was further forward, or because he was concentrating on an unfamiliar task, had somehow missed this friendly exchange and, at the precise moment that I opened the throttle and turned to starboard, leapt bravely aboard the now receding trawler,.. or rather he didn't. He hit the water still reaching for the trawler and paying out the warp, and disappeared in a huge eruption of oily flotsam and jetsam.

"Oh, shit," muttered Frazer, then at the top of his voice, "IDIOT OVERBOARD! WARP TRAILING! STOP THE FUCKING ENGINE!!", and he heaved the life-belt towards the now surfacing Les. I knocked her into neutral and dived to the rail.

"Les, are you all right?"

"Been better, thanks Tom. This some kind of initiation ceremony is it? I mean, can I come back on board now? This water's a disgrace, you know. I think I've just swallowed a used french letter."

"Doubt it mate," remarked Frazer conversationally, "Irish waters, remember, not allowed here, are they?"

Les glared a SAM missile out of oil-sticky eyes.

"Tie that warp round your waist, Les, and we'll winch you out." I suggested hastily.

"Thanks, Tom, but I can manage myself," snarled Les and bugger me if he didn't walk up the side of the boat, hauling himself up by the warp which was still firmly attached to the samson-post. I heard Frazer gulp from the length of the boat.

"Bloody hell, Les, I've never seen anyone doing that before. You sure you're not James Bond?"

"No, Tom, I'm not James Bond, just fighting bloody mad. It's bad enough to get dropped in the shit...."

"I didn't mean it, Les, honest!" I protested.

"I know you didn't mean it, Tom, but that bastard's tongue is going to get him hospitalised before this trip's over."

"I'm sorry, Les, I'm sorry," Frazer gushed as he picked his way back to the cockpit, "here, let me help you out of these wet clothes."

"Get your hands off me, you...you...."

"Queer?"

"I wasn't going to say that!"

"Was!"

"Wasn't"

"Was!!"

"Jesus Christ! Will you two knock it off!" I pulled them apart. "We're adrift in a fishing harbour with one wet crewman and half the Irish fishing fleet pissing themselves with laughter beside us. We're trailing warps and probably contravening a bookful of regulations. Do I have to remind you that this is supposed to be an undercover operation, for Christ's sake?"

"Sorry skipper," Frazer mumbled and nudged Les.

"Oh, yeah, sorry skipper," and he sniggered. Then Frazer sniggered, and then, God help me, I sniggered. Then Frazer started to shake with laughter, causing Les to giggle, and still we were drifting across the harbour.

"When you ladies are quite finished playing skipping ropes you could come alongside me if you want! We're not all like that cunt O'Driscoll"

A large fisherman with a face like the proverbial halloween cake was waving to us from one of the trawlers.

"Thanks very much, we'll be right there!" and warps were retrieved engine engaged and a modicum of seamanship restored to the situation.

Our second attempt at mooring was successful. We made fast. I cut the motor. We had arrived. We were in Ireland at last.

"See!" said Frazer," just goes to show what a difference a bit of practice makes!" and Les threw him into the harbour.

"No hard feelings, mate?" enquired Les with a smirk as we hiked up the hill to the pub. Frazer was still scowling, hands stuffed deep into the pockets of a fresh pair of jeans.

"I'll tell you after you've bought me at least a couple of pints, you vindictive bastard. Christ knows what I've caught from swallowing half that harbour!"

"I got a gut-full of it too, remember," Les pointed out.

"Yes, but you fell in accidentally, AND it wasn't even my fault!" Frazer shot an aggrieved look in my direction.

"I'll say this, though, Frazer, you're lighter than you look, mate. Must be all these bulky clothes you wear. You went over the rail easier than I expected you to."

"I wish I'd bust your truss, Rambo. I should never have gone on that diet."

"I think we're here!" I called to them from the door of O'Sullivans. They had been so deep in acrimonious argument they had completely failed to notice that I had stopped.

"FRAZER! LES!"

They turned round in mid-snipe. I made pint-drinking hand signals and pushed open the door of the public bar.

The few customers in the bar eyed me without much curiosity and carried on with their conversations, pints, dominoes or newspapers. I walked over to the bar where the barman was heavily involved in decanting three bottles of stout into straight glasses.

"Good afternoon. Could I have three pints of Guinness please?"

The barman looked up slowly. He was a small wiry man of indeterminate age, his one noticeable feature being that he appeared to have just had the most meticulous shave possible. His pink face shone. His chin glistened. He was immaculate. He leaned across the bar and looked me up and down. A grin further lit his face.

"You'll be from the yacht down at the fish-quay that had the spot of bother earlier?" he announced to the entire bar in a voice which belied his stature.

"Er, yes, I'm the one that didn't go for a swim."

He grunted in reply suggesting the opinion that a ducking might have improved me.

"There's yer Guinness," he said pointing at the three glasses he had already poured, "are these your crew?" He nodded in the direction of the door where Frazer and Les were in danger of becoming wedged shoulder-to-shoulder in the door-way, such was their rush to slake two harbour-water aggravated thirsts.

"Yes, that's them. I take it then, that we were expected?"

"Oh, yes," winked the barman, "and Brendan there reckoned you might be needing a gulp of something pretty urgent when you got here!" He nodded towards the corner of the bar where a large man in tweeds, cords and brogues sat nursing a pint of stout obviously enjoying our bewilderment.

"Come on over, lads. I've kept a seat for you."

"Brendan McCaulay?" I ventured.

"The very same! Delighted to make your acquaintance!"

He shook each of us violently by the hand, his great paw engulfing our normal-size arms almost to the elbow. I made the necessary introductions and we sat down. Serious inroads were made on the Guinness before the silence was broken.

"So, lads, ye made it!"

"Evidently," muttered Frazer into his pint.

"Yes," I agreed, "we made good time. The weather was kind to us."

"Ahh, God be praised for that!" said Brendan with genuine sincerity, "I'm told 'tis a woild ould place out there past the Rock.

You wouldn't catch me going out there. Oh, no, oi prefer to keep good Oirish sod under me feet, thank you."

"You a farmer, then, Brendan?" guessed Les.

"A farmer? Me??" roared Brendan." No, begod, oi am not! No, oi'm a chartered accountant by profession, and when oi'm not doing that, I help me brother at the brewery up the road."

Frazer's eyebrows shot to his hairline but his nose stayed in his pint.

"Oh, ah, yes, a chartered accountant," Les was struggling, "you're not what I'd expect a chartered accountant to be like, somehow."

"Is that roight, now?" said Brendan, apparently genuinely surprised, "and what would your chartered accountants be loike in England, now?"

"Well..." Les was obviously choosing his words with care. He certainly couldn't explain that they didn't usually look like over-upholstered farmers on an away-day break.

"They're, ah, usually rather smaller people," explained Les, "with striped trousers..."

"Yes, and rolled umbrellas, and bowler hats!" Frazer helpfully contributed.

"Well, not necessarily," said Les, "but they're usually rather dull sorts who probably wouldn't drink pints of Guinness in public bars..." Les was running out of ideas.

Brendan was doing a very good job of looking interested, but was obviously very sceptical about the rather unsavoury picture of English Chartered Accountants that was being painted for his benefit.

"Is that roight, now, boys. Sure oi don't think oi'd like to be a chartered accountant in England, then, if that's the case, begod no!" He shook his head in deep sympathy with all the poor, grey, unlovely English chartered accountants which were at that very moment forming such a forlorn image in his mind's eye, "begod, no indeed!"

I felt that this totally bogus gloom which had descended upon the group at the thought of a nation of suicidal chartered accountants should be dispelled before we got into the realms of English beer, weather, or, God help us, politics.

"Well, Brendan, I gather you've got a cargo of fine Irish Ale for us to take back to England?"

"That oi have Tom, that oi have, but ye won't be wanting to rush into things will you? No, you'll be wanting a bite to eat and a few jars, and be then you'll probably feel loike a snooze before yer tea. What with that and the sing-song tonight, you'll be worn out! No, tomorrow will be time enough. Whose shout is it?"

"Mine, I think." said Les pushing back his chair and smirking at Frazer.

"Bloody right it is." said Frazer.

"You don't happen to know if the Harbourmaster is around, only he asked us to let him see our documents, and he said he'd probably see us in the pub."

"Oh he's here all roight, but he doesn't loik people talkin business with him in the pub, see."

"Takes his drinking seriously, does he?" I tried to be flippant in the face of Brendan's apparent seriousness.

"No, Tom, he takes his work seriously," Brendan scolded.

"Sorry, Brendan, It was a joke."

"Ah, Tom, it's a serious business running a pub, you know. Got to be done right. Big responsibility it is!"

"I thought we were talking about the Harbourmaster, Brendan."

"We are, Tom, we are. Pat O'Sullivan. That's him over there serving your mate. Pub's been in the family for years, of course, and he's our harbourmaster when it's shut."

"Christ, no wonder he knew all about us when we turned up. He does commercials for this place over the V.H.F. you know. Had us all drooling down our oilskins out there this morning."

I turned towards the bar and caught Pat O'Sullivan's eye. He gave me a wave and a knowing wink.

"Sure I know it," admitted Brendan, "sure you should see it when the fleet comes in, the drinks are seven deep along the counter before the first boat has tied up. He's got a wee radio under the pies over there. Saves time when it's busy."

"Four pints of Guinness!" announced Les dumping his round on the table, barely managing not to spill the lot.

"I'm not very good at carrying four pints all at once, sorry lads, but I asked the barman for a tray and do you know what the silly bugger said? 'Sure you've got more than enough to carry without a tray as well' ...bloody hell."

"Ah," said Brendan in all seriousness, "you should have said you wanted to put the drinks on it, see, he maybe thought you wanted it for something else."

We all looked blankly at Brendan. No one wanted to be the one to ask what else you could possibly want to do with a tray. No doubt we'd find out soon enough.

"Er, yes, so Brendan," Frazer was coming up for the third and final time in this conversation, I felt. If he couldn't grasp a floating log of reality soon he would sink without trace. "I don't suppose there might be a place we could all have a shower and a shave? I know these two certainly need one. Ha ha..."

Brendan sniffed in our direction like he was sampling a fine wine.

"No, no... ye'll do a day or two yet. No you don't want to be worrying yourselves about that now."

Frazer offered up a silent little prayer.

"Actually, Brendan, a wash would be nice, ah, whether we need it or not," I tried.

"Well now, that's different," said Brendan, "you should have said you actually wanted to wash. Sure you can come up to my place and have a nice hot bath if you want. No bother!"

We were all going to have to get used to the local somewhat disconcerting habit of literal interpretation and stop using our self-conscious English euphemisms.

"Thank you, Brendan, that would be lovely. Would one each be too much trouble.....?" I shouldn't have said it...

"Well I only have one bath Tom.....but you can each have your own water. We're not unhygienic here you know." Brendan looked quite offended, "but let's have another pint first, your round Frazer."

Frazer wandered meekly over to the bar. He knew when he was beaten.

CHAPTER 13

"Why, in the name of God, have we stopped now?"

Frazer was becoming exasperated by the rather leisurely progress of the last load of beer towards the boat. This was because the brewery had insisted on producing a particularly venerable dray, pulled by an even more venerable, but admittedly enormous, horse.

This together with the not infrequent stops at aunty's houses, water troughs, pubs, and almost any irregularity in the road surface, (of which there were many) "to save the axles", turned a two-mile trip into a day-long trek. We had finally come to a standstill in a narrow street within sight of the boat, but at the top of a rather steep hill, leading directly to the dock-side.

The previous three loads had been accomplished relatively easily by rather fresher rigs than ours under cover of darkness, and I had my suspicions about the source of horse-power. These horses didn't eat hay. The pile of boxes on the fish quay was evidence that the purity of the enterprise had been slightly compromised in the name of expediency. This pile was being reduced at a steady rate at this very moment by many willing hands. The boxes were fitting nicely into Sligo's hold and promised pints of Guinness were looming large in the minds of the worthies fitting them.

Now we were in charge of the token 'traditional' load and things were not going well.

"The brakes don't seem to be working roight", declared Brendan, who had taken on the task of piloting the rig.

"Brakes!?" Frazer was getting into his stride, "Jesus Christ Almighty!"

Brendan hastily crossed himself.

"We've done nothing but stop since we bloody started," he bawled, "what do you mean, the brakes won't work?"

"Well, Frazer, it's loike dis," started Brendan as if he was talking to a three-year-old.

"Look, Brendan, this had better not be another of your Irish sayings, because if it is..."

"No, no, Frazer, oi'm just trying to explain about de brakes on de cart. See, when we're going along on de flat, loike, de horse here,..." and at this point he patted the horse's rump, in case Frazer had failed to notice the motive power of the vehicle upon which he had spent a very long and frustrating day.

"I know what a horse is, thank-you, Brendan!"

"Well, not many people from England use horses dese days, you know, it's all cars and lorries, and...."

"God almighty!" sighed Frazer.

"Anyway," Brendan ploughed on regardless, "loike I said, on de flat bits de horse can stop de cart by himself, see. But on a steep hill loike dis one, you need de brakes too or de cart moight push de horse over and de whole lot would run off and end up in de harbour, and we wouldn't want dat now, would we?"

"Wouldn't we?" said Frazer with a maniacal grin.

"No, we wouldn't," Brendan affirmed, "so we'd better unload here and take de boxes of beer to de boat a wee drop at a time."

"What!? Tom, tell this lunatic that there is absolutely no way that I am going to man-handle even one of these boxes down to the boat. Tell him also that I am saving my energy in order to be able to kill him in a particularly gruesome and painful manner when this lot is finished."

"Ah, Frazer," laughed Brendan," sure you're a great man for de jokes!"

"Tell him I am not joking, Tom."

"He's not joking, Brendan."

"Oh, bless you, Frazer," giggled Brendan, "sure oi wouldn't dream of asking a gentleman loike yerself to lug great boxes down dat hill, no, what we do is get some of de lads to unload most of de beer, and then de horse'll be able to manage it, see, an' den we come back for some more,..." Brendan is nodding at Frazer and pointing up and down the hill as if Frazer might have difficulty grasping such an intricate strategy, while Frazer is staring wildly at Brendan as if he had just proposed a public evisceration of the horse. After a minute Frazer seemed to regain control, however.

"Brendan, wouldn't you think that perhaps that idea would take rather a long time? I mean, it'll be dark in about six hours, and there's a bank holiday coming up at the end of the month, and, gosh, I really would like to die in England AND NOT IN THIS LUNATIC ASYLUM YOU CHOOSE TO CALL A TOWN!!..."

Brendan was beginning to get the message and was casting sidelong glances, looking for a bolt-hole, should the need arise.

"Maybe there's a quicker way, Brendan." I said, taking him as far away from Frazer as possible. "If we could tie a rope to the back of the cart and take a couple of turns around that tree there, we could slowly let the horse guide the cart down the hill and there would be no danger of him getting overtaken."

Brendan gazed at me in dazed admiration.

"By God, Tom, that is a darlin' of a plan! Now why didn't oi t'ink of dat, me bein' used to carts and hills and de loike? Oi'll tell you why, Tom, because oi don't have brains loike you have! Dat's why!"

"Oh, God," moaned Frazer, "tell me something new."

"Ah, but wait a wee minute, Tom," said Brendan, "where do you suppose we moight lay hands on a bit of rope long enough and strong enough to reach all the way down de hill? Its a quarter mile if it's an inch!"

"No problem, Brendan, we've got miles of warp aboard Sligo Bay. Frazer'll go and get some, won't you Frazer?"

"Yes, Tom, willingly, anything to get away from this pantomime for five fucking minutes!" and off he trotted.

"Maybe we should have a wee drink while we're waiting," suggested Brendan and lifted one of the boxes off the dray," the brewery said we could have a case to ourselves for our trouble," and he proceeded to break open the lid.

"Er, I don't think you should do that, Brendan..." I started, but Les, who had been a very subdued spectator of the days proceedings so far grabbed my elbow and hissed, "leave it, Tom, you'll only arouse suspicion!" and looked around, casually.

"No, Tom, it'll be all roight, really, it's the custom, you know. De brewery always loads an extra crate. It's a gratuity, loike," and he unscrewed a cap and pulled deeply at the beer, "here, have one yerselves," and he handed us a bottle each. We sipped guiltily in silence.

"Owld Neddy there certainly seems to have taken quite a likin' to that box," remarked Brendan, conversationally, "sure oi've never seen a horse eat cardboard before!" He reflectively nipped his Woodbine and wedged it behind his ear, prior to another gulp of his fourth bottle of Bantry Bitter.

"What!? Oh Christ, Brendan, take it away from him, quick!"

"Not on your loife! He's fokin' huge...and mean lookin' with it...you take it away from him! Anyhow, who cares if he eats an owld box, sure it'll soon be empty. If we take the rest of the bottles out they'll be nothin' in it to spoil."

"Not exactly...Oh my God, I think he's smiling!"

"Don't be daft," said Brendan, "horses don't smile...mind-you, he has got a queer sort of look about him...kind of wobbly, loike...he seems to be leaning on dat wall."

"Don't let him fall, Brendan," I begged, wrenching the remains of the carton from the slavering jaws of the patently inebriated horse, "I wonder if he'll drink some black coffee?"

"Coffee is it now?" roared Brendan, hugely amused, "B'jasus you'll be offering him a smoke next...he's a bloody horse, man."

"I'm serious, Brendan, we've got to sober him up quick!"

"Sober him up? Christ it would take seventy-odd pints of best stout to get that big bastard pissed. The only drink he's had recently was out of my aunty's trough and I assure you that there's nothin' in it but God-given rain water!"

Neddy was by now doing a wonderful impression of a badly operated pantomime horse. His back legs wanted to go for a walk while his front ones seemed to be getting ready for a rendition of 'Climb Upon My Knee Sonny Boy'. The dray was more or less anchoring him in place, but as Brendan had so colourfully observed, the horse was enormous and sooner or later something had to give.

"What do you do to sober someone up quick?" I asked no-one in particular.

"Tell him you lost the lottery ticket?" ventured Frazer who had reappeared with a length of anchor warp, "This ought to do it...what the hell is going on now!?"

"Yer man Tom here has only slandered this good honest working beast. He says it's an alkyholic!" Brendan struck a pose of righteous indignation.

"The horse ate one of the boxes," I explained.

"And...?" asked Frazer.

"And...he's pissed as a fart."

Frazer's face lit up.

"It bloody works, by God, not, ahem, that I am normally in favour of experiments on animals, you understand, and,..." and this for Les's benefit, "and, purely out of professional interest, of course, I am pleased to say that Trigger here has confirmed for us that these boxes do in fact contain what they are suspected of containing".

Brendan ignored this peroration, thankfully, as he now ignored most things Frazer said.

"Put the warp on the dray, for now, maybe if we can get him to drink enough water he'll snap out of it," I suggested.

But by this time the horse had sunk with a dreadful finality between the shafts of the dray and loud, happy snores were rattling nearby windows.

"Aw, he's toired, bless him," said Brendan.

It's at times like this one tends to ponder not only the snap-shot of one's present situation, but the broader brush-strokes of ones life, so to speak.

Here we were, in charge of a ramshackle brewer's dray, loaded with boxes, the fabric of which was soaked in enough illegal substances to keep most of the Home Counties off work for a week, and filled with bottles of beer which was destined to be flushed down the toilet without the customary intervention of the human kidneys. The horse which could pull it but not stop it on a hill was now terminally rat-arsed and blocking the only route to the harbour available to us. Brendan was rapidly approaching a similar state of intoxication, and Frazer had gone off in a huff leaving Les and I to survey the wreckage and suffer the withering scorn of a rapidly expanding audience of school-children and small dogs.

"Phone the fire-brigade mister! They'll shift him!" one helpful youth suggested.

"My dad drives a JCB," announced another, menacingly.

"Call the vet," said a little girl with carrot-coloured pigtails, "he'll have a pill that will sober him up!"

"If he does, I'd love to know about it," muttered Les wistfully.

"This is ridiculous," I pulled Les away from the throng, "We can't wait until the stupid thing wakens up, it could be out for hours! There must be something we can do."

"Well I'm buggered if I can think of anything. Even if we could get the horse out of the way, we still have to get the cart down to the quay-side. I'm not convinced this rope-trick of yours will work."

"Not without something substantial between the shafts to guide it, it won't. What we need is another horse. We could hitch him up to sleeping beauty here and drag him out of the way, then get him to guide the cart down the hill."

"With respect, Tom," moaned Les, "if I don't see another horse for the rest of my life it'll be too many. Surely there's a lorry somewhere we can borrow."

"My dad drives a JCB!" piped the lad again.

"Look, piss off, son, I don't give a shit if your dad is J C Bamforth himself. Christ, the last thing we need here is a hole dug."

"I don't know about that," I said looking at Neddy who seemed to be more or less painted on the road by now, "I think he may have had rather too much, ah, cardboard for his own good....Les?"

Les had wandered over to the front of the cart and was minutely examining the mechanical intricacies.

"Tom, Come here a minute! Where's the kid who's dad had the JCB? I think we have the answer!"

"Oh good, we dig a big hole and bury the whole mess and go home and forget about it. When do we start?"

"No, silly bugger, I reckon a JCB could gently, sort of scoop the horse to one side, and then, well, you know how the bucket-bit opens up like jaws?OK...He could grip the shafts of the cart and reverse the whole thing down the hill to the quay!"

"Brilliant! Where's the kid? Hey son! Does your dad really have a JCB?"

"Yes he has!" the lad admitted proudly, "and it's big and yellow!" he elaborated, "AND it's the bestest JCB in Manchester!" he concluded, proudly.

Les looked like he was torn between killing the lad and bursting into tears.

"Jesus H Christ!" he groaned.

"That's great, son," I said moving the boy out of range of Les's boot, "you don't happen to know if there is a JCB like your dad's nearby, by any chance?"

110

"No...no..." the boy seemed to be mentally sifting through a vast databank of earth-moving equipment.

"Well fuck it," said Les, "that's it then. We're fucking royally fucked, might as well go home and face the music. I'll be drummed out of the brownies for this, you can bet your arse on that, oh yes, I am well and truly shafted, my friend..."

"..no...none of them are as new..." the lad continued, unperturbed by Les's announcement, "they're all a bit older I reckon."

Les took a firm grip of his temper.

"Just tell us where they are," he hissed through clenched teeth, "there's a good lad!"

"Over there!" and he pointed to the high gate behind us on which was written in large brutal letters:

MICHAEL O'DAY--PLANT HIRE
AND FUNERALS
NO JOB TOO BIG

Les goggled at the gate against which he had been leaning and intermittently kicking to relieve his frustration for the past few minutes.

"It's going to be a toss-up which branch of Mick O'Day's organisation we are going to need first!" I quipped.

Les honoured me with one of his best glares.

"OK, don't take a vote on it! Only trying to bring a little levity to the situation."

"Please spare me your incisive wit at this juncture, Tom, I think my supply of self-control is about to run out. If we open that gate and find nothing but navvies' shovels I shall not be responsible for my actions. I shall demand immediate access to Frazer, whose vitals I shall use to decorate this poxy street."

"Maybe we should leave it 'till tomorrow, eh? I'm sure things'll look a lot better in the morning."

"Open the fucking gate, Tom."

"Look, Les...."

111

"The gate, Tom, now, please."

"Oh, well, since you asked nicely...but listen..."

"OPENTHEFUCKINGGATENOW!!!"

I slid the gate a foot along its runners and peered into the yard. The sight of a gratifyingly huge excavator in the JCB idiom met my gaze. Bits were lying round it and oil was dripping from it but it seemed to be complete. A large man was wielding a spanner in the guts of the thing.

"Mr O'Day?"

"Come in and shut the gate! I'm catchin me death in here!"

We entered and slid the gate shut. Quite how that helped to prevent his early demise was unclear since the yard was open on the other three sides to rolling fields, apart from the odd low hut and a large barn-like structure. "What d'yes want?"

"We would like to hire your JCB for a short while."

"Ah, well, that's different gentlemen, and when would you be wanting it?"

"Well, now, actually, if it's not too much trouble."

"Ah, urgent job is it?" he asked conspiratorially, tapping the side of his nose.

"Well, yes, fairly urgent."

"No problem, always happy to help the cause," he said winking in a stagey way. I was beginning to think that perhaps he was getting the wrong message.

"We've got a problem with a horse," I said.

"Course you have," he agreed, "and where would you be wanting the 'horse' buried, sirs?"

"Look we don't want to bury it, actually, it's only a bit drunk. We just want it shifted a bit so that we can get the cart down to the quay." Les suddenly realised that this particular explanation without the accompanying scenario outside the gate probably sounded a bit strange.

"What he means is..."

"No need to explain, boys, I know you lads have codes and things. The less I know the better. Just show me the job and I'll do it."

Mick was clearly becoming agitated and equally clearly thought we were involved with the IRA or some affiliated organisation.

"Ah, look, Mr O'Day, maybe if you took a look outside your gate you'll get a better idea of the problem."

Mick reluctantly approached the gate wiping his hands on an old string vest. He slid it open a crack and peered out.

"Holy Mother O' God!" he exclaimed, "what dirty bastert has killed Clancy's horse?" He withdrew his head from the opening and glared at us in rage.

"He's not dead, Mr O'Day," I corrected, "only asleep. He's a bit drunk, actually."

"Jesus Mary and Joseph, it would take seventy pints to get that big...."

"Yes, yes, Brendan McCaulay has already pointed this out..."

"McCauley? Brendan McCauley? That eedjit? Sure he knows nothing about horses. Was it him got Nellie drunk? Let me get me hands on him..."

"Look, Michael," Les calmed him, "may I call you Michael?"

"Hrmph!" growled Michael.

"You see Michael, we don't actually know how, ah, Nellie got into the state she's in, but it's important that we move her and get the cart down the hill to the quay, and what I thought we could do..." but Mick was already doing it.

He started the digger with a roar and a huge cloud of black diesel smoke.

"Open the gates!" he ordered.

"Open the gate, close the gate, open the gate," I muttered, "bloody hell, now I know how the policeman at the end of Downing Street feels."

The JCB lurched out into the street and confronted the stricken Nellie.

"Undo the harness and raise the shafts!" ordered Mick like a Household Cavalry officer astride his steed. We obeyed.

"Right, stand well back!" and he gave Nellie a mighty prod in the rump with the edge of the shovel. To our astonishment Nellie gave a snort and staggered to her feet.

"There, I thought that would shift her. She'll be right as rain now! Close the gates behind me lads, thanks very much!" and he reversed back into the yard.

Les and I were once again left with our mouths hanging open as Brendan, who also seemed to have made a miraculous recovery proceeded to re-hitch Nellie to the cart.

"Rioght!" he beamed, "where's dat rope?"

Well, much to everyone's astonishment except mine the rope-trick did work. Sligo was soon floating comfortably down on her marks and we were anchored off the fairway supposedly getting organised for the return trip.

Our departure from the fish-quay had been accomplished with rather more aplomb than our arrival, albeit with a degree of unseemly haste since our exploits with the dray had lent us a degree of notoriety, not to say glamour. We had become something of a focal point within the harbour. Indeed the gathering throng was beginning to cause problems for the fishermen, who, while being as polite as circumstances allowed, had a job to do, and were beginning to make it clear to us that if we didn't shift our poncy Tupperware boat from their jetty they'd sink us, cargo and all. The last straw took the form of a coach party from the next town who insisted that the price of their ticket included a guided tour of our ship and tea with the captain.

Hence our anchorage well out of reach.

"This is more like it!" sighed Frazer, stretching out luxuriously on the hatch-cover, "look at that scenery! Listen to that silence! Smell that fresh air!"

"Yes, well, I must confess I'm very tempted to hang about and enjoy the peace out here myself," I admitted, "but with all due respect to Les, I'd much rather get shot of this cargo and get this over and done with."

"Yes, I suppose you're right, Tom. Mustn't keep our friendly pushers waiting. I'd love to be a fly on the wall when Les and his boys finally round them all up. I must say, though, they can't be very bright, I can't imagine a dafter, more complicated way of smuggling drugs into the country, can you?"

"It did seem a bit of a shambles. What do you reckon, Les?"

"I was thinking about that," he said thoughtfully, "I reckon that they took the calculated risk of losing control in the mid-stages in order to 'break the chain', if you follow me."

"Hmm, you mean, the fewer people who know what's going on in the middle, the less chance there is of you lot tracing them back from the end user?"

"Precisely! Although I reckon that there was probably someone keeping an eye on things from a safe distance, just in case. For instance, I don't suppose you noticed that during all the kerfuffle with the horse the remains of the empty box magically disappeared?"

"No, I must admit I didn't notice," I said. Frazer seemed to be very busy with a lashing on the hatch cover.

"What about you, Frazer?" Les tried.

"What?"

"You didn't see what happened to the rest of the box back there after we moved the horse, by any chance?"

"Me? No mate, we were all a bit busy, if you will remember. Not really in the 'Keep Ireland Tidy' mode if you get my drift. I assume it's still lying in the gutter."

"You assume wrong, Frazer. I hunted high and low for that box and I assure you that it was no where to be found. Someone removed it and I'd love to know who."

I knew who, and so did Frazer but I realised that any revelations in that department could cause me considerable grief from two directions.

"Don't suppose we'll ever know," I said, "everything lashed Frazer?"

"All ship-shape and Bristol fashion Cap'n."

"OK, we can sail her out from here. Frazer, you raise the fore-sail. Les, you hoist the main."

The sails were soon slatting in the light air and the anchor came up cleanly. Sligo Bay bore away and headed for the open sea.

"Give me a course for the Bristol Channel Frazer; we have a cargo to deliver!"

I could have killed Frazer when I realised that he had managed to salvage the remains of the box and smuggle it aboard without Les noticing, but every time I tried to challenge him about it HM Revenue & Customs seemed to be within earshot. Eventually, however, Les went ashore at one point to telephone his masters in London and I collared him.

"What the hell do you think you're doing, Frazer? We're supposed to be the good guys, remember?"

Frazer looked at his hands defensively.

"Look, Tom, I only borrowed it to try with my brew. I'll be very careful with it. I won't let anyone else have it. It's exactly what I've been looking for, you know that!"

"Yes, I know that, Frazer. I also know that it's a bloody powerful drug with God knows what side-effects. It might be highly addictive for all we know. Alcohol is bad enough."

"Yes, I know that, Tom...I know. I just couldn't resist the opportunity when I saw the box there in the road, forgotten. Seemed a shame not to borrow it."

"Listen, Frazer, I like a drink as much as the next man. I'm used to alcohol in all its forms, and as you know its effect is limited to some extent. It can only be concentrated so much...but this stuff..."

"OK, Tom...OK. I know what you're saying. I suppose in my heart of hearts I agree with you. I know what all the other nasties do to a man, or a woman for that matter," he looked at me for a reaction, "I'm as agin it as anyone can be. I suppose I have to reconcile my desire to innovate with beverages with my attitudes on chemical abuse."

"The whole beauty of booze is its self-limiting properties, I suppose. It's the one aspect of it which sets it apart from other drugs, with the exception of marijuana, perhaps."

"Yes, I've got nothing against a chap smoking the odd joint either. No one ever OD'd on grass. Did they?"

"Not that I know of, but you can be damn sure someone could OD on this stuff. Did you see what it did to that horse?"

"Dropped him like a sack of spuds all right," admitted Frazer, "but he seemed none the worse afterwards."

"How does a horse explain that he has a stinking hangover, may I enquire? He could have been vowing to sign the pledge for all you know. Anyway that's got nothing to do with it. I do happen to know that large animals have a much better tolerance of drugs than people have. So don't even think about trying that stuff...you haven't have you!?"

"No I haven't. To be honest I'm scared to. I've no idea of the concentration or the purity or anything. I was going to try very small concentrations at first..."

"Forget it Frazer, if you don't chuck that stuff over the side, I will, and you'll go with it...I mean it Frazer. Get shot of it...all of it...now...before Les gets back!"

And that's how Frazer abandoned his dream of becoming a coin-in-the-slot drinks tycoon. Morality triumphed over avarice. The torn-up bits of box floated away on the morning tide to sink out at sea and give the local shoals of herring the biggest piss-up they were ever likely to enjoy. God knows what the fishermen made of it next day when half their catch had hiccups and the other half were spoiling for a fight right there on the deck.

Frazer was very subdued for a while after that and we obviously kept it to ourselves. He hadn't reckoned on Les looking for the remains of the box, but his theory about a fifth-columnist in the crowd with which, of course, we agreed wholeheartedly, came in handy under the circumstances.

The sail back was as uneventful as the outward leg. Sligo was heavily laden and felt like a floating cottage and although the sea was, if anything, bumpier you could have comfortably eaten soup off the saloon table.

By two o'clock the following morning we were safely tied up at the small ship quay at Avonmouth, and apart from a somewhat diffident port controller who after asking us if we were sure we were in the right place, and shouldn't we be looking for the marina, showed us where to 'park', as he put it, no-one seemed to be much interested.

"What do we do now?" Frazer whispered.

"We go to sleep and wait until morning," Les whispered back.

"Why are we whispering?" I asked, in a whisper.

"Dunno, really," admitted Les, in a slightly more normal, but still pretty 'sotto voce', "it's just so sodding quiet."

"It is two a.m. remember. All the little truck and crane drivers will be well tucked-up by now. Like I should be," I said, "anyone for a night-cap?" and I waved the rum bottle.

John Paton

CHAPTER 14

"Cath?.....Yes, it's Frieda.....yeah, fine....me and Carol are going for a 'henny' drink at the Marine tonight. You coming? .....No nothing posh, just jeans and sweater.....no, we won't be late......your mum will be fine Cath.....about 7.30?......OK, eight.....I know, she can be difficult......OK, see you there, 'bye."

The lounge bar at the Marine Hotel actually had a few customers for a change. They looked dishevelled enough to be the crew of a recently berthed yacht, plus a couple of mature locals who were regarding them with deep suspicion.

"You'd think they'd never seen 'yachties' before the way they're glaring at them!" Carol sipped at her Gin and Tonic as she watched the scene in the bar, "they're such an insular lot here!"

"I think maybe something was said," Frieda observed. "The language is a bit ripe and you know how they feel about 'language' in here.

The 'yachties' were certainly pretty rowdy. Nothing threatening, but the combination of several pints and the obvious effects of having just stepped off a cruising yacht after many days at sea meant that any attempt by any one of them to move about the bar was a somewhat unsteady business. One of them had already fallen quite suddenly sideways off his bar stool much to his surprise and to the huge amusement of his pals.

"Hey, barman, can't you keep this fucking place on a steady course? My mate here spilled his pint!"

Tables had obviously been bumped and harsh words of complaint spoken.

"What's happened to Cath? I thought you said she would be here at eight?"

"Oh, you know Cath. She won't leave until her Mum is comfy in front of the TV with an evening's supply of tea and bikkies. She'll be here soon, I'm sure."

One of the wobbly crew emerged from the gent's toilet still zipping his fly as Cath entered the bar.

"Ooops! Sorry love, bit of a problem with the old 'pub door'.....wouldn't like to give me a hand, would you?"

Cath's look froze the guys smile on his lips and he slunk back to his stool. He sat down carefully and buried his nose in his pint. One of the older crew said something in his ear. He shrugged and grinned. It got a bit quieter.

"Well, really...." was Cath's reaction as she plonked herself down beside the other two.

"What'll it be Cath? Double Vodka and Kahlua? Champagne Cocktail?"

"No, really Carol, I don't drink, just an orange juice please.....but could you maybe ask the man to put some of that nice red stuff in the bottom? I think that looks so nice!"

"OK Cath, I was joking. One 'Nothing' Sunrise coming up!"

Once Cath had her drink in front of her she dared to look around.

"Oh, look, it's Mr and Mrs Green from the shoe shop.....cooee!"

Then Greens acknowledged her wave stiffly, still casting dirty looks at the yacht crew.

"What's the matter with them?" she asked.

"Oh, I think that they feel that the high standards of the Marine Hotel have been compromised somehow."

"Hmmm..." Carol was smirking, "Could it also have something to do with the poster over there by the door?" and she nodded in the direction of a small A4 coloured poster stuck at eye level next to the fire exit.

"What is it?" asked Cath brightly as she stepped over to it for a closer look. "Oh, oh dear! Er, oh my goodness!"

"What the hell's wrong Cath? You're red as a beetroot!" and Frieda joined her.

"Bloody hell! I don't believe it! Carol, you've seen this?"

The poster featured a very burly looking guy in a strange space-man type costume, which showed more than it covered.

"ONE FOR THE GIRLS!"
"BILL AND BEN THE SEXPOT MEN"
"MOVE LIKE NIJINSKI AND HUNG LIKE HORSES TOO!"
"FRIDAY NIGHT AT THE MARINE CLUB"
"BE THERE OR BE SQUARE!!!!"

Carol and Frieda howled in hysterics.

"Really, you two, I don't think it's anything to laugh about...that's rude, isn't it?"

"Oh, come on Cath, there's no harm in it. I'm sure it's all pretty tame. Why don't we go along for a look? It's tomorrow night. What a laugh!"

"Yes, I'm game. Come on Cath.... be brave!"

"Oh, I really don't think......"

"Right, that's settled. I'll get the tickets now. Reg! Three tickets for the stripper night!"

"Oh, Carol, I couldn't...."

"I'm paying and you're coming.....no arguments!"

The Greens huddled in shocked conference. The yachties were taking a great deal of interest in this latest development.

"Won't your fellas object ladies?"

"They wouldn't dare..... and Cath here is a free woman!"

"Frieda!" Cath hissed, "Don't tell them that! I don't want to be chatted up by that lot!"

A big cheer rose from the yachty table. However, to the girls' relief, they left it at that.

"I wonder how the men are getting on with the boat?" Frieda had been putting off broaching that subject and was glad Carol was the instigator.

"I'm sure they're fine. Last I heard they had arrived in Ireland OK. Tom said he'd try and phone me from Avonmouth when they got in."

"Where's Avonmouth anyway?" Cath's grasp of matters geographical was sketchy to say the least.

"Near Bristol, Cath. Up the M5 and turn leftish."

"Is it very far?"

"No, a couple of hours maybe, why?"

"Well, I was just wondering if maybe we could go and meet them. Take some fresh stuff.... food and things..."

"That's very thoughtful Cath." Frieda seemed genuinely pleased.

"Actually, it had occurred to me to go as well, but I didn't think anyone else would want to come."

"Well, I can't. No reason to anyway." Carol tried to look indifferent. Cath and Frieda exchanged glances.

"OK, that's settled! Me and Cath will go and meet them when they get in. I'm looking forward to that!"

The Marine Hotel was buzzing and already groups of women of vastly varying ages were jostling through the ballroom door. Vaguely suggestive music could be heard coming from within and the room was in relative darkness.

"I think I'll go home actually, mother......"

Frieda and Carol took an arm each and frog-marched Cath towards the ballroom.

"You're going in Cath. Look on it as an important part of your lifestyle development! Don't worry, we'll look for somewhere near the back."

Cath gave in and allowed herself to be propelled to a table on the periphery of the floor. The room had been decorated, for want of a better description, in mock-bordello red drapery, which on closer inspection turned out to be bed sheets dyed scarlet. Gold highlights had been added using old Christmas tinsel, but in the general gloom, the effect was quite reasonable. Each table had been set with a red tablecloth and a somewhat rustic candle in a wine bottle.

At one end of the room, an impromptu stage had been organised by means of sheets of plywood set on beer crates. A tasteful fringe of green material, tartan for some obscure reason, had been tacked in place to hide the undesired 'Worthington' logos. Spotlights on poles had been set up, as had a very weary looking set of public address speakers. A shaven-headed and much pierced youth crouched in a corner fiddling with a number of boxes of electronics, which, judging by the assorted squeaks and bangs, and rising and falling illumination, controlled the lights and sound.

The noise level in the room was pretty high, and it was apparent that many of the ladies had been building up a considerable quantity of Dutch courage. Most tables were well stocked with glasses, and commodious handbags containing an assortment of liquid containers were tucked, ostensibly, out of sight of the bar staff who were shimmering from table to table.

After half an hour or so of rising mayhem, it was becoming clear that some of the audience were becoming restive. Shouts of 'Where are they?' and 'Get 'em on!' were becoming more frequent and the bar staff were being exhorted to get up on stage to 'show 'em how it's done!'.

The room was suddenly plunged into darkness. A hush fell. A single spotlight was switched on, illuminating an apparition on stage, so bizarre, that the hush continued for a few breathless seconds. Then mayhem!

A very large person, dressed in a lurid yellow, halter-neck party frock and wearing a huge curly blond wig stood before them. The makeup, which had apparently been applied by a team of plasterers, barely disguised the considerable blue shadow covering its jaw. Eyebrows had been applied somewhere near the hairline in two black arcs. The front of the dress had been padded out with what could easily have been two official size footballs. The apparition held up a massive bejewelled paw in an effort to quell the riot.

"Good evening ladies!!"

The din subsided a little.

"I said Good Evening Ladies!!!!" and he held the paw to his ear.

"Fuck me, audience participation at a strip night!" Frieda whispered to Carol.

"I hope that's as far as it goes!" They both giggled. Cath hadn't moved since the spotlight came on. She was transfixed. Her mouth was opened a fraction and her blink rate could be measured only with a calendar. Carol nudged Frieda and nodded in Cath's direction. They raised eyebrows at one another.

The audience attempted a feeble 'Good Evening' back.

"Can't hear you!" More pawing of ear and craning of neck.

"Get bloody on with it, you tosser! Can you hear that?" The audience was clearly not in the mood for this brand of childish pantomime banter. The grotesque looked offended as he adjusted his bosom, which was already anything but symmetrical.

His subsequent attempts to warm up the audience with a succession of bawdy jokes simply met with increased hostility, so he eventually gave up.

"Laydeeesss! The time has come I know you've all been waiting for with baited vibratorssssss!"

"Hoooray.....'bout bloody time......do get on..."

"The first act tonight, our very own Bill, for your delectation......"

The room was once more plunged into darkness. The sound system gave out a loud pop and the strains of a rather childish tune emerged.

"Oh, my, God.....," Carol choked back a howl, "It's the theme tune from Fireman Sam! I remember it from when the kids were little!"

The spotlight lit the centre of the stage where the grotesque had been replaced by a rather over-dressed fireman. His uniform was clearly that of a much bigger man.....he was barely as tall as Carol.... and he stood, legs apart, arms outstretched with a huge grin on his face. Fireman Sam ground on remorselessly. His grin began to slip and he shot a glance at the sound man. Clearly he was expecting the tune to change in some way.

The audience started to take an interest in the direction of his gaze, and in the gloom, could clearly see that the sound man was engaged in some sort of private struggle. He appeared to have got his pinkie ring caught up in his nose ring and had completely lost interest in the on-stage proceedings. Fireman Sam faded. There was a moment of silence. The strains of Postman Pat tum-te-tummed into the hall. The audience exploded in helpless laughter.

"This is fabulous!" Frieda was practically on the floor.

The sudden outburst distracted the soundman from his naso-digital battle. He quickly took in the general situation, and one-handed changed the sound track. The fireman on stage was visibly sweating profusely. A vaguely familiar slow dance number blared out. Rather too hastily the fireman started to remove his clothes while mincing around on the stage. A jacket was tossed up stage, a shirt was whirled into the audience revealing a baggy singlet. He had obviously not been let into the secrets of the velcro assembled trousers, as he was now having some difficulty getting them off over his boots. As he hopped around the stage to hoots from the crowd, some wag threw a very large pair of pink knickers which flopped at his feet. He smiled a dubious thank you to the donor. Finally he was in vest and pants and the serious grinding began. To rhythmic clapping from the hall, the vest was removed and whirled to another corner of the audience, and finally the boxers were dropped. He stood there in shiny splendour. A vision of shaved manhood, fully five foot six, reasonably well built, Carol had to concede, wearing a leather posing pouch somewhat loosely filled. Much bumping and grinding followed, and selected members of the audience were invited to rub baby oil on various body parts. This was done with a somewhat inappropriate degree of seriousness on the part of the stripper, and a total lack of inhibition by the rubbers!

Carol and Frieda were becoming restless. Cath continued to stare in silence.

"I've had more fun in the dressing room in GAP."

"Wow, really?"

"He's no Swarzenegger, is he?"

The stripper returned to the stage. The music faded to be replaced by a slowly developing drum roll. He reached for the sides of his thong. As the final cymbal crash exploded, he turned his back and bent suddenly forwards, taking the thong with him. His arse shone out in the spotlight. The crowd roared approval.

"More...More...More..." as he turned slowly to face the audience still bent double. Finally, with a non-verbal 'Ta-Daa' he stood up straight, arms outstretched, thong round his feet. The audiences cheer was less than deafening. The naked member was longish, but rather disappointingly snake-like.

"Dear me, poor lad....."

The lights went out suddenly. A series of thuds, followed by curses were heard from the stage as the poor sod obviously tripped over his thong in his haste to escape the less than enthusiastic crowd, who were even now slow-hand clapping him. Frieda looked at her watch.

"We're missing Eastenders for this."

"Yes, I think it's not quite what we were expecting. Let's slip away. Coming Cath?"

"Er, actually, I think I might just wait a bit longer. See if things, you know, get better...."

Frieda and Carol did a slow take.

"Yes, er, OK then Cath. We'll, er, see you tomorrow?"

"Hmmm....'bye."

Two very surprised women left the Marine that night. One somewhat preoccupied one stayed to the bitter end.

CHAPTER 15

"Bugger this for a game of regular conscripts!" Frazer complained from his self-imposed look-out position on the hatch-cover, "they're not bloody coming, I tell you. Someone has tipped them off. We can't sit here like a bunch of lemons for ever!"

"We've only been here a few hours, for God's sake, Frazer. They'll be here soon enough. And sitting up there like an old broody hen won't bring them any faster. Come and help me with the lunch. Make one of your famous salads, that'll pass the time."

I was becoming exasperated with Frazer. He had been like a cat on hot bricks since we got up that morning, admittedly rather late, a lot of serious sleeping went on once we finally turned in, and from the moment Les disappeared with the documents in a generally building-ward direction, he had maintained a vigil on deck, huffing and puffing, and complaining loudly about Les wandering off and him having to wait around.

"I just hate not knowing what's going on, Tom. And let's face it, here we are with a hold full of beer, not to mention the drugs, with no papers, no Les to vouch for us. What are we supposed to say if someone official starts asking questions?"

"Who's going to ask questions, for God's sake, Frazer? There's been no-one near us since we tied up. It's pretty obvious that no-one gives a toss what we're doing."

"I still say that one of us should have gone with him."

"You still don't trust him do you?"

"I didn't say that, Tom, I've no reason to believe that he is anything other than what he claims he is, I've seen his ID and his passport, and I'm sure he's trying to catch some nasty villains and no, I don't trust him if you must know."

"Bloody hell, Frazer, why not?" I had good reason to take Frazer's gut feelings seriously. He had a nasty knack of being right.

"He's a Customs man, Tom, a policeman with teeth. A lot of power and no sense of proportion. A gorilla with toothache and a chainsaw. Have we got garlic or not? I'm quite sure he's not above using any convenient chicken, i.e. us, as bait to catch the fox, i.e. the drug barons in question. We could be sat here right now, about to be descended on by gun-toting hoodlums bent on retrieving their dope at any cost. By the time the cavalry arrive, we could be dog-meat. Pass me the mustard, the Dijon. The first thing we'd know about it would be a gentle rock of the boat as they crept aboard..."

The boat rocked gently. Frazer dropped the mustard in the salad bowl. I think I screamed, I'm not sure.

"Is anybody home?" sang a light female voice.

"Bastards are using women as decoys," hissed Frazer, "keep quiet and slug them as they come down the steps."

"Hang on, Frazer, that voice is awfully familiar. It sounds like Frieda to me, what's she doing here?"

"You mean they've got Frieda?! My God it's worse than I thought!"

"Fuck off Frazer, you daft bugger, I'm going up."

"Surprise!" sang Frieda.

"Surprise!" sang Cath.

"What the f..., what are you two doing here?" I demanded, much less gallantly than was obviously expected.

"Charming, I'm sure. That's a lovely welcome after we drove all the way here to welcome you all back home. We thought you might be slightly pleased to see us, female company after your long hazardous voyage and all that stuff, and all we get is '...what the fuck are you doing here!', really lovely that is!" Cath flushed at Frieda's expansion of my welcoming speech.

"Frieda, I'm sorry, really I am, and you Cath, honestly. You've no idea how glad we are that it is you two and not someone else," I shot a black look at Frazer, "come on aboard and have lunch, it's nearly ready."

"Were you expecting someone else, Tom?" asked Cath, "'cos if it's not convenient..."

"Bugger off, Cath," said Frieda, heading down the companionway steps, "I'm starving and I need a drink. I'm sure there's plenty for everyone, eh, Tom? We've brought some goodies too, as it happens."

"Sure, Frieda, of course, thanks, come on Cath, welcome aboard. We're actually waiting for Les to come back with the truck to take our cargo away, that's all. Shouldn't be long now."

Frazer huffed.

"Tom!" Cath hissed tugging my sleeve, "where's the ladies? Tom! The loo?"

"Ladies is it you want, Cath?" boomed Frazer. Cath winced. "No ladies room on this boat, Cath you'll have to go over the rail. It's quite safe. I'll hold you!"

Cath beheld Frazer with horror and loathing.

"Bloody hell, Frazer, you silly sod," Frieda protested, "she'll wet her pants in a minute! Where's the loo!" Cath found Frieda only slightly less embarrassing than Frazer. I put her out of her misery.

"Over there, Cath, behind that wooden door. Do you know how to use it?"

"What?" Cath was beginning to panic.

"It's a sea-toilet, Cath, first you lift the lid and make sure there's some water in it. If there isn't just give the pump a couple of strokes with the lid down, then after you're finished..."

"For God's sake Tom!" exclaimed Frieda. Cath was seriously beginning to consider the rail option. Frieda bundled her into the head. "Just pee Cath! Tom can sort out the plumbing details later!" Cath stopped her slamming the door.

"But Frieda, it's not just..." whimpered Cath.

"Better still!" declared Frieda glaring at me with, I thought, unnecessary malice. She pushed the door shut.

"Right you two, on deck, give the lady some peace."

"Just let me switch on the extractor fan..." I reached for the switch panel.

"Tom!"

"OK, OK, I'm going."

The sun had come out and it was quite pleasant sitting out on deck while Cath made herself comfortable below us.

"I honestly thought Cath never did that." mused Frazer.

"Did what?" asked Frieda.

"Crapped. You know, I thought she was like the Queen. Had the operation. The crapectomy. You live and learn."

John Paton

"Boats are like that," I reminded him, "you learn a lot you didn't expect about people on board boats, eh Frazer?"

"Hmm," Frazer grinned and checked the horizon.

"Silly sod," said Frieda.

"So what are you two doing here, really?" I asked.

"Well, I was missing you, Tom..."

"Yes, but listen, Frieda, this isn't exactly a jolly with the lads, or had you forgotten all that?"

"No, Tom, I hadn't forgotten..."

"Jesus, I hope you said nothing to Cath about it!"

"Of course I didn't, what do you take me for?"

"Thank God for that."

"As I was saying, I was missing you and I thought it would be a good idea if we could be here to meet you as you came in. Actually, Cath thought of bringing the food and stuff, you know, a welcoming committee. I asked Cath if she knew where you were docking and she dug out the details. When we phoned the port authority this morning they said you were already in so we jumped in Cath's car and here we are!"

"You really shouldn't have, Frieda, we'll be back home pretty soon, and the fewer people we have around here the better. We may have to get out fast."

"If we ever get rid of this bloody beer," grumbled Frazer.

"Well, we won't hang about if you think it might be a problem. We can give you a second welcome when you arrive back home! A proper one!"

"I'd much prefer an improper one." I was warming to this theme.

"Oh God, here we go!"

"Sorry, Frazer, we'll behave. So when do you think they'll come for this cargo, Tom?"

"I'm buggered if I know, Frieda, I just hope it's soon. This isn't exactly my idea of a cosy berth. There isn't a pub for miles."

Cath appeared in the companionway and looked at me meaningfully.

"Hi, Cath...oh, yes...OK...finished are you? Yes, well, I'll just sort things out, shall I?"

"I actually think it's all OK, Tom. I read the instructions on the lid. I think it worked.

Frazer stuck his head over the side.

"Yep, all away Cath, you shouldn't use so much paper,

128

though, tends to clog the pump. By jove you were desperate, weren't you?"

"One of these days, Frazer..." snarled Frieda. Cath retreated in embarrassment.

"Let's have some lunch." I suggested wearily.

"It really is amazing how a good tasty salad can make even corned beef taste good," announced Frieda, wiping her lips.

Her effort to restore a modicum of good-will with Frazer, however, seemed to be lost on the man in the shell-suit who had suddenly appeared in the companionway and was pointing a very realistic machine-gun at the group round the table.

"Nobody fuckin' moves!" he said.

Thankfully Frieda smothered the impulse to turn round to identify the source of this interruption.

Cath put her hand to her mouth and uttered a tiny bleat.

I glanced at Frazer, who had gone chalk white. He put down his fork, very slowly.

This was a very nervous gun-man. He was sweating visibly and the muzzle of the gun vas vibrating like a tuning fork.

"Put your hands on your head and follow me up these stairs. No funny stuff now, this isn't a replica!"

We followed obediently to find another armed shell-suit on the dock-side. This one was black and looked about twelve.

"I thought it was the policemen who were supposed to look young as you got old," Muttered Frazer.

"Fuckin' shut it you!" barked the kid.

I scanned the dock-side for possible help, but as usual there was no-one about.

"Just walk quickly over to that container and get in," the frightened one ordered, poking Frazer with the muzzle of his gun.

"All of us?" asked Frieda.

"Yeah, all of you! Move it!"

We trotted off in the direction of an old rusty unmarked container. As we got near, the rear door swung open and two men jumped out. They were wearing jeans and leather jackets, but didn't appear to be armed. Our boys were obviously the soldiers of the group.

"Get in!"

We clambered into the darkness of the container. There seemed to be someone else inside, but the door slammed shut before we could see much.

Apart from Cath's quiet sobs, none of us seemed to want to break the silence. I could hear a muffled conversation outside followed by retreating footsteps.

"Sorry folks, this is my fault, I'm afraid," Les announced from the darkness. Cath screamed.

"Les! What the hell..."

"Bit of a cock-up. Sorry."

He sounded funny, like he was having difficulty talking.

"Are you all right? Where are you?" I reached out in the direction of the voice.

"I'm OK mainly, Tom. Just missing a couple of teeth and I think my arm's broken. Can you undo my wrists and ankles? Bastards tied me up with gaffer tape. It's a sod to get out of."

I found him lying in a corner with his back to me. I fumbled around his arms trying to find the end of the tape to unwind it. He jerked violently.

"Sorry, Les!" I stopped tugging.

"Don't stop, Tom, just get it over with as quick as you can, please hurry."

I managed to remove the tape from his hands as gently as possible. He was sweating buckets and obviously in a lot of pain. He lay down flat as I worked on his ankles.

"Jesus, mate, they really did a number on you, didn't they?"

My eyes were becoming accustomed to the dark, and by the little light that got in through small holes here and there in the container, I could make out Frazer kneeling next to Les's head wiping blood from his face with a handkerchief.

"Always carry a clean hanky, my mum used to say, never know when you might need it!"

"Thanks, Frazer," Les sat up and took the proffered handkerchief, "you make a lovely nurse."

Frieda was comforting Cath in the other corner of the container. Les's face looked like it had been used to tenderise a house-brick.

"Tom, could you reconstitute some of that tape and splint my arm with these bits of wood over there?"

There were bits of what looked like broken orange-boxes scattered about and the baddies had used about a mile of tape on

Les. He was soon suitably splinted, after more wincing and sweating and he once more lay back to recover.

"Jesus, what a cock-up!" he groaned.

"Quite," remarked Frazer, "I take it you've noticed that we have female company?"

"What!?" Les sat bolt upright. "What the hell are they doing here?"

"Good question," I replied looking over at Frieda who looked back unhappily. Cath's face was buried in her shoulder.

"Christ, that's all I fucking need!" said Les as he flopped back on to his back.

After a few minutes uncomfortable silence he sat up again.

"Right, this is the situation..."

"Can I just interrupt you for a moment, Les? There is one among us who knows not what transpires." Frazer looked over at Cath.

"A..and I d..don't want to know, either," she sobbed, "just get me out of here, Tom, I'm very frightened."

"Yes, OK, Cath, we'll do our best. I'm sure everything will be all right."

"Might not be a bad idea to keep her in the dark about this, Tom," said Les, "as long as she does what she's told she should be OK."

"OK, then, you were saying?"

"Yes, the situation is this. Our friends caught me sniffing around for clues. It was pure bad luck, really. I had got all the paperwork sorted out and was coming back to the boat when I decided to have a quick look round the nearest warehouse, just out of curiosity..."

"What do they say about feline fatalities?" Frazer was doing his irony-ing.

"Yeah...anyway, I had a look around and found nothing suspicious, and I was just leaving through a side door when who do I walk slap into but one of the villains we've been nearly catching for years...and he made me!"

"Made you?"

"Recognised me, you know, so he shouts for his heavies and I leg it...right into the bastards. One of them did the bridge-work with his gun-butt and the other one broke my arm with a pick-handle."

"Charming!" Frazer shuddered.

"Quite! Anyway, it seems that the truck they were going to use has broken down, or something, and they had decided to put the stuff in this container until tomorrow and move it then, but of course they now have another problem. Or to be pedantic, five problems."

"What do you think they'll do?"

"I don't know. They could just decide to abandon the lot and bugger off in the hope that by the time we get out of here they'll be long gone. Or they might decide to get another truck and take the stuff anyway, again leaving us here..."

"Let's hear theory number three, then," I prompted.

"Well, they might just be stupid enough to think that a murder rap is worth risking to get clean away."

"Personally I don't like that particular theory," Frazer said, "it has a finality about it I'm not prepared to contemplate at the moment."

"We have to take it into consideration, though, Frazer," I said, "they look to me like they wouldn't grudge the ammunition."

"Correct, Tom. I'm quite sure these two soldiers are itching to try out their new toys, but we do have one thing in our favour."

"Oh? What might that be?"

"Guns make a hell of a din. They won't shoot us here. They'll have to move us. While we're here we're safe."

"Suddenly this crate has become terribly attractive somehow," said Frazer.

"So what do we do now?" asked Frieda sounding more in control than I felt.

"We wait," said Les.

"Until they shoot us or until we die of starvation?"

"Well you can if you want, Frazer," Les's love for Frazer's wit was showing no signs of growing, "I however will wait until dark and hopefully get out of this box."

"It's pretty substantial, Les, we won't be able just to burst through the doors and we don't have as much as a tin-opener between us."

"I'm working on it Tom," said Les, "I'm working on it. This container is pretty old. With luck it was abandoned because it was damaged."

"I can see out!" Frieda was in the corner nearest the doors, "there's a little hole here you can look through and I can see the boat...there's somebody on it...I think it's one of the shell-suits."

"Let's have a look," Les was struggling to his feet. Frieda

yielded her spy-hole and came and sat beside me. Cath seemed more composed and was fussing with her somewhat rumpled dress. Frieda slipped her arm in mine and smiled.

"This is another fine mess you've got me into, Stan!"

"Sorry Olly," the words came naturally enough but I hadn't the heart for the full impersonation.

"We'll be OK, won't we, Tom?"

"Sure we will. Les is a lot more capable than he looks, believe me. He's got a gun if the worst comes to the worst..."

"Correction, Tom, HAD a gun, they found it on me and decided it might be wise not to let me keep it," Les grunted from the spy-hole.

"Oh, well, if he ever gets another one he'll know what to do with it, then, which is more than I would."

"I wish Andy was here," said Frieda.

"I know what you mean," I agreed, "we could use his expertise if it comes to a ruck."

Frazer was silent during this exchange, but we both knew what was going through his mind.

I held out my hand and found his. He gripped it and moved closer. I realised he was near to tears.

"Silly sod!" he muttered thickly. But he held on.

"There are two or three of them prowling about the boat now," announced Les, "I think they're trying to start the engine."

"They'll have a job," I replied, "I've got the keys in my pocket, and I kicked the knob off the battery isolator switch on the way out of the boat. They'll need a new one."

"I wondered what you were doing, Tom," said Frieda, "I thought you had tripped on the steps."

"That's what you were supposed to think."

"Good man, Tom...yes they've abandoned that. Now they're undoing the hatch cover...one of them is going in."

"I hope he falls and breaks his stupid neck!" Cath was obviously feeling better.

"Well said, Cath," I gave her a little clap, "we'll have you home in no time, you'll see!"

"Oh, I do hope so, Tom. Mum'll be terribly worried."

"She knows where you are, then?" asked Les.

"Well, no, not really, I told her we were going to Truro for the day. She wouldn't like me going to Bristol."

"Great! What about you, Frieda, did you tell anyone where you were going?"

"I don't think so, Andy's in London today, we just came on the spur..."

"Terrific! So no-one will be looking for you?"

"No, I suppose not..."

"OK, look, I reckon that they plan to move the stuff either tonight or tomorrow. We'll keep an eye on what's happening at the boat and meantime try and figure out how to get out of this sardine tin. Cath, you take first watch."

"OK, Les...oooh!"

"What."

"I can't get up!"

"What do you mean?"

"I mean I can't get up! My dress seems to be caught at the back. See if you can free it, Tom, but carefully, it's a good one."

I went to her and started fumbling behind her back.

"Has this dress got buttons down the back?" I asked.

"Yes, it has little pearly ones with a sort of swirly..."

"Yes, never mind that now, Cath, it's just that they seem to be caught between two of the panels on the container. You could admire them from outside right now."

"How did that happen?"

"Presumably when you flopped down there you bumped the side hard enough to force the panels apart and they trapped the buttons. Now when you try to get up they get caught tighter."

"Can't you force them apart again, Tom?"

"Not really...tell you what though, can you sort of slide up the crack? I think I could get a big enough opening further up."

Cath slowly struggled to her feet. I could see that it was doing her precious dress a power of no good, but at least the buttons were still attached, all but one, maybe. I prised a gap between the panels.

"OK Cath, try now!" She lurched forward and was free, minus yet another button, and a bit of dress, "sorry."

The dress slipped off her shoulder showing a chaste bra-strap.

"Oh, Tom, you ripped it!"

"Sorry Cath, I'll buy you a new one when this is over, I promise."

She glared at me and took up her look-out position holding her dress in place.

"Let's have a look at that crack, Tom," said Les, "how wide do you reckon we could force it?"

"Not much down here. Maybe a couple of inches further up, though, there's nothing holding this seam together. I think we've found that damage you were hoping for."

"Tsk, tsk, British workmanship!" Frazer was feeling better.

"Start packing these laths into the gap and see what we can do. Maybe we can force it enough..."

"Shouldn't we wait until it's a bit darker? I mean they might see what we're up to."

"That's true, Tom, OK, let's get some rest. We'll take turns keeping an eye on what they're up to on the dock then make a start when it gets dark." Les took little persuasion to flop to the floor. He was obviously in considerable pain.

Dark seemed to take forever to arrive. The bad guys had apparently decided earlier on that they could do nothing without transport and headed off in the direction of the main buildings, leaving one of the shell-suits on guard, perched on the bonnet of Cath's car. Of course even moonlight was considerably lighter than the gloom of the container, but Les eventually decided it was dark enough to give us cover. We were soon packing everything we could lay our hands on into the widening gap in the container wall. The men's shoes were most successful, and with brute force we were able to create a gap of about nine inches wide over a couple of feet. The only snag was that it was about four feet up the wall.

"We'll never get through that, Les," Frazer complained.

"You certainly won't, that's for sure!"

"Bog off Les, no-one'll get through that gap."

"Someone really slim just might..."

We all turned to look at Cath who was simultaneously trying to disappear and look fat.

"No! No! Absolutely not! It'll ruin my dress totally! Look at all these sharp edges! No!"

"Oh, well, that's it then. We wait until they come and massacre us with those machine guns..."

"Tom Morton...! Two dresses then! Good ones! From London!"

"Cath, if you pull this off you can have a whole wardrobe from Paris," said Les, "I happen to know where I can get a hold of some haute couture which no-one seems to want to admit to owning."

"OK, what do I do?"

"Well, you'll need to climb on someone's back and somehow try and squeeze through the gap. The drop to the ground will be quite tricky, so be careful. Then it's simply a matter of opening the doors from outside. I'm pretty sure they're not locked."

Frazer volunteered to be the step-up and Cath clambered up rather shakily. She got one leg through the gap.

"Ohhh...my dress keeps catching. I think I can get through, though!"

"Good girl," encouraged Les, "keep trying."

"Nearly there...oh something else is caught now, there's nothing this side to step on! ...umph ...I...think... I'm...through!" and she disappeared through the gap. Her dress, however did not, nor, we noted with interest did her bra. There was a muffled thud from outside.

Seconds later a knock came to the door.

"Yes?"

"Tom! Can you hear me?" Cath hissed.

"Yes! For goodness sake open the door!"

"Not until you give me my clothes back!"

"Christ Cath, we're trying to escape here! This is no time for false modesty!"

"I am practically starkers out here! I'm not having you lot ogling me no matter how desperate the situation! I'll open the door a bit and you can pass me my clothes, then you can come out."

"Just do it, Tom," said Les, handing me the remains of Cath's attire, "we'll be here all night!"

"OK Cath, open the door!"

The door opened a crack and a hand appeared. I thrust the rag into it.

"Hurry up Cath!"

"Ok you can come out."

We emerged cautiously on to the dock-side. In the dim light we could make out the boat, Cath's car near it, and Cath, totally bedraggled, half naked, bleeding, with tears painting tracks of mascara down her cheeks.

"Tidy yourself up a bit girl," said Frazer, "you look terrible!"

CHAPTER 16

We were out of our prison, but we were by no means certain we were out of trouble. Cath had recovered her composure to some extent after having scrounged a tee-shirt here and a belt there, and pieced together an outfit which covered what the remnants of her dress plainly did not.

Frazer was keeping his distance in case she found a heavy object with which to strike him, but he needn't have bothered as Cath's general state of saturation panic more or less swamped any other emotions she might have felt.

"OK we're out, now what?" I asked, as we seemed to be frozen in a bunch behind the container.

"Check out the sentry, Tom," Les was retrieving his shoes from the escape hole," is he still there?"

I sneaked a look round the end of the container. The guard was still there, but he had managed to break into Cath's car and was in the passenger seat with the interior light on.

"He's inside Cath's car. He seems to be reading a book," I reported. Cath whimpered slightly.

"Good, nice bit of shoddy sentry duty. Just what we need."

Frieda helped Les into his shoes.

"I reckon the others are still around, waiting for transport. Probably sleeping in their cars over by the warehouse there."

Cath let out a loud sob.

"Shh! Cath," said Les, "I'm going to try to get to a phone. If we can get some troops here quickly we might just be able to round this lot up. Could be some shooting, though, so I'd like to get you lot, especially the girls, away first."

Cath decided to have hysterics.

"Jesus Christ Cath," hissed Frazer, "could you please can it? There's a bunch of homicidal maniacs with machine guns trying to catch a few winks not a hundred feet from here. Have some fucking consideration!"

"Th-there's no need to s-swear, Frazer," wailed Cath, "I'm frightened. We could be killed. What's going to happen?"

Her misery reached a soft spot in Frazer's heart.

"I'm sorry, Cath, really I am. Look, I'm frightened too if it's any comfort. I didn't mean to be rotten to you. Here, take my hand."

Cath hesitated at first, then decided that Frazer was being sincere. She caught him in a death grip and closed her eyes.

"Christ, girl, I didn't mean you to take it off at the wrist, relax, you'll pull a muscle!"

"Could you two shut it and listen!" Les was getting ready for action. "Tom, you and I can jump the guard in the car, I reckon. That'll let you lot get away in Cath's car..."

"Oh, sure we can!" I wasn't keen, "and he gets to his gun and blows our heads off! No way, Les, I'm no guerrilla fighter and you've only one good arm, remember?"

"Have you got a better idea?"

"I have, as a matter of fact." I had, too.

"Do you see how the tide has gone out and the boat has dropped down below the harbour wall? Remember we left slack on the warps to allow for it?"

"Tom, this is hardly the time or place for a lesson in seamanship!"

"Shut up and listen. I reckon we could get aboard Sligo and get away in her without the guard seeing us. He probably wouldn't notice until we were well away from the dock."

"But he's between us and the boat, "Les pointed out, "how would you get past him without being spotted?"

"We don't need to. There's bound to be a few dinghies at the slip. We can easily get there without being seen, then we row round and climb aboard from the sea!"

Les thought about it for a few seconds.

"Yes, that'll work. Good thinking, Tom. OK you and Frazer take the girls and I'll see you when this is over...I hope!"

"Wait a minute, Les, why don't you come, too? You can radio for help from the boat."

"No, Tom, I need to be here to help round up the gang, much as your suggestion appeals. No, you lot get the boat away from here, you don't need to go far, somewhere busy would be best, and report to the nearest Customs or police. Give them my card." And he thrust a business card into my hand.

"Ah, Tom," Frazer tapped my arm, "I take it you've forgotten that you effectively disabled the engine earlier on."

"We can sail her out."

"I think our sentry friend, sloppy as he is, might just notice a few hundred square feet of white canvas rising from the sea in the moonlight and decide to turn it into net curtains with his pea-shooter."

"Look, Frazer, let's just get aboard. We can work out the details once we're there." I had an overpowering urge to get on board Sligo. I just knew that I could do something constructive once I was there. Here, I could do nothing.

"OK, go for it," Les said, "I'll keep an eye on our studious friend. One at a time, keep low, not too fast, Tom you go first...OK, NOW!"

It's difficult to run not too fast, at a crouch, when you're trembling with fear and your eyes are shut. I soon realised that I would have to look where I was going or I would end up in the harbour. To my utter relief and amazement I found myself on the sloping ramp of the slip and was soon below the level of the dock. I sat down to get my breath back. Frieda fell over my feet and let out a tiny scream.

"Ow! Shhh! Jesus, look where you're going! Are you all right?"

"Yes, I was frightened to look!"

I smiled a little condescending, but understanding 'women, bless 'em' type smile and was glad Frieda hadn't gone first to witness my arrival.

"Here's Cath!"

"Catch me, catch me, catch me..." she was muttering as she hit the slip. We caught her and she fainted.

"Cath! Wake up!" hissed Frieda slapping her gently.

Cath stirred.

"Sorry Frieda, I feel OK now, you can stop hitting me," she whispered.

Frazer arrived like a charging bull.

"I'm getting too fucking old for all this James Bond stuff," he gasped, "let's find that dinghy and get out of here."

I was staring at the end of the slip. There was something wrong. Who ever heard of a slip with absolutely no dinghies of any kind tied up to it. Nothing. Not so much as a bit of drift wood sullied the water's edge.

"What the f...!?"

"Oh brilliant," Frazer groaned, "what now professor? Any other bright ideas?"

"I'll swim round to the boat," I reluctantly volunteered, "her tender is in the water, I'll be back in a tick, don't worry."

I stripped to my underpants and waded into the water. It was filthy and freezing.

"Be careful, Tom!" was what Frieda should have said.

"God, Tom, you've got a hole in your pants!" is what she actually said. I took a deep breath and pushed off. I couldn't help feeling that at a time like this I could have done with a little more moral support. Sartorial criticism was decidedly de trop.

It seemed like miles before the friendly bulk of Sligo Bay's stern loomed over my head. I quickly found the tender tucked in between the hull and the dock-side and scrambled aboard. I decided to have a quick look to make sure there was no-one aboard and carefully folded down the stern boarding ladder. I climbed until I could just see over the stern. The boat was in darkness. It seemed to be deserted. I could make out my sweater on the cockpit seat where I had left it earlier. I was freezing. I reached over the stern and picked it up. The beer bottle that was hidden in its folds hit the cockpit floor with a heart-stopping clatter. I think I may have wet myself, but I'm admitting nothing. After about a minute I dared to move. No one had heard the noise. At least I now knew that there was definitely no one aboard. No one alive at any rate.

"What the hell kept you?" Frazer demanded on my return, "I thought you had decided to swim to Wales!"

"Sorry, folks, just stopped off to collect a sweater. Bit cold after that swim."

"You were away long enough to knit the bloody sweater, and what was that clatter? Sounded like a bottle. "You didn't stop off for a drink too, by any chance?"

"Sod off Frazer, help the girls into the dinghy and push us off." I was in no mood for Frazer's sarcasm.

I rowed us back to Sligo to the accompaniment of Cath's teeth chattering.

"Well, we've got a nice night for it," quipped Frazer.

No one seemed to be caring much.

Frieda tapped me on the knee, "Tom!"

"What is it love?"

"Have you forgotten that I don't like boats?"

"I must confess that it had slipped my mind, my darling. I recommend, however that you come with us. The alternative could be unpleasant. It's a bit like reminding the surgeon you don't like general anaesthetic, really."

Frieda sat back and thought about this.

"Anyway, it's like a millpond tonight, you should be all right."

"Tom, I get sick thinking about boats, remember?"

"Look, you'll be OK. I've been thinking about where we go from here. Going out to sea would be the obvious thing to do, but it's quite a way to the nearest safe haven, so what I thought was we could go up-river to Bristol."

"Can you s-sail to Bristol, Tom?" Cath was taking an interest, "I thought it was miles from the sea."

"The river is navigable all the way to the shops, Cath."

"Gosh!" The word 'shops' had the desired effect on Cath and she almost smiled.

"Also, we're more likely to find a policeman in Bristol than in the Bristol Channel."

"True, Tom, true, but we are painting ourselves into a corner, rather," said Frazer.

"I know, Frazer, but so are the baddies, if they decide to follow us."

"Oh..!" Cath yelped.

"...not that they will," I added hastily.

The dinghy nudged Sligo's stern. I shipped the oars and grabbed the boarding ladder.

"You first, Frazer, and help the girls."

Frazer shinned up the ladder and took up position in the cockpit.

"C'mon Cath, you first."

"Keep your voice down Frazer!" I hissed nodding in the direction of the dock.

"Oh! Yes, OK, skipper, forgot, sorry, I'll be quiet..."

I drew my finger across my throat and he got the message.

We all scrambled aboard and I put the dinghy on a long line.

I noted with satisfaction that it drifted slowly on the tide in the general direction of Bristol.

"Well, Tom, the tide's on our side, but I'm afraid the wind's not." He was right. We were hard against the fenders. We would drift nowhere.

"Damn!"

"I suppose we could row her out?"

"Too heavy. Never get her moving." I was casting around for inspiration. "Tell you what, though, we could warp her out!"

"Now you're talking, skipper, how?"

"D'you see that channel marker out there? We could row a line out to that and pull her up to it. We would be well out in the stream by then and we could drift from there."

"Have we got a line that long?"

"As long as an Irish hill."

"So we have begorrah..."

"Is that one of these sailing terms, Tom?" asked Frieda.

"What?"

"As long as an Irish hill"

"No it's more of a horsey term, really."

"Is it? I've never heard it before."

"No, you won't have, I just made it up."

"Really, Tom!"

"You row out, Frazer, I'm knackered."

"What if the sentry spots me, Tom? He's likely to start taking pot-shots. He might puncture my dinghy!"

"Wear something dark, then. Here, have my sweater."

"It's all wet."

"God almighty! Get a dry one, then."

"No, I'll wear yours, I might get shot and I'd hate to get blood on my own stuff."

He retrieved the dinghy and tied the long warp to the thwart.

"Right, you pay out the line. If you think you're going to run out just make it fast. I'll get the message. You can tie another one to it then, OK?"

"OK, good luck." He struck out strongly for the marker.

It would be a good few yards before he was out far enough to be seen from the car and I could see him craning his neck to see over the dock-side. After what seemed like an age he reached the channel marker and I could make him out tying the warp to it. It passed through my mind that what he was doing was strictly illegal and it would be just like our luck to be caught. Then I realised that being caught would be quite handy under the circumstances, so I decided that it was therefore most unlikely to happen, knowing our luck.

He was soon back at the boat. I took the dinghy line and made it fast.

"OK, let's go for it, Frazer, slip the mooring lines and come back here and help me. We'll have to hand the line; the winch will make too much noise."

Just to be safe I took a turn of the line round the samson-post and we started to pull. At first it seemed like we were getting nowhere. She was a big boat, and heavily laden into the bargain, but sustained heaving soon had some effect. Not quite the effect I was hoping for, however. Why I imagined we would move crab-wise out into the river, I'll never know, but that's exactly what didn't happen. As soon as Sligo unstuck from the dock she headed off up-river with the tide in a huge crazy arc, with the channel marker as a pivot. Soon we were on the end of the line downstream of the marker, but pointing the wrong way.

"Let her go, Tom!"

"But we'll go backwards!"

"Who gives a shit? Let her go damn it!"

"But the line, it'll be a hazard..."

"Soddit Tom, there's a bigger bloody hazard on the dock over there! The sentry's seen us!"

I let go.

Now as every yachtsman knows, drifting with the current is a free ride, but as the man said about free lunches, there ain't no such thing. The bill arrives in the form of the realisation that as far as the body of water in which you are floating is concerned, you are stationary and therefore by definition, you cannot steer, change the direction in which you are facing, or more importantly, avoid large, hard obstacles. In order to achieve these desirable capabilities you have to arrange to either go faster than the water, difficult without some form of motive power, or alternatively, slower. The immediate threat from the shore had receded with the hasty withdrawal of the sentry in the direction of his masters. A more solid threat, however, presented itself in the shape of the next channel marker down the line, now approaching out of the gloom.

"Let go the anchor, Frazer, quick!" I yelled.

"How much chain do you want?"

"Never mind all that, just let it go. As soon as it hits the bottom stop the chain. If we drag we can at least steer round this bloody marker!"

Frazer freed the anchor and yards of chain rattled out of the pipe. As soon as I saw wake from the stern I spun the wheel to turn her away from the marker. We slipped past by inches.

"Could do with a coat of paint, that marker," Frazer remarked.

"We can't go on like this forever, Frazer, sooner or later we'll snag something big on the bottom..." Sligo pulled up with a lurch. Frazer and I looked at one another.

"D'you think we've snagged something big on the bottom, skipper?"

"Shit, shit, SHIT!!"

In the ensuing silence the unmistakable sound of a powerful outboard came across the water. A large inflatable was heading our way from the dock. Somehow we could guess who was in it.

"Isn't that just typical," said Frazer, "how come they can find a boat and we couldn't?"

"Never mind that, what the hell can we do? We're caught like a rabbit in a snare, here. They've got guns and we've got nothing....Frazer?"

He had suddenly dived below and I could hear him rummaging in the flag locker.

"What the hell are you up to?"

"Ta-Daaa!" he sang, brandishing the old Very pistol, "drop one of these babies in their laps before they reach us and they'll have something else to think about!"

"Jesus, Frazer, I suppose it's worth a try. You'll need to wait until they're really close, though, to make sure. Keep it out of sight for now."

The boat was closing fast and we could make out three men aboard. We stood at the bow trying to look casual, Frazer holding the pistol behind his back like a paramour with a bunch of daisies.

"Right, Frazer, NOW!" I yelled, and he let fly with a red flare.

And it would have hit it's mark, too, if what now happened, hadn't.

The roar of the outboard suddenly stopped with a strangled yelp and the boat nose-dived to a halt pitching it's passengers unceremoniously into the river, guns and all.

"Bugger me!" said Frazer.

"The rope!" I pointed at the boat, "the one we left tied to the marker! It caught his prop!"

The three gangsters were clinging to the stationary boat like drowned rats, obviously thinking nasty thoughts in our direction.

"Told you that rope was a hazard to shipping," said Frazer, blowing across the muzzle of the pistol like a B-movie gunslinger.

"You told me....!" I cuffed his ear and we burst into relieved laughter.

"What are you two laughing about?" Frieda enquired from the companionway steps.

"Oh, nothing much, three bad swimmers and a cowboy mainly."

"Why have we stopped?"

"We're anchored to the bottom, actually," I admitted.

"Yes, what are we going to do about that, by the way?" asked Frazer.

"The easiest way would be to motor her round and see if she'll come free. I'll rig a connection to the battery and get the engine started, now that we've got a breathing space. I don't imagine our friends over there feel like continuing the chase."

"No they look like they wish they had kept up their subs to the RAC."

The men had climbed back into the boat and were fishing around the stern, trying to untangle the rope. Having had to do this myself on previous occasions, to which I would not normally admit, I knew it would take them more than a few minutes even with the aid of a very sharp knife. When a big outboard grabs hold of a strong rope it grabs good. We would be sipping ale in Bristol before they got going anywhere.

Chugging up-river through the Avon gorge is an impressive trip by any standards, particularly where you pass under Brunel's lovely Clifton Suspension Bridge.

"Watch out for falling bodies!" quipped Frazer. I looked up

automatically. I could see how it was a popular suicide leap. The sheer height made it a cert and the scenery lent a high degree of drama. I'd never heard of anyone actually scoring a direct hit on a passing boat, though.

Once we had got the engine started we freed ourselves from the bottom relatively easily. The alternative would have been to leave the lot behind, chain and all, with a marker buoy, hopefully to retrieve it at a later date. I hadn't been too keen to do that.

"D'you think we'll make it to the town before closing time?" Frazer asked hopefully.

"Well, considering that it's half-past midnight now, no, I doubt it."

"Is it? I hadn't noticed the time. Doesn't time fly when you're enjoying yourself!"

"Any chance of a cuppa, Frieda, I'm gasping...and frozen!"

I was beginning to take an interest in things like cold, hunger, and all the little things you take for granted when people are not actually threatening your life.

"Keep it down, Tom, Cath's asleep. She's absolutely whacked, poor thing. I'll put the kettle on."

"Dig out the rum bottle, too, there's an angel, I need something right now."

I decided to motor right into the town. With any luck they would let us through the lock into the floating harbour. I planned to tie up next to the Watershed. I wanted to see Cath's face next morning when she found herself in among the shops. But mainly I wanted to get my head down. I felt more tired than I had ever felt in my entire life.

CHAPTER 17

What Cath wore to go shopping next morning will remain a secret between her and the nearest Dorothy Perkins, but suffice to say she returned before most of us had done more than think about having a stretch and a scratch.

I woke to find her standing over me at the cooker. I had spent the night on the cabin sole, there being only three bunks and me being too tired to climb into any of them.

"Hi Cath, nice shorts!" I remarked from my low-level vantage point.

"Don't look up my legs, please Tom, surely you saw enough of me last night."

"Sorry Cath, but you do look rather fetching." She was wearing a pair of flowery bermuda shorts and what I believe is known in fashion circles as a 'body' in dazzling white. It fitted very well indeed. "I've never seen you in anything quite so...ah...so..."

"Revealing?"

"I think flattering was the word I was searching for, but yes, I suppose revealing is appropriate. You getting all daring in your old age?"

"I just thought it was time I modernised my image a bit. I think last night made me grow up very suddenly. I've never had to face a scary situation before and I think I coped with it rather well, really. I always wanted to wear nice sexy clothes but I was too scared to before. But I reckon after last night it'll take a lot to scare me."

"Steady on, Cath you'll be sunbathing topless, next!"

"Oh I don't know if I could do that...yet."

"Good girl. What's in the other bag?" I asked, although I had guessed from her manoeuvrings around the galley.

147

"Breakfast. I got bacon and eggs and tomatoes and sausages and..."

"Poetry!"

"...and croissants and fresh coffee..."

"I've died and gone to heaven, haven't I, you're actually an angel, go on admit it!"

"Oh, Tom!" Cath giggled and fussed among the shopping bags.

"What's going on here then?" demanded Frieda emerging from the pilot berth, barely knickered and shirted and looking very cuddlable in an untidy sort of way.

"Cath is trying to turn my head, Frieda, by talking about food. I reckon she's trying to muscle in on your territory."

"Is she indeed? Good grief, Cath, if I didn't know for a fact that I hadn't brought it with me, I'd have said you had pinched half my wardrobe as well! What's come over you?"

"I don't know why you're making such a fuss, Frieda. You're not the only one who can wear sexy clothes and attract the odd wolf-whistle, you know!"

"Oops, sorry, Cath," Frieda put up her hands in surrender, "no offence meant, honestly, you look really nice...really!"

"Thank-you, do you want sausages and bacon for breakfast?"

"You bet, the works! I'm absolutely starving!"

"Coffee won't be a minute. What d'you think Frazer will want, Tom?"

"Same as Frieda and me but more, I should think." I got up and sat on the sleeping form of Frazer to attract his attention.

"You'll burst my bladder doing that you sod," he muttered from the depths of his pillow.

"Your bladder is on your back?"

"No, but it's really full!"

"This is a charming conversation, I must say," said Frieda, "Here's Cath trying to cook breakfast and all you two can talk about is bladders."

"OK," said Frazer, turning over and stretching, "I'll have everything that's going, thanks. I feel like I haven't eaten for days."

"Yes, when did we last eat?" I wondered.

Four large breakfasts were devoured in unseemly haste and in relative silence. Frieda had contrived to sit next to me and as the meal progressed, she pressed closer, putting her leg over my leg, until she was practically sitting on my knee. By coffee she was snuggled well in to my chest, and Cath and Frazer were becoming painfully aware that their presence was becoming surplus to requirements.

"Well, Cath," Frazer announced, "that was a magnificent meal! I reckon that it's Tom's turn to wash up, don't you?"

"Oh, yes Frazer, definitely Tom's turn."

"And, Frieda should probably help him, don't you think?"

"Absolutely, Frieda should help."

"Shall we go for a stroll around the sights of Bristol Docks then Cath? I must say I could use a leg-stretch, and the atmosphere in this boat is becoming distinctly oppressive."

"Yes, Frazer, most oppressive, let's go."

They both disappeared out on deck, closing the cabin door behind them. We both knew what we had to do, and without a word, set about it with a will.

"I suppose we should do these breakfast dishes before the others get back," I suggested without much enthusiasm after about an hour.

"Sod the dishes," murmured Frieda, "there's bits of you I haven't licked yet. Turn over."

"Bloody hell, Frieda, you may not like boats, but they don't seem to put you off nooky."

"Nothing puts me off nooky."

Some time later there was a thud on deck.

"Sounds like they're back," I suggested trying to sound disappointed. I had to admit that when Frieda was in full flood she was a bit much for me. I could get used to it though, I could certainly get used to it. "And the dishes still aren't done."

"Mmmmm," said Frieda.

"We should at least get dressed."

"They won't come down, Tom, relax, you're so up-tight."

The cabin door swung open and a man's face appeared.

"Oh, sorry, I didn't think there was anyone aboard."

"Evidently!" said Frieda grabbing her shirt. "Do you normally just wander about other people's boats unannounced?"

He backed up the steps out of direct line of sight.

"No, sorry, I'll explain when you're, ah, decent. I'm actually a colleague of Mr Dawson."

"Oh, I see!" I pulled on my shorts, "that's OK then."

John Paton

"No it bloody well is not OK, Tom," Frieda was still miffed, "being Les's mate doesn't give him the right to come barging in here without so much as a polite cough. These Customs people think they can do what they like."

"Actually, I think they can."

"Can what?"

"Do what they like."

"Well he can wait until I'm good and ready to be seen. And if he thinks I'm making him a cup of coffee he's got another think coming!" and she shut herself in her cabin.

I went up on deck.

"Sorry about that, mate," said the visitor, "there really didn't seem to be any sign of life. She a bit upset is she?"

"Oh, don't worry, she'll get over it, what can we do for you?"

"Well, actually, we came to relieve you of your cargo, if it's no trouble. Mr Dawson suggested we might find you around here. The villains have all been rounded up and all we need now is the evidence."

"Thank God for that! Is Les OK?"

"Oh, he's fine. He said to tell you he'll be in touch when you get back to base."

"I suppose we'll be needed to give evidence and all that nonsense? Oh, and what about the small matter of the reward?"

"'Fraid I don't know anything about all that. I'm sure Les will sort all that out with you later. So, can we get started?"

"Sure, help yourself, is that your truck?"

There was a large blue van parked on the quay-side with several boiler-suited men standing next to it.

"Yes. The lads'll do all the work. Have you got a hoist of any kind?"

"Yes, there's a derrick you can rig on the fore-mast. It runs off an electric winch on deck."

"Fine, leave it all to us. I'm sure you've got other things to do," and he gave a knowing smile in the direction of the cabin.

"Oh, yes, the dishes, I'd forgotten about them."

"It was actually the dish, singular, I was meaning. Some people have all the luck!" and he climbed ashore to organise his troops.

Unloading was well under way by the time Frazer and Cath returned.

150

"Thank God for that!" exclaimed Frazer surveying with obvious satisfaction the growing pile of boxes on the quay-side," I've never been so glad to see the back of a year's supply of beer in my life."

"Are they from Customs, Tom?" Cath asked climbing on deck.

"Certainly are, Cath, our part in this little drama is now officially over."

"That's nice, Tom, only I was wondering what had happened to my car. You don't suppose they might know, do you?"

"God, Cath, I'd clean forgotten about your car. I suppose it's still on the dock at Avonmouth. Why don't you ask that chap over there in the suit? He seems to be in charge."

Cath clambered ashore and accosted the Customs man. It was clear from all the head-shaking going on that he had no knowledge of Cath's car, no matter how elaborate her graphic and sweeping manual demonstrations of it's size and shape.

"Stupid man says he doesn't know anything about a car, but if I left it there, it'll probably still be there...says he!"

"Yes, well, he's probably got a bit more to think about than parked cars, Cath. He'll be making press statements about drug-hauls and the like soon. I doubt if that will include references to the security of your Metro."

"But I'm worried about it, Tom; it's not even locked up."

"Look, Cath we'll be passing there on the way home, we can drop you and Frieda off on the way past."

"But that could take ages, Tom, I want to see my little car now!"

"Tell you what, Cath," Frazer interceded, "why don't you and I take a taxi out to Avonmouth now, and fetch it, then you and Frieda can drive home from here. How does that sound?"

"Oh, yes please Frazer, that would be wonderful!" and she actually gave him a hug.

I found this turn of events somewhat perplexing.

"I must say, I'm a bit surprised at this sudden rush of helpfulness, Frazer. I thought you two were sworn enemies?"

"Not any more, Tom, old mate. Cath and I have come to an understanding, haven't we, Cath?"

Cath answered with a little smile and a little shrug, and started busying herself around the galley. Frazer gave me a knowing look and indicated with his head that a stroll on deck would be appropriate.

"What was all that about, Frazer, I hardly dare ask?"

"Don't get the wrong idea, mate, I haven't seen the light, sex-wise or anything, but I've felt closer to Cath these last few days. She seemed to be so out of place among us three and yet she mucked in and did things so against her nature when the chips were down, I realised just how plucky she really is. Anyway, we had a long chat while we were walking, and do you know what she asked me, Tom?"

"No idea, do tell."

"She asked me if I was a homosexual! Came right out with it. No beating about the bush. I was, for once, almost lost for words."

"What did you say?"

"I asked her what made her think that, and do you know what she said?"

"Look, skip the question and answer bit Frazer, just get on with the story."

"Oh, OK, sorry, anyway, she said I reminded her sometimes of her uncle Peter and he was one. What do you think of that?"

"What am I supposed to think?"

"I don't know, really, but it makes you think, you know, Cath being so, well, straight...oh I don't know."

"Frazer, with respect, you're not making much sense. What makes you think that you've got the monopoly of hiding dark secrets behind a facade of normality? Just because Cath keeps herself to herself doesn't mean she's a total innocent. She could be a reformed hooker, for all you know."

"She isn't though, is she?"

"I doubt it, but who can tell?"

"Who indeed. I must confess, Cath's the last person I would have expected to force me to examine my multiplicity of standards. I'm not doing very well in the growing up department, am I?"

"I think you're doing fine, Frazer, considering."

"Considering?"

"Considering you only started last week."

"You mean that night at Frieda and Andy's? Yes I've got that to go back to, haven't I? What do you think I should do, Tom?"

"Look, Frazer, all I think you should do right now, is take Cath to get her car. No doubt we'll find plenty of time during the sail home to discuss the many facets of your personal life, if you want to, that is."

"Hmm, OK, Tom, point taken, but I do value your opinion, you know that, don't you?"

"Yes, Frazer, I know that, I'm sorry, I'm just not in the mood right now, that's all. Bear in mind I have my own little upheaval to deal with as well."

We both looked over to where Frieda was pinning an assortment of singularly un-seamanlike undergarments to an impromptu clothes-line rigged between the two masts.

"Don't need 'Reid's' to interpret that set of signal flags, at any rate," quipped Frazer, "I don't imagine the average Bristolian sees the likes of these every day!"

Indeed a small crowd was gathering, but it wasn't the spectacle of Frieda's frillies that seemed to be absorbing their interest, but the rather odd behaviour of the men loading the boxes into the van. There had obviously been a slight miscalculation in the logistics department, and there was just not enough room to fit them all in. Consequently and much to the public amusement, the customs men were removing the bottles from a dozen or so boxes, flattening the boxes and squeezing them into the spaces available. The resultant ranks of beer bottles left standing on the quayside they were ignoring completely, and indeed the odd one or two had already been accidentally toppled into the harbour. As the doors of the van were finally closed on the load one of the onlookers overcame his natural West-country reticence to enquire as to the fate of the surplus refreshments.

"You comin' back for these 'uns later then?" he enquired cocking a thumb at the ranks of bottles.

"Nah, we don't need them, no room in the van, you can have them if you want."

"Cheers, mister!"

You'd be amazed how many pint-bottles one man can carry. In a matter of seconds the quay-side was totally devoid of bottles, and even the ones that fell off the quay were being searched for by a small boy in a rowing boat, but they had disappeared in the murky waters of the harbour.

The crowd dispersed and the van pulled away leaving us wondering if it had all really happened.

CHAPTER 18

The taxi-trip to Avonmouth had found Cath's car safe and relatively sound where she had left it on the quay-side.

It had collected a few dog-ends, a beer-bottle and what Cath described as 'an extremely nasty magazine'.

"Even Frazer thought it was nasty!" Cath confided in a private moment back at base. I was amused by the 'even' and wondered what Frazer would have said in his defence, if anything.

The sail home had been uneventful and our eventual arrival in our home port was greeted with so little ceremony that it was disappointing.

"What did you expect?" demanded Frazer, "the band of the Royal Marines playing Hearts of Oak?"

"Well, no, but the odd waving granny or toot of a siren would have been nice."

"Tom, you're a merchant ship now, you'll have to get used to the hum-drum routine like all the others. You don't imagine that the captain of the Normandy ferry gets all huffy when no-one waves a granny at his ship docking, do you?"

"No, but this is a first, you know, pioneer stuff, I thought maybe I'd be interviewed by the local paper."

"Yes, well, every cloud has a silver lining. If you'd leapt ashore drunk and exposed yourself to a schoolgirl you'd have been all over the front page for sure. They don't want to print happy things these days. If it's not a disgrace or a disaster they're not interested."

Frazer's dilemma over what to do about Andy was conveniently, if not satisfactorily solved by Andy's sudden long-term posting overseas. In fact he was gone by the time we got back. This led to a certain amount of speculation by Frazer about the government's motives and I confess I had to agree. It all happened too soon after the investigation recently admitted by Dawson.

And speaking of Dawson, we had heard absolutely nothing from him since the night of the great escape. All phone calls to the number on the card he gave me were answered by a particularly surly machine which sounded like a Dalek impersonating Windsor Davies and no-one ever returned my calls.

We had more or less given up on him and written off any hope of collecting the reward money until one evening two or three weeks after we got back.

I had moved in with Frieda to the unanimous unconcern of the local population. I must say I really had expected the odd raised eyebrow, whispers in the post-office queue, you know the sort of thing, but all I got was my mail redirected without asking by the postman and a 'lucky bastard' from the Harbourmaster.

"It's almost as if you felt guilty, Tom, you should be pleased," Frieda said, "I am a single woman, after all, you're not stealing anyone's wife, remember."

"No, but they don't know that! They should be a little bit shocked, surely."

We had invited Frazer round for a curry and we were going over the events of the last few weeks for the umpteenth time.

"I do think it's a bit thick of Dawson not getting in touch though," said Frieda, "I mean he did promise a reward, and they got their baddies and the drugs. It's really not good enough."

"Yes it is a bit off, that," agreed Frazer, "something I meant to ask you, Tom, were those guys who unloaded the stuff from the same branch of Customs as Les?"

"Damned if I know. They just said they were from Customs, I think."

"Didn't it say on the papers or somewhere?"

"Ah...what papers?"

"The receipt, or orders, or whatever he waved at you...he did wave papers at you, I take it? Tom!"

"Now let's not get all worked up, Frazer, he was obviously from Customs, he knew all about it after all."

"Bloody hell, Tom, you don't mean you just took his word for it, do you?"

"Well, yes, actually, he sort of caught me on the hop, like."

"With your trousers down, so to speak," said Frieda.

155

"Yes, well, anyway, I'm sure he was who he said he was."

"Who did he say he was?"

"Ah, I didn't catch his name, actually.

"Or you didn't ask, more like!"

"Look, I..."

The phone ringing saved me from further attack.

"I'll get it!" I volunteered leaping from the table. I recognised the voice immediately.

"Hello, Tom, is that you?"

"Yes, is that you Les?"

"Yes it's me, where the hell have you lot been? I've been trying to get you for ages. The yard phone doesn't seem to be working..."

"No, it's broken..."

"...and you're never at home. The man in the hotel finally suggested I try here."

"Well, yes, here I am." I tried to sound cheerful and unconcerned.

"Look, I'm trying to salvage what I can from that cock-up, can you come up to London to give evidence next Tuesday?"

"All of us?"

"More the merrier!"

"Yes, I suppose so, but I thought it was a success."

"It may have looked like a success from where you were standing but I can assure you it was a total disaster. I got tied up again, all of the gang got clean away, and they even nicked my wallet this time!"

I felt queasy.

"But the bloke said you had rounded them all up," I said lamely.

"What bloke? Oh never mind, at least they didn't get the stuff."

"No," I breathed again, "at least that's safe."

"So we'll have to come and get it from you soon then. Tomorrow be all right? I'll send some blokes with a truck. Make sure the sloppy buggers show you their warrants, by the way, there's been too much slackness about this whole operation in my opinion, OK Tom?...Tom?"

CHAPTER 19

"OK, let's go over it all again." Les was nothing if not persistent. We had answered all his questions about the shambles in Bristol about a dozen times already. Even I was beginning to doubt my memory of what happened. At least he hadn't actually arrested us.....so far.

The sequence of events after the phone call was something that will stay with me a very long time. Within the hour a large black people-carrier was parked in front of the house and two determined men were helping me, Frieda and Frazer into it in the time honoured, head-dipping fashion. No amount of light hearted banter from Frazer elicited any more than a grunt from either of them. Brutally polite was an excellent description of their demeanour.

A few hours later we pulled up outside a somewhat unprepossessing building somewhere in Bristol. The familiar figure of Les met us at the front door.

"I don't fucking believe you, I really don't!" were his first and last words to me before we reached his office somewhere several floors above. We stood looking at one another, feeling vaguely sorry for ourselves.

Finally Frazer snapped, "Fuck it, Les, don't blame us for your total cock-up. You're supposed to be the fucking trained professional. Mr fucking competent and all that shit. We....."

"Shut it Frazer."

Frazer shut it.

"Right, the truck. Think hard. Was there anything at all distinctive about it?"

"It was big....biggish, you know about the size of a normal delivery type truck. I'd say possible about a three to five tonner." I was guessing, but it was my best shot. "Dark blue, but with no writing or anything on it."

"Make?"

Head shakes all round.

"No clue as the number plate I suppose?"

"No, it was side-on all the time....it wasn't an old truck....quite shiny and new.

"Could it have been a respray maybe?"

"Yes, I suppose so."

Les had stopped taking notes some time back.

"And the blokes. The main man. Can we agree on a description?"

"About 40, I'd say. Heavy set but not tall....about Frazer's height. Fair hair cut very short."

"Quite good looking....." was Frieda's contribution.

Les shot a look at Frieda then at Frazer.

"Not my type, mate. Too chirpy by far."

"Chirpy."

"Yes, I prefer the cool, silent type," and he winked at Les.

This didn't seem to improve Les's mood in the slightest.

"The others? Anything you remember?"

"Well, as I said, I think one of them could have been Asian, but I can't be sure."

"Not Chinese?"

"No, not Chinese.....Indian, Pakistani, that sort of thing. Listen Les, are we arrested or anything? I mean it's bloody late, we're all tired......"

"OK, sure, we're not really getting very far. No, you're not arrested..... just helping with enquiries. It's too late to take you back home so we'll put you up next door for tonight. It's a nice hotel. I'd like to visit the dock where you berthed tomorrow, just for a look round. I'd appreciate it if you hung around. You can do any phoning you want to do from the hotel. They're expecting you anyway. I think there will be food laid on if you're hungry."

"I'm not hungry," Frazer grumped, "but I could use a stiff drink. I take it there's a bar?"

"Of course, on the house. In fact, if you don't mind too much, I'd quite like to join you."

"Get us off-guard, eh?"

"No, bugger it Frazer, I really need a drink. This mess has dropped me right in the poo, to be honest. I was angry with you lot at first, but I understand what you had been through and how maybe your guard might have dropped. Believe it or not, I'm on your side on this. I just want to try and rescue something good from the wreckage."

"Fair enough. I just hope you've got over the butch 'bad-guy, bad-guy' interrogation bit. It doesn't suit you...."

"Watch it, sweetheart. I'm not in the mood!"

We were shown into very well appointed rooms in the hotel next door. Frieda and I got a room together, I was gratified to discover. Frazer was next door. Someone had provided a remarkable array of night attire, socks, jocks, slacks, shirts, an entire wardrobe in fact. The bathroom was stocked with the best of cosmetics, shaving gear, everything, in fact that we hadn't been permitted to pack in our hasty departure.

We had arranged to meet in the bar at midnight. I had fifteen minutes to freshen up.

"Listen, Tom, if you don't mind, I think I'll turn in. I am absolutely exhausted with all this. You go and have a drink if you want."

"Yes, OK, love. I don't intend to make a night of it." I kissed her and headed for the bar.

"Ah, there's nothing to beat the healing qualities of a good malt!"

Frazer was on his second Glenfiddich and was beginning to relax at last. I sipped at a Laphroaig. I'm more of an Islay Malt man myself. Les had plumped for Black Label. This was quite a well stocked bar, tucked away discreetly at the rear of the hotel, and as Les had promised, on the house. In fact the complete lack of any bar staff had placed Les behind the counter, administering booze like a pro.

"Has any of the stuff actually appeared on the streets yet?" I asked. There seemed to be too many blanks in this whole thing.

"That's the odd thing. We've had no reports of it anywhere. I can't understand it. You'd think that after all that bother they'd be wanting to cash in. There has to be enough gear in these boxes to show up somewhere."

"How would it normally be used? I mean, it's unlikely to be cheaper than booze."

Frazer was right. Who'd bother paying for an illegal designer drug that mimicked booze when booze was easily available?

"That's the nasty aspect of this one. It's being used as a date-rape drug. It's completely tasteless. Pop a tiny amount into a girl's coke and she's off her head in seconds. Everyone assumes she's hammered, Prince Charming offers to see her to a taxi......"

"Fuck me. That's not nice. And I suppose it's a bastard to detect afterwards?"

"Almost impossible. The only sure sign is that the kid has no alcohol in her bloodstream."

"And so you're saying that there have been no date rapes with drugs reported recently?"

"None with this drug, no. All the other drugs people use can be detected."

"What about the beer? Has it shown up anywhere?"

"Yes, that's interesting. The beer has turned up around the Bristol and Cheltenham areas on the black market. Just few bottles here and there. No boxes of course."

"How would the drug normally be recovered? From the cardboard, I mean."

"Not sure. I assume the boxes would be shredded and soaked somehow, to remove the drug. It's normally found in pellet form or on a tiny piece of rice paper. It's hard to say what they'll do this time."

We sat quietly for a while, each with his own thoughts on the matter. Finally Frazer drained his glass and stretched.

"Right, I'm turning in. I don't know about you two but I'm wiped out by all this."

"Yes, good idea Frazer, I'll finish my drink. I won't be long behind you."

I wanted a quiet moment with Les. We watched his retreating figure. He looked as tired as I felt.

"Listen Les. I want you to get Frazer and Frieda out of this mess right now. It's nothing to do with them and it's not fair that they have become involved. I can assure you that if it wasn't for the fact

that we are best mates, they would certainly have been a lot less co-
operative with you than they've been up to now."

"Yes, Tom, I know. I'll get the lads to take them home
tomorrow. They can't really add anything more now, anyway I
reckon. I'd appreciate it, though, if you hung around a bit longer."

"I've got no problem with that, but please, no more cloak and
dagger stuff. I'll show you where we berthed, but I really don't
want to have any more to do with this. I volunteered remember. I
would like to un-volunteer now, if it's OK with you."

"Yes, fair enough, Tom. I'll get you back after we've been to the
harbour tomorrow. Listen, I really appreciate what you've done to
help me. I have to tell you that this has been one of my worst
operations. I'm not exactly flavour of the month with the boys
upstairs. Frankly, all we can do is have a fairly hefty post-mortem
and move on. Maybe when the stuff finally surfaces on the street
we might be able to re-open the case, but for now it's a dead duck."

"Why do you think it hasn't appeared?"

"I do not know. I can't figure an organisation that goes to all this
bother, but doesn't seem to want to make money from it. It just
doesn't make sense. Not in the normal run of things anyway. I
mean, if it was explosives or guns I would think terrorists, but not
drugs. Even terrorists sell drugs to get cash."

"But surely we don't have terrorists in Bristol?"

"We have terrorists everywhere, mate. Don't kid yourself on that
score. But, no, I don't smell terrorist in this one. It's too messy."

"Well, I'm off up. See you tomorrow."

"Yes, good plan. Breakfast at eight OK?"

"Great. 'Night Les. Thanks for the drinks."

"You're welcome. Courtesy of Her Majesty." He flicked off the
bar lights, had a last look round and followed me out of the bar.

"You here tonight too, Les?"

"Yes, later mate. I've still got some work to do next door. See
you in the morning."

At the rooms I bid Frazer a silent good night as I passed his door
and slipped the key-card into 'our' slot. The door swung open
without the usual click. I could see that the light was still on.
Stupidly in my tiredness I assumed that Frieda had simply left the
door unlocked for me. I crept in quietly in case she was asleep. She
wasn't. At least not in that particular room. The beds were unslept

in and nothing had been moved. My tired brain told me that I had stumbled into the wrong room by mistake and went out into the corridor to check. Of course it was the right room. Next to Frazer and he was already inside his.

"Frazer!!!!" I was hammering on his door. Somehow I knew she hadn't just popped out for a few ciggies. The door swung open. The room was as empty as mine.

Now I was really scared.

I took the stairs two at a time and hit the pavement running. I soon found myself outside the building we had left an hour ago. It was in total darkness. I hammered on the door in the hope of attracting a security guard, but it was pretty plain that the place was locked up for the night. Nothing short of a direct hit by one of these tank-busters would have opened these doors.

I beat my time back to the hotel. As before there was no one at the reception. I hammered on the bell. A half asleep night porter stuck his head round the office door.

"My friends! Did you see them leaving? Were they with anyone?"

"Er, no, I've been busy...." and he nodded in the direction of the office. The sound of a TV movie reached me.

"Police. Call the police. My friends have disappeared."

He picked up the phone in a daze.

"Maybe if you'd been here at the desk and not watching bloody movies, you might have seen what happened! Get a bloody move on!"

He dialled nervously.

"Yes.....police......yes, Cameron Hotel.....yes that's right. Next to Revenue and Customs.....yes, some people have disappeared suspiciously..... What?.....no, I'm the night porter.....one of the guests reported it."

He handed me the phone.

"They want to speak to you."

I grabbed the phone from him.

"Listen, three people have disappeared in the last few minutes. I think something terrible has happened to them. You need to get someone over here fast."

"Calm down, sir," came the voice from the other end, "is there any sign of a struggle? Any evidence of violence?"

162

"No, but..... look I'm sure there's something wrong. I, that is we've been helping Revenue and Customs next door with enquiries into a drug ring and they put us up here for the night, and my friends have simply vanished!" I suddenly realised how ludicrous this sounded.

"Listen, Mr.... ah, what did you say your name was?......Sir?"

"Never mind. False alarm. Sorry to have bothered you!" I hung up. It was dawning on me that there was no way I was going to get the police out here at....what time was it?....Christ it was three in the morning!

The night porter was looking at me very strangely. I turned on my heel and headed back to my room....*our* room! Where the hell were they? What had happened? I was in a complete funk. Who could I phone? Who could I phone at this time in the morning? The two people I wouldn't hesitate to phone at this time in the morning had disappeared. Could I get a taxi? Would it take me all the way home? I had no money on me!

There was a polite knock at the door. I nearly had a heart attack. It took me a second or two to find my voice.

"Who's there?"

"Tom, it's me, Les.....you all right?"

I wrenched the door open and Les leapt back like he had been struck.

"Wh....?"

"Frieda and Frazer! They're gone!"

"Gone?"

"Fucking gone Les! Not here! Not next door! Vanished!! When I got back up both doors were unlocked and the rooms were empty."

Les sunk wearily on to the bed.

"Shit. SHIT! SHIT!! SHIT!!!.....I'm sorry Tom. I don't know what to say. Let me think."

I gazed at him frantically.

"Well?"

He had his head in his hands.

"What made you come back anyway? How did you know....?"

He looked up as if in a daze.

"Eh? Oh, well, I had nipped round the corner to the all night shop for the morning papers and a few fags. When I got back the guard inside said some nutter had been pounding on the door while I was out. It just occurred to me that it might have been one of you so I thought I'd check."

I was beginning to have a rather bad feeling about this conversation.

"Les. Is there some small detail you are keeping to yourself in this deal? Something perhaps it's time you told me about?"

His head was back in his hands.

"We had a sort of tip-off. I thought it was bollocks and ignored it."

"What kind of tip off, for fuck sake? You fucking ignored it?"

"Calm down Tom, it's not what you think."
"Calm down?! How can I be calm when you ignored a tip off about our safety?"

"It wasn't that kind of tip-off. What we got was a whisper that your friends Frazer and Frieda were somehow on the other side in this mess."

He looked up at me. I stared back. I was dumbstruck.

"I know, Tom. I thought it was utter bollocks. I still do to some extent, but now...."

I felt as if I was going to faint. I sat down. I fainted.

CHAPTER 20

"Tom! Wake up! Come on man, get a grip!" I thought I was drowning. The jug of water Les had thrown on my face had gone up my nose in its efforts to bring me round.

"Let's get the fuck out of here. I don't know what the hell is going on, but I don't think it's a good idea to hang around here much longer."

He was dragging me towards the door. I grabbed at a towel and a sweater as I passed the wardrobe.

"Come on!"

"I need something to wear. I'm soaked. Couldn't you have used a bit less water?"

"Sorry. Get dried quick...."

I towelled down the best I could and ditched my wet shirt. I struggled into the sweater and headed for the elevator.

"No, Tom, the stairs. I want to make sure there are no surprises waiting for us in the foyer."

We ran down the three flights as quietly as possible. Les peered through the glass panel on the door at the foot of the stairs.

"OK, all clear. Let's move."

We scurried across the foyer. The porter was still tucked away watching his movies.

"If that's a Western, it's a bloody modern one." The sounds of synthetic orgasm reached us.

The street was deserted and around the corner of the building a well-concealed keypad released a side door into the Customs building.

"I should have realised the front door wouldn't be used at night."

"This is the garage entrance, Tom. My car's down here," and he led me down a flight of concrete steps to a vast underground car park. I recognised the black MPV that brought us here. There were other anonymous saloons and vans and in the corner was a gleaming red Morgan two-seater. The hood was up. Les opened the unlocked door and climbed behind the wheel. Not without effort I squeezed into the passenger seat and buckled in.

"Les, this is a bloody great car! I've always wanted one of these! I ...." the rest of my sentence was drowned by the roar as Les fired up the engine.

"Sorry, Tom?"

"Never mind!" I shouted.

We headed for a ramp where a huge roller door was opening. We barely cleared it as we shot into the empty street and turned right.

"Where are we going?"

"I'm taking you home. It's time you were out of this mess, as you said."

"What about Frieda and Frazer? We can't just abandon them!"

"I'm not abandoning them, but until we get some whisper of where they've gone, there's not much we can do. Trust me, they'll surface."

"Well, the police weren't much......." my head hit the dash as Les slammed on the brakes.

"Police? What police?"

"Well, when I found them missing and I couldn't find you, I phoned the police. I...."

"What did you tell them? Tell me!"

"Well, I said we had been helping you guys....."

"Did you mention drugs?"

"I might have.....I....."

"Fuck......."

"What? Les, I didn't know what to do. I was frantic."

"Oh........sorry Tom. It's just that, well, I could really do without these buggers nosing round this."

"Look, Les, if my friends are in danger, I think we should get all the help we can. I don't think this is the time to start fighting a turf war."

Les had driven off again and the Morgan was waking the residents of Bristol with it fruity exhaust note echoing in the sleeping streets. He drove in silence for a few minutes.

"Right. This is the way I see it. They either left of their own accord or they were taken."

I nodded. Short of spontaneous evaporation, I certainly couldn't think of an alternative.

"If they left of their own accord, they're probably OK, but with an agenda we can only guess at."

"They're not mixed up in this, Les."

"OK, so they were taken. Presumably by the drug people. But why? They've got their stuff. They must think your friends can finger them in some way. If that's the case, then things do not look good for your friends. But I don't get it. Why take them and not you? Presumably you know as much as they do. No, there's something we're missing here. My guess is we're going to hear from the kidnappers. And not before too long."

I let us into my house and collapsed on the armchair.

"I'll catch a few winks on this very attractive looking sofa, if you don't mind, Tom. I am shagged out."

"Me too, Les. Make yourself at home. There are blankets and stuff in the hall cupboard. I'm off up."

As I moved towards the stairs I noticed the light on the answering machine was blinking.

"Les."

"What?"

"The answering machine. I've got a message."

"It's probably nothing important, but you'd better check it."

I hit the 'play' button.

"....Tom? Sorry, Tom, er, it's er, ten thirty..." it was Cath's voice. We both relaxed. "I've been trying to get you. I don't know if it's important, but someone has been here looking for Frazer and Frieda. They don't seem to be at home. I thought they might be with you. Anyway, never mind. See you tomorrow?"

"So they don't want Cath either. Maybe we're getting somewhere Tom. What do Frieda and Frazer have in common, that you and Cath don't?"

"Andy?" We both got it together.

"But why Andy? What the fuck's going on?"

"Look, Tom. I know I can't think straight right now. I don't know about you, but I think the best thing we can do is try and get a few hours sleep. We'll talk to Cath in the morning and maybe we can get some more information to work with."

I was in no state to argue. I felt wearier than I had felt for years. I don't remember getting into bed. I slept like the dead.

"Coffee?"

Les was at my bedside with a large steaming mug of fresh coffee in his hand.

"Oh, cheers, Les. What time is it?"

"Eight thirty. Thought you needed a bit of a lie in. How do you feel?"

"OK, I think. Have you been up long?" He was fully dressed if not shaved.

"Nah, half an hour. Took the liberty of phoning round a few contacts."

"And?"

"Nothing. Not a whisper. Come on, let's see what Cath has to say."

I slugged half the coffee as I got showered and dressed. It was a miserable morning. Steady rain and a blustery wind. I grabbed a couple of oilskin jackets as I left the house and handed one to Les.

He examined them approvingly.

"We'll need these. Bloody hood leaks like a sieve."

We drove round to the office. It was locked.

"Funny, Cath should be here. Maybe she's sick."

I picked up the phone and dialled her house.

"Hello?" Her mum's shaky voice.

"Oh hello Mrs Chalmers, it's Tom. Is Cath there?"

"Oh, hello, Tom. Nice to her from you dear. How are you?"

"I'm fine, Mrs Chalmers. Could I speak to Cath please?"

"She's not in dear. She's at work at that boat place. Left about eight I think.....no maybe it was quarter to. No, I tell a lie it was eight because the news......"

"Thanks Mrs Chalmers. Take care." I hung up. Les was staring at me.

"Well?"

"She's not there. Left for work as usual."

"Does she live far away?"

"No, five minutes walk, max."

The phone rang. I picked it up.

"We've got your Miss Chalmers. She's OK...so far....aren't you dear?.....Tom! Tom!! It's me...they....OK now listen to me Morton. We want our stuff. Tell us where it is and little Cathy here keeps her good looks. Fuck us around again and she's fish food......"

I looked frantically at Les who was mouthing 'what??'

".......be at the dock at Avonmouth tomorrow at noon. On your own. Don't fuck up." The phone went dead.

"They've got Cath! They want their stuff! I don't get it. They already got their stuff!"

"Well, someone certainly got it. And what's more to the point, why didn't they mention Frieda and Frazer?"

"Hello, Dawson? We think we've found your cardboard."

Les and Tom had returned to Tom's house to try and make some sense out of the information they had so far. They weren't doing too well. They were roused from their deliberations by the beep of Les's secure cell-phone.

"What's the story?"

"Well, we got an odd report of strange behaviour of wild animals around a land-fill site near Gloucester. It started with dead rats, then seagulls and finally apparently inebriated foxes, dogs, stuff like that."

"Just a minute...." Les turned the phone a little from his ear and beckoned me over to listen in. "....go on."

"OK, well we didn't really pay much attention to it.....you know, filed it under 'miscellaneous odd reports' that sort of thing. But then we got another report from the environmental boys saying that none of the animals tested showed up with any known toxin. They did more tests and found your stuff in minute quantities. We popped up to the dump and came across a mass of what looked like pulped cardboard bagged up in polythene. It tested very positive indeed. There was still a huge amount of the stuff still in it. Looks like your smugglers weren't very good at the recovery process. It had killed the small animals outright and then when the bigger animals ate the carcasses they got pissed. You don't want to meet a pissed fox, believe me."

"Any lead on who dumped it and when?"

"Only that it was a couple of guys in a blue van. Last Tuesday week. We got the number from the watchman, but it came up as a moped in Stornoway."

"Descriptions of the guys?"

"Nothing useful. Driver was medium build, white, wearing overalls and a woolly hat, his mate was Asian, same overalls."

"Sounds like the same blokes. Have you got the stuff?"

"Yes, we recovered as much of it as we could. Some of the bags were pretty well ripped up. We got the dump people to bury the rest."

"OK, listen. I want you to get a team up there to try and get tyre prints, shoe prints, anything."

"Forget it mate. There are bloody hundreds of vehicles in and out of there every day. We had a look ourselves. Not a hope in hell."

"Shit! OK, what about the bags? Anything there?"

"Nah, usual black garbage bags you can buy anywhere. Lab boys are looking, but don't reckon they'll get anything useful. I'll keep you posted though."

"OK, mate, cheers.....oh, listen, before you go....has there been any more on the other two.....yes, the Prentice woman and....."

"No, not a dicky bird. It all sounded a bit doubtful anyway. Just something that got picked up at GHQ in the course of normal traffic apparently."

"GHQ? Cheltenham? Can you get me a transcript?"

"I'll give it a try, but you know that lot....."

"Yes, thanks anyway, cheers."

"Curiouser and curiouser."

Les had poured himself another coffee and sat at the table in the kitchen. He pulled out a note pad and started flicking through it as if looking for something that rang a distant bell.

"So now we know that the stuff was taken by what appears to be a second group. Either that group are associated with Frieda and Frazer......"

I began my protest.

"I know, I know, you say they're clean.....or they are the ones who have kidnapped them from the hotel. Please Tom, let's keep an open mind on this. I know they are your friends, but there still remains a tiny element of possibility I can't afford to ignore. This second group have now reclaimed at least some of the drug and dumped the debris. None too carefully at that. The first group don't seem to be aware of the second group and have taken Cath on the assumption that you still have the stuff. What we need to find out is how the second group got to know about the shipment."

"Well, we didn't tell anyone...."

"I know, Tom. You're the least of my worries. No I reckon either it's been a gang tip off or someone inside our organisation. Either way it'll be like looking for a needle in a haystack to find him."

"So what do we do about finding Frieda and Frazer?"

"Bugger all we can do but wait. Barring the possibility that we've got a lunatic collector of people whose names begin with 'Fr' we can only assume they've been kidnapped as some sort of leverage. We'll hear soon enough I reckon."

"And meanwhile?"

"Meanwhile we concentrate on getting Cath back. Somehow we've got to convince her kidnappers that some other gang took the stuff. Hopefully they'll buy it and sort it out amongst themselves. It's not going to be easy though. Who's going to believe that you simply let an anonymous gang unload tons of booze from your boat on a busy dock in broad daylight."

"Yes, well, don't rub it in....."

"And then continue to watch them, along with a bunch of tourists, dump half of it in....."

"The camera!!"

"What?"

"Cath's camera! She had a little disposable camera with her on the trip. We had forgotten about it until Bristol and she had us take pictures of one another on the boat while all that nonsense was going on! There's a good chance that some of them have shots of the van in the background!"

Les looked as if he was going to hit me, then a huge grin split his face.

"Christ, Morton. Could you please try and make your memory work a wee bit faster in future. Where are the pictures?"

"Well, that's just it. She never developed them. At least I don't think she did as I've never seen them. They, or the camera must be in her house somewhere."

Fortunately for us, the sun had come out earlier and Les had taken the hood off the Morgan. We leapt over the doors simultaneously and were on our way before you could say 'cheese'.

CHAPTER 21

The camera had been there, sitting quite innocently on Cath's dressing table. There were still a few shots left on the roll, so, Cath being Cath, obviously hadn't wanted to get it developed until it was full. The lab had produced good quality A4 prints and Les was busy spreading them out on the sail table in the boat shed when I arrived next morning.

"I think we've got what we're looking for, Tom! Look, there's the van with a clear shot of your blond guy. There's another with the other guys. This is brilliant. They even got a rough take on the number plate and it looks similar to the plate on the van at the dump."

There were several shots taken that day as well as some taken around Bristol, obviously during the shopping trip and one or two local shots. The last shot on the reel was of three men neither I nor Les had ever seen before. They were dressed informally, like any typical holidaymakers. They were clearly aware that they were having their picture taken as they were hamming it up in a half-hearted sort of way. The big guy was bald as a coot.

"Who are these guys Tom? Do you know them?"

"Never seen them before in my life. The picture seems to have been taken on the harbour here, though. I recognise the breakwater. They're a miserable looking bunch."

"Hmm....I think I'll hold on to this one as well. Just in case. We could be looking at our kidnappers."

"Somehow I doubt it Les. I mean she obviously took the photo with their permission or the camera wouldn't be sitting on her dressing table. I don't imagine kidnappers would take the trouble to return someone's camera to her house, particularly if it had a picture of them in it!"

"No, I agree, but still.....I mean, it's just not like Cath to take pictures of strange men, now is it?"

"No, I'll give you that."

"So, do you think the kidnappers will let Cath go when they see these? I mean, they're pretty conclusive."

"We'll just have to see, won't we?"

I arrived alone at the dock in Avonmouth a few minutes before noon. I parked the car outside the gates and, with the prints carefully tucked inside my jacket, I headed for the dockside. The place was more or less as I remembered it. The rusty container was still there looking even more decrepit than before. A small coaster was tied up where Sligo had been. It seemed to be unloading bags of cement or something similar. I sat on a bollard and waited. I had no idea what to expect. Would they simply approach me in broad daylight? Surely not. They'd hardly leave themselves open to identification with a drug scam and now a kidnapping to their credit. I personally felt relatively safe as I, theoretically, had information they wanted.

Minutes passed. The guys unloading the coaster ignored me studiously, and sweatily continued with their work.

A few minutes later a motorcycle appeared from behind the nearest warehouse. It appeared to be heading for the dock gate, but at the last minute it turned sharply and pulled up next to me.

"You Morton?" The motorcyclist wore a full face helmet with a completely black visor. That answered my question about identification.

"Yes. Have you got Cath? Is she OK? Can I see her?"

"Get on."

I clambered on to the back of the bike and we roared off towards the warehouse. The bike pulled up next to a barred window at the side of the building. The biker nodded that I should look inside. Cath was there, sitting at a table with her chin in her hands. If she recognised me at the window it didn't show as she simply looked up and then down at the table again. The bike sped off before I could shout or react to seeing her. We turned at the end of the building and entered the open warehouse door.

"OK, where's the stuff. And no fucking me around."

I pulled the envelope of prints from my jacket and handed it to the biker. He walked to the end of the building and slid the prints out. As he examined them I had a look for the door of the room I reckoned Cath must be in.

"What the fuck is this shit? Holiday photos? I told you not to fuck me around Morton!"

"That's where your stuff is. These guys unloaded it from the boat. We thought they were Customs men."

"Do you expect me to believe this shit? Customs men? Showed you their badges did they?"

"Well, no, actually......"

"What?! You just took their word? Are you mad? You're fucking me around, ain't ya?"

"Look I've already had a bollocking from Customs over that. I don't need one from you."

The biker, who had forgotten to lower his visor and whom I could now see was black, studied the prints again.

"So who are these guys? How do I know they're not your people?"

"You'll just have to take my word. I assure you I have no idea who they are."

"My people ain't going to like this. Not one bit. I mean..... just handing the stuff to complete strangers. I'm bloody shocked, I really am......" and he wandered off dialling his cell-phone.

"....yeah.... handed it over to a bunch of guys in a blue fucking van...... thought they were Customs...... no I couldn't believe it either, bloody disgraceful...... what? I dunno." He looked over to me.

"Who took the pictures? How do we know this ain't staged?"

"Cath took them. Ask her. There were other pictures on the roll. Some shopping in Bristol and one of three guys at the seaside."

"I'll call you back....." and he snapped the phone shut. "Wait there cunt!" This man was charm personified.

He crossed the floor to a door at the end of the warehouse. He undid a heavy padlock and entered the room. After a few moments he re-emerged with the prints.

"She says yes, she took them, and some stuff in Bristol, but she don't know nothing about no blokes at the seaside."

"Well, it was the last picture on the roll. Maybe she forgot."

"Hmff....." he redialled the phone. "....yeah, seems kosher.... yeah, OK.....nah, I'm wearing me helmet, oh fuck!" he snapped the visor down, ".....what? Oh nothing......yeah, OK." He shut the phone. "Mind if I keep these? Might come in handy like."

I was hardly in a position to protest. "Yes, fine, er, can I go now?"

"Yes.....listen; you didn't see my mug, ok? I know who you are remember. Don't fuck me around!"

This man's obsession with 'fucking him around' was beginning to get on my nerves. However, I was certainly relieved to see him climb aboard the bike and roar off out of the warehouse. I was left standing alone in deafening silence.

Cath! I ran to the door which was only bolted. I shot back the bolt and entered the room.

"Go away! I don't want to talk to you. It's nothing to do with you being black and for the last time, I'm not fucking you around!!"

"Cath, it's me."

She stiffened, she turned as far as the ropes tying her legs to the chair would allow. Her jaw dropped.

"Tom! Oh Tom! What.....how?"

I ran to her and held her. She grabbed my waist and buried her head in my stomach. I could feel her tears wetting my shirt. After a few minutes I prised her away from me.

"Here, let me untie your legs. You look rather uncomfortable."

"I tried to untie them myself, Tom, but I couldn't. He kept my hands tied most of the time anyway."

I had a sharp pocket knife with me and as I sawed at the heavy ropes I tried to find out what had happened.

"How did they take you, Cath? I mean, did they hurt you?"

"They grabbed me on the way to work. One minute I was walking along and the next I was bundled into the back of a car by two men with knitted masks like the ones you see the terrorists wearing on TV. They didn't hurt me though. They were quite gentle really. The frightening thing was they never spoke. Not a word for the whole journey here. They left me here with the motorbike man. It was him who phoned you."

"Yes, I remember his turn of phrase. " 'Don't fuck me around' seems to be his favourite expression."

"Oh, yes, I'm sorry Tom, I didn't mean to swear at you. I don't usually....."

"Yes, I know, Cath.......there, you're free. You can get up."

"I don't think I can Tom. I can't feel my legs. I've been tied up since early when he let me go to the loo. I think he overdid the knots."

I took one limp calf in my hands and started massaging. She had nice calves. I had never noticed before. After a few minutes I tried the other one. "How's that feeling?"

"I'm getting terrible pins and needles now.....oww, it's really sore Tom!"

"That's a good sign. Try and walk. I would really like to get the hell out of here if you don't mind."

"Yes, me too. I think I'm OK. Is it far to your car Tom?"

"No it's just outside the dock gates. I'll help you."

And arm in arm we slowly made our way out into the afternoon. It had all seemed too easy somehow.

"He was actually quite nice....."

"Who?"

"The black bike man, you know...."

"Oh. OK, that's something to be grateful for, I suppose." I was having difficulty agreeing with her with the memory of what he called me still niggling.

We were making our way out of town in light traffic. I wanted to get on to the motorway before the rush hour made it unbearable. Cath had been quiet and was clearly emotionally drained by the experience of being kidnapped and then tied up for a day. I was happy to let her sit quietly and recover.

"He didn't seem to know much about what was going on. What *is* going on, Tom? Is it the same people as before?"

"I do not know, Cath. There have been some strange developments lately, but we'll talk about it once we get you home and comfy, eh?"

"Yes, I suppose so......why did he ask me about my pictures though. I never got that camera developed."

I explained about the pictures and how they were instrumental in obtaining her release. The traffic was slowing in front of us, however, and I was having to concentrate on my driving. Soon we could see that the hold up was due to an accident up ahead. Cars were being diverted on to the opposite pavement to get past. It looked nasty and I was trying to distract Cath from the scene. Clearly a car had pulled out in front of a motorcycle and the rider was sprawled on the road. I saw some bloke trying to remove the victim's helmet and rolled down the window quickly.

"Stop! Don't touch him! Leave his helmet on!" the samaritan hesitated and looked up.

"What? He needs to breathe.....I think he's unconscious."

I pulled over and got out. There was something familiar about this biker. I raised the black tinted visor. It was our friend of earlier.

"Well, my friend, you've been fucked about good now, eh?"

"What?!" the samaritan looked shocked.

"It's OK, he's, er, a friend. Let's get him into the recovery position until the ambulance comes."

We tried to organise his limbs as gently as possible. He was beginning to come round. It didn't look as if he was too seriously hurt.

"Is he all right, Tom?.......oh! It's Ben! The bike man!"

"His name's Ben? OK, Cath, just wait in the car......Ben! Ben! Can you hear me?"

He mumbled something but clearly wasn't completely conscious.

An ambulance was making its way through the traffic towards us, it's lights on and siren beeping spasmodically as if to say 'Scuse me! Pardon me!' Soon the paramedics were beside us with oxygen and a stretcher.

"Oh, good. You've left his helmet on. Thank God!"

The samaritan glanced at me, approvingly, I thought. The paramedics worked efficiently on Ben, easing his breathing, checking for injuries and generally being capable and efficient just like the ones on TV. They eased a split stretcher under him and gently lifted him into the back of the ambulance. Across the road the police were busy taking statements, calming the lady driver and generally tidying up the traffic jam.

"Do you know the victim sir?" I was caught off guard by the young lady constable behind me.

"Eh?   No!   Well,   yes,   I   suppose....."

"Either you know him or you don't sir. It would be helpful if you could accompany him to the hospital and maybe help us identify him.....to inform relatives?" I had been looking particularly blank and she must have thought I was slightly mad. I was, in fact trying to think fast and furious about what to do next and what to say.

"Yes, yes, of course. I'll come along with him. He's a, er,

business associate actually." The constable looked doubtful. I told Cath to follow the ambulance to the hospital.

"But Tom......"

"Please Cath. It won't take long. I promise."

I climbed into the ambulance with Ben and the paramedic. The door was shut firmly behind us. Through the little window I could see Cath struggling with the driving seat of my car while trying to avoid losing the ambulance in the traffic.

"Do you think he'll be OK?"

The paramedic had taken blood pressure and pulse. He had rigged up a breathing tube and was setting up some sort of drip.

"Yes, he doesn't look too bad. A bit of concussion maybe. Once we get him to hospital they can have a good look at him. Bloody motorists. I can't tell you the number of times that's nearly happened to me."

"You a biker?"

"All me life. Me dad bought me my first bike when I was four. I was motocrossing competitively when I was six. I love bikes. I bloody hate motorists. Think they own the road. They can't stand it when we go past them in a traffic jam. D'you know, one bloke actually deliberately opened his door on me on the M4 last week? I nearly took the bloody thing off at the hinges. A Honda Goldwing takes a bit of stopping I can tell you. He won't try that stunt again." He chuckled at the memory. "That was a nice bike your friend was riding. In a bit of a mess now, though. Might have a problem with parts. Morinis ain't that common. I'll find out where the cops took it, later, and maybe have a chat with the guy..... see if I can help. Us bikers have to stick together."

"I must say, I've never ridden a bike before. It looks too cold and uncomfortable most of the time."

"Nah, not if you've got the right gear on. I ride mine every day, 365 days a year. I love the cold weather. The bike seems to go better. Mind you, the big Honda's a bit of a gin palace. The wife likes her comfort. I used to ride an old Triumph Thunderbird. What a machine. No protection from the elements though. I was much younger then."

"When you say big, what do you mean?"

"Big! Big frame, big engine....1200cc mine is."

"1200cc! That's bigger than my bloody car!"

"Yes, and I bet you a fiver it was a bloody sight dearer too! Right, here we are. Time to get this man into bed."

He flung open the door to be met by a team with a trolley. I glanced around to see if Cath had been able to keep up with us. There was no sign of her. We followed the trolley into the Accident and Emergency Department. The paramedic was reciting vital signs and injuries to the hospital people. Soon Ben was lying on a bed, still fully clothed.

"I see you kept his helmet on. Good" The doctor was shining a light into Ben's eyes. "OK, you can take it off now nurse." I was beginning to feel like some sort of war hero. I'd be getting a medal soon from the motorbike safety committee.

Ben was coming round quickly and was clearly agitated by the predicament he found himself in.

"What the fuck.......? Shit! Me head!"

"OK, Ben, calm down. You're in hospital. You've been in an accident. We just want to check you out and make sure nothing is broken. Your friend Tom is here."

"Eh, who?" He found me at his side, "oh, yeah, Tom. My friend Tom. Good old fucking Tom."

I smiled upon him indulgently. The team worked efficiently, stripping off his obviously expensive leathers by the simple expedient of cutting them to ribbons with scissors.

"'Ere, fuck it! Stop! Me leathers! They cost a fucking fortune!"

The nurses worked grimly on. Soon they were down to his underpants. He was a well-built lad, was Ben and I caught a couple of the nurses exchanging knowing looks. One arm looked a bit odd, but apart from that he seemed OK.

"He might have a fracture there, and I'm pretty sure he's dislocated his thumb. Pretty common in this type of accident. OK, get him warm nurse. Organise an X-ray and give me a shout when it's done. You can stay with your friend if you want, Mr.......?"

"Morton, Tom Morton."

I sat on a stool next to the bed.

"Fuck me, I'm fucked!"

"They say you're actually not bad considering......"

"No, I mean I'm fucked....you know, in trouble like. If the boss doesn't get these pictures soon, I'll have a lot more injuries than this."

"Hmm....I see what you mean. I must say, I was surprised he took our word for the pictures. I mean if he really thought we stole his stuff, I'd have thought he'd be much tougher."

"He never thought you 'ad it. Are you serious? Plonkers like you lot? Don't make me laugh."

He didn't look in the least like he was going to laugh.

"Well, why did you kidnap Cath?"

"I never kidnapped her! Not my scene! I never hurt her neiver! You ask her!"

"Yes, she did say you were very kind. But why the kidnap thing?"

"Well, we figured you must know sumfink, like, so we had to get you to tell us what you knew. We could hardly bring you in for questioning, like the fuzz, could we?"

"No, I suppose not."

"We never reckoned on the pictures though. That was a bit of luck, that was!"

"Do you know who the people were then?"

"Nah, I don't, but we'll find them. You can bet on it, and when we do.......oh, fuck!"

"What?"

"The fuckin' pictures! Where are they?"

"There's a bag here I think your stuff is in........yes, here they are." I dug out the envelope and showed it to him. He pulled me close.

"Listen, mate. I suppose you couldn't do me a favour, like. You couldn't maybe get these to the boss for me. I mean, I didn't hurt your girl. I could 'ave done anything to 'er, but I never did, so how about it?"

"Are you serious? You want me to deliver information to a criminal which may well lead to serious repercussions for another criminal when I do?"

"S'all right. Crim against crim. Fair game that is!"

"Also, he's not exactly going to say thanks, tip me a fiver and send me on my way when he realises who I am, is he?"

"He don't know you from Adam. He wasn't involved in the Avonmouth mess. Neiver was I, fank fuck! These guys are still in 'ospital."

"Oh, God. OK, anything to get this over with. Where do I take them?"

"Good man, Tom. I won't forget this. I promise. I owe you one."

"Look, I don't want any favours, OK? Just tell me the address."

"OK, take them to the Aragon Bar in Clifton. Ask for Mr Lacey. Just say I got detained. You don't need to say anyfing else."

"OK, now, listen. I want no more to do with this, you tell your people. No more kidnaps, OK?"

"Yes, mate, you 'ave my word."

"Oh, by the way, the ambulance bloke is a biker. He admired your.....Moroni, is it?"

"Morini, Moto Morini. It's an Eye-tie bike. Lovely little machine. How is it? Have you 'ad a look at it?"

"Yes, well the front looked a bit bent, to be honest, anyway this ambulance bloke says he'll find out for you where the police took it and get back to you. He seems to think he can help with spares too."

"Oh, fuck me, Tom. You're a bloody gentleman you are. Not enough like you in the world mate. Straight up. Enough to make a guy lead an honest Christian life you are!" An improvement on being called a cunt, I thought.

"Yes, well, I never had any illusions of sainthood. Just trying to help. Anyway, must go. Good luck, Ben!"

There was no sign of the policewoman who wanted the statement and I sure as hell wasn't going to wait around for her! I hurried out of the A&E to look for Cath. She was having an argument with a traffic warden who seemed to be objecting to her parking in the ambulance bay. I strode up waving the envelope of prints.

"Doctor! Excuse me! Thank you driver! Quickly, we have to get these X-rays to the airport pronto! Thank you officer!" and I leapt into the passenger seat and slammed the door. Cath smiled a weak smile at the warden and climbed behind the wheel and drove off.

"Why do we have to take X-rays to the airport Tom? Why did you say you were a doctor?"

"Just get out of here Cath. Park as soon as you can do so without getting into a fight."

Cath found a quiet side street with no yellow lines and pulled over. I lay back with my eyes shut.

"Tom? You all right? Is something the matter?"

I handed her the envelope. She took it from me like it was an award.

"Why do we need X-rays, Tom?"

"Just have a look at the pictures in the envelope Cath"

She drew the prints from the envelope and as she absorbed them I explained about the significance of them and the delivery I had promised to make.

"I must say, I'm a bit worried about this guy remembering me in future."

"OK, Tom, I'll take them in. I'll say I'm Ben's girlfriend."

"No way, Cath! You've been through enough!"

"No, it's all right Tom. I want to do it. You've done enough."

"Well, if you're sure........" I was anything but sure. I changed places with her and we headed off towards Clifton. I had no idea what was waiting for us in the Aragon Bar.

CHAPTER 22

Unconsciousness left Frieda gradually at first and then suddenly, horribly. Her first sensation was blackness, closely followed by the realisation that she was tied up somehow, her mouth was taped and she was extremely uncomfortable as she seemed to be lying on a very cold hard floor. She wriggled to try and ease the pain in her side. This made things worse. Her full bladder now made its presence known. She tried to make a noise but only managed a muted squeak. She tried moving again, but realised that the body next to her was preventing her from turning over. The body next to her! Who?...

Frazer had wakened earlier and had managed to get a little more comfortable by rolling over. That's how he discovered he was not alone. He figured that the other person was female as he was able to feel her hands, which were bound behind her. He tried to remember what had happened, but he could recall nothing much after leaving the bar for his room. He hoped that the person next to him was Frieda and then immediately, guiltily, for her sake, hoped it was not. He felt the hands again. No rings, short nails. It could be Frieda. The person wriggled. Good, she's OK. She made a squeak. Frazer held her hands and squeezed gently. Must try and reassure her. He grunted a hello.

They heard the noise of a lock being turned and footsteps entering the room. The light level improved. They must be hooded in some way as the light was filtered through thick cloth.
Frieda felt strong hands on her, yanking her up to a sitting position. The hood was removed. She found herself looking into the eyes of.....Tony Blair?? No, eye-holes. This joker was wearing a

John Paton

mask. Nice of him to keep the party light, she thought. She looked beside her. Frazer was being similarly propped up by George Bush. He was blinking and sniffing as his hood was removed. He saw her and tried a reassuring nod.

Tony Blair picked up a video camera and George Bush held a newspaper in front of them showing the banner headline. Tony filmed for a few moments and they left. George returned with a tray of food and two cartons of juice. He cut Frieda's hands free. He left and locked the door. Not one word was spoken.

Frieda and Frazer looked at one another and it was a few moments before Frieda realised that with her hands now free she could remove the gags. She ripped hers off first and then carefully removed Frazer's.

"Thank fuck for that, I was about to asphyxiate! My nose was all blocked with muck from inside that hood."

She threw her arms about him and hugged him.

"Oh, Frazer, I'm so glad it's you!"

"And not Tom?"

"No, I don't mean that.....I mean a friendly face. This is awful! What's going on?"

"Well, I assume it's something to do with the drug thing, but beyond that I haven't a clue."

"What are we going to do?"

Frazer looked around the room, then at his bonds. They were heavy plastic ties of the sort the police use to restrain people. He knew that they couldn't be removed without heavy duty cutters.

"Well, I'd say, not a lot right now. Do you feel like eating?"

"I don't know. Maybe something to drink. I've had nothing since the hotel."

"Me neither. That complimentary drink was foul, but at least it was wet."

"Yes, I had one....... you don't think......"

"Oh, fuck. Of course. Drugged. I wonder if it was the boat stuff. It sure as hell works."

Frieda was suddenly aware that she didn't need the toilet any more.

"Oh, Frazer.....I....I think I wet myself when I saw Tony Blair."

Frazer couldn't hold back a chuckle.

"I don't blame you, love. You're lucky it wasn't Cherie. You might have been in an even worse mess!"

Frieda surveyed her wet pants. She plucked at them tentatively.

"You might as well get used to it love. I don't think we're likely to be offered a shower and change of clothes for a bit yet."

"Shit! Fuck!.....Oh, I don't know.... Arsing bollocks! I hate having a wet bum!"

"That's the Frieda I know. Let's have a drink. We need a plan."

Frieda opened a carton of juice and helped Frazer to drink. She had a huge slug herself.

"Not too much. We don't want a repeat...." and Frazer nodded at her little puddle.

"Yes, but let's at least move a bit. At least to a dry patch."

"Bloody women, always complaining about getting the wet patch!"

They shuffled sideways along the wall to the far corner of the room. The floor was covered in ancient worn linoleum which didn't quite fit.

"How long do you think they'll keep us here?"

"Haven't a clue. Presumably the little filming session was to show someone that they have us, and the paper was to prove we are still alive, today at least."

"Is it the drug gang?"

"Must be. I don't think it's the Inland Revenue."

Frieda started nibbling on some cheese and offered some to Frazer. They ate a little in silence.

The door burst open suddenly and Frieda choked on her food.

"OK, lights out. We'll be back in a few hours. Have fun."

The door slammed shut and the light went out. Total blackness. The sound of retreating footsteps. A car starting up. A retreating engine, then nothing.

Frieda had nearly coughed herself sick. Frazer tried his best to comfort her, but with his hands tied behind him, it was unsatisfactory to say the least. Frieda got the message and put her arms around him more for her comfort than his.

"OK, it's OK. We're still alive. Relax."

They stayed that way for a while until Frazer eased himself away.

"The way I see it, and I don't want you to think I'm a total pessimist here, is that we don't have a huge chance of coming out of this unharmed. We need to figure out some sort of plan."

"Yes, I know. But what? We're tied up, locked up, we have no clue where."

"OK, OK, listen. I looked at my watch.....thank God they didn't take it off me.... and it's just after nine. I reckon we're here for the night. Let's see if we can at least get out of these handcuff things. The door looks pretty solid, but.......well, anyway, lets take it one step at a time. That tray of food. There's a plate there, isn't there?"

"Yes, but....."

"Get it and try and break it clean in two. That should give us a good cutting edge"

"OK, great idea. I have it.....er, Frazer.....it's plastic."

"Shit. Bastards aren't as stupid as I thought. OK, let's think. Frieda, can you reach into my trousers pocket. I think I might have a lighter. We might be able to melt these plastic things. I can feel my keys, so maybe they didn't bother to empty my pockets."

Frieda fumbled in Frazer's pockets as he wriggled around to give her access.

"I have your keys......and a hankie....and some change.....turn over...maybe the other side."

Frazer did as he was told.

"Yes, there's something.... feels like.....a packet of polos!"

"Where's my bloody lighter then?"

"I thought you'd given up smoking?"

"Yes, well, I just got into the habit of carrying a lighter. I must have dropped it though. Look behind me Frieda....maybe it fell out of my pocket."

Frieda fumbled behind him.

"No....I don't feel anything......Ow! Shit! I think I've cut myself!"

"Cut yourself? What on?"

"I don't know....feels like....just a minute.....it's between the lino and the wall. It's a broken hacksaw blade I think."

"I don't believe you. They lock us up and leave us a hacksaw blade? Is this some sort of initiative test?"

"Well, I don't think it was deliberate. It was pretty well buried back there."

"Thank you God! Who'd have thought it? This must have been some sort of workshop. The blade got missed maybe during a clear-out. Right, try and cut through the band tying my hands. Put that hanky round it first though, we don't want you cutting yourself more."

186

Frieda wrapped the hanky round the end of the blade, and fumbling in the dark, started sawing away between Frazer's wrists. The blade was pretty blunt and rusted, but it wasn't long before the band parted with a satisfying pop.

"Thank fuck for that! My bloody hands were dropping off! Right give me the saw. I'll cut our feet free."

Soon they were both stretching and rubbing sore wrists and ankles. The main problem now was the total lack of any light.

"Can you find my keys, Frieda? Give them here."

Frieda retrieved the bunch of keys from the floor between them and handed them to where she assumed Frazer to be. They finally found one another's hands and suddenly a little red light cast a dim glow in the dark. Frazer held it up to his chin and leered.

"Fuck off Frazer. You look stupid!"

"Sorry, only trying to cheer you up."

"Well, don't. So now that we've got enough light not to do anything with, what do we do?"

"I thought I'd have a closer look at the door. It's worth at least trying to break out, although I'm not too hopeful. It looked pretty thick. One thing in our favour is that it opens outwards. I might be able to break the lock. You hold the light near where the lock is and I'll have a go at kicking it open."

Frieda stood to one side of the door and held the little light as near as she dared. She didn't relish being crippled by a Frazer wielded Doc Marten. Frazer took a step back and swung a huge kick at the door. It popped open almost without protest sending Frazer sprawling with a crash into the darkness outside.

"Frazer?? Are you....."

"I'm fine. Find the light switch."

Frieda stifled a guffaw. Frazer was in a heap on the floor covered in an assortment of masks, wigs, Christmas crackers and paper hats. He looked like the aftermath of a huge kiddies party.

"Help me up please. Now we know where they got the masks from. This must be some sort of warehouse."

Frieda tried to help him but with little success as she was giggling hysterically.

"Sorry Frazer, it's the relief of being out of here...."

"We're out of *there* Frieda, but I don't know about *here*. Let's have a look around. I assume this whole place is locked up."

They moved away from the store and by the light they left on

187

could see that the warehouse seemed to be a standard industrial unit of the type you would find on a thousand industrial estates all over England. At one end was a large roller door in which was a small wicket gate. Frazer tried it and found it locked.

"Padlocked on the outside, I'd guess."

"Look at this, Frazer!"

Frieda was holding a bottle. A bottle of beer to be more accurate. A bottle of Bantry Bitter beer identical to many they had seen on the dockside at Bristol to be absolutely and nit-pickingly precise.

"Well, well. That answers your earlier question I reckon."

A few more bottles were scattered around the floor in a corner. As Frazer was poking among them the sound of a car approaching reached them.

"They're coming back Frazer!"

"Keep calm. It might not be them......listen, just in case it is, I can see a way out. It's risky, but worth a try. Come on. Stand over here just inside the wicket door. I'll put the store light out. As soon as they open that gate and step inside we make a run for it."

"Where to?"

"Fuck, me, Frieda, bloody anywhere. Just bloody run!"

Frieda positioned herself as ordered and Frazer killed the light. With difficulty he reached the door beside her just as it swung open. A single figure stepped inside and walked towards the store room.

"Now!" Frazer ordered and shoved Frieda through the door. She ran straight into the arms of.......

"Les! Am I glad to see you!"

"It's OK Frazer, you can come out!"

Frazer stepped out to greet his friend. The gun Les was pointing at Frieda's head, however, looked very unfriendly.

"Couldn't wait to see me again ladies? How nice."

CHAPTER 23

"Is this it?"

"I think so, that little plaque beside the door says 'Aragon'. This is Clifton, so I suppose we must be in the right place. I must confess it's not quite what I expected."

After a great deal of, well to put it in Cath's words, 'faffing around', we had finally asked a local for directions and here we were parked in front of what I can only describe as a very respectable looking establishment. You know the sort of thing..... cool modern exterior. Plenty of glass and chrome. Nice fabrics in evidence in the windows, no brass lamps, no fake Edwardian glass, no Guinness adverts, and certainly no drug dealers hanging around the doors. I was particularly gratified, indeed relieved to note that the management had decided to forego the use of bouncers. At least not out in the street. This was the type of place where the bouncers gave you the benefit of the doubt and waited until you disgraced yourself inside and *then* threw you out. Classy.

"OK, what do we do now?"

Cath was examining the place with what I thought was uncharacteristic professionalism.

"Right, Tom, give me your jacket."

"My jacket? What for?"

"I need to look hard. You, know, a biker's bird."

I happened to be wearing my faithful leather jacket, but not really what would normally adorn the shoulders of a Hell's Angel. More a Wimbledon Cherub, really. I gave her the jacket after removing the cell-phone and wallet from the pockets.

"Right, give me the envelope. What was the guy's name again?"

"Lacey. Mr Lacey. Look Cath, do you think.....?

"I'm going in, Tom. I can do this." And she stepped from the car. Feeling slightly guilty, I watched as she moved towards the door. Two paces from the car she paused and put the envelope between her teeth. She started rolling the waist band of her skirt with a degree of hip-gymnastics, until the hem was a good six inches above her knee. She stepped up to the door. She hesitated. I thought she was going to change her mind, but once more she gripped the envelope in her teeth and furled the skirt to quite the most revealing level I could ever have imagine possible. Not for the first time it struck me that Cath had a cracking pair of legs. With a quick glance back at me she entered the bar.

Time passes remarkably slowly when you are sitting in a car staring at a pub door. The mind plays interesting games involving all sorts of combinations of situations involving, well, booze, mainly, but also possibly, encounters of a vaguely socio-sexual nature. However in this case I was more concerned about encounters of psycho-sadistic nature to be completely relaxed about the fact that after ten minutes she had not emerged, scathed or unscathed. I decided it was time I took a more pro-active part in this episode. I locked the car and, trying to look as cool as possible in my Budweiser tee shirt, I developed my role as 'bloke finding a nice bar and deciding to pop in for a drink'.

The interior was every bit as tasteful as the exterior, and I was beginning to think that maybe we had got the wrong place. I couldn't immediately see Cath, but this was mainly because I still had my Oakleys on. I decided to keep them on in the interest of 'cool' and felt my way to the bar. The stools were chrome-leather concoctions, designed to be just the right height to give most women under six feet tall trouble getting on to them. Perfect in fact. I chose a perch and surveyed the room. After some difficulty and by dint of reluctantly shoving the Oakleys on to the top of my head, I found Cath apparently deep in what seemed to be very familiar and jocular conversation with a bunch of smartly dressed young men. Two were black, in the sharp, yuppie idiom and the other three were white and looked as if they had just arrived, fresh and scrubbed from the gym. She seemed to be enjoying herself and was clearly the centre of attention. Now, don't get me wrong, Cath's a pretty girl, but more in the Doris Day than the Madonna idiom. I was somewhat bemused.

"Er, we appreciate you honouring us with your presence sir, but patronage in the form of the purchase of a refreshment, alcoholic or otherwise, would make us feel so much more valued. You may not be aware of this, but we are not, nor ever intend to be affiliated to the social services department."

I turned to find a remarkably handsome, and frankly glowing specimen of the barman genre. He was dressed entirely in black which contrasted starkly with his, well, I suppose, for want of a better description, albino physiognomy. His smile was beautific.

"You will find that our range of comestibles is extensive and, dare I say it, imaginative in a suitably tasteful manner, I hasten to add. I'm sure I can find something to amuse your, obviously sophisticated palate." This last pronouncement made, of course, while eyeing my less than sophisticated tee-shirt. I liked this guy.

"You, don't, by any chance, happen to have on the premises, a Laphroaig more than twelve years old?" I decided to enter into the spirit of the thing, in more ways than one.

"Would fifteen be an adequate accumulation of antiquity, sir? The deeper reaches of the cellar may possibly yield a distillation in years nearer the score, however the journey may delay, for as much as three minutes, the provision of a refreshment I feel must adequately satisfy your immediate requirements."

"Fifteen years would be perfectly acceptable. Thank you."

A generous shot of the 'cratur' was duly delivered in what I swear was a Caithness glass on a spotless coaster. A tenner changed hands.

"Slainthe!"

"Nasdorovje!"

"Ah! Sir is familiar with the Russian language?"

"Not really, but I just thought I'd get my own back. You don't really expect me to believe that you speak the Gaelic?"

"Of course. I am fluent in sixteen modern and five ancient languages."

"Bollocks. OK, say something more than 'cheers' in Gaelic."

"Very well....er.... '*Is truagh nach tainig Minig Nach Tig Leath cho minig 's a thainig Minig a Thig*'

"Bloody hell! What does that mean?"

"It's a pity that the things which don't come often don't come half as frequently as the things which do."

"Fuck me......"

"Not tonight, sir, I'm working. But if you'd like to give me your phone number......"

"No, I'm not.... I mean I'm......"

"If you mean you're more interested in the lady with the skirt round her neck, she's just left." He nodded towards the door.

"What? Oh, right! Cheers!" I downed the whisky and fled the bar. Cath was trying to break into the car, but thankfully with little success.

"Watch it! You'll break the lock!"

"Get me out of here, Tom! Now!"

We were well down the Exeter road before she would say a word. Ever since we left Clifton she had been locked in some sort of creative time-warp which involved silent mouthing of what I could only assume was a run-through of the conversation she had with the guys in the bar. I couldn't stand it any more.

"Cath! Please tell me what happened in there! This is driving me crazy! What did you tell them? Who were they? Oh, and by the way, I can see you pants."

That did the trick.

"What? Oh! Oh dear!" She unfurled her skirt to a more modest configuration. "Sorry Tom, I'm still....what is it actors say? Coming down?"

"Bloody hell, Cath. What's happened to you? You've turned into some sort of Jekyll and Hyde character. I'm not sure I like it."

"Get used to it! This is the new Cath!"

I goggled at her. She tried to keep a straight face, but after a few seconds she broke into a fit of giggles.

"Sorry. Errmm. Oh dear. It's not me, is it?"

"No, not really. So what happened??"

"Well, I went in and asked the man at the bar if Mr Lacey was in. He asked me who wanted to know and I said 'me!' He's a bit funny that barman. He does go on a bit. He said 'Madam, now that we have clarified the source of the enquiry, the purpose and provenance would in all likelihood improve the realisation of a satisfactory rejoinder' or something like that. So I said that I was Ben's girlfriend, and he said 'no'."

"No? No what?"

"That's what I said...no what...and he said 'no to your first question', and I said..."

"Cath, for god sake!"

"Oh, sorry, anyway, Lacey wasn't there but the barman told me that the guy in the black suit was his 'main man' and I should talk to him."

"Bloody hell. Wasn't that a bit risky? I mean, you just took his word?"

"Tom, think. If he had told me the man was Lacey how would I have known he wasn't?"

"True. So......?"

"So, I went over and introduced myself as Ben's bird and said I had something for Lacey. The guy in the black suit said that he was glad I'd arrived as he had been waiting for some time.... well that isn't exactly what he said, but it's what he meant."

"I can imagine...."

"Yes, well, so then they offered to buy me a drink. I didn't want to 'blow my cover' so I ordered a 'Slow Screw Against the Wall', Carol had one the other night at the stri.... Marine Hotel, and I remembered the name. They all seemed to think this was terribly funny, but they ordered it anyway. The barman seemed to enjoy making it. Actually it was really nice. I should try it again some time."

I was having trouble concentrating on the road by now. Cath's inner mind was a place I was reluctant to explore, but I felt I owed it to myself to hear the end of this saga.

"So, anyway, I gave him the envelope and he had a look at the pictures, but didn't seem too interested. He asked why Ben hadn't come and I told him that he had been unavoidably detained. He said something about Ben unavoidably having his legs broken if he didn't get his act together in future and his friends laughed. I don't think he's very nice, really. I didn't notice you coming into the bar Tom. Why did you come in?"

"Bloody hell, Cath! I was worried! I didn't for one moment imagine that you were going to enjoy social intercourse with a drug gang!"

"I had nothing of the sort, Tom! How could you think of such a thing! I was just chatting."

"Yes Cath, of course you were. Sorry. By the way, where's my jacket?"

The rest of the journey passed in uncompanionable silence. I couldn't believe she left my jacket in that pub. To be honest, I was equally furious at myself for not noticing she wasn't wearing it when she left. There was obviously no way we were going back for it.

It was quite late when we got home so I dropped her off at her house and headed off to my place for a bath and a stiff drink. I was hoping there was some news about Frazer and Frieda from Les, but there was nothing. Not even a phone message.

I lay in the bath sipping my malt until the water began to get cold, thinking over the latest developments. Where the hell were Frazer and Frieda? Why hadn't we heard from them? I was pretty sure they weren't with the drug crew that took Cath, so they must be with the other lot whoever they were. I knew that Les's theory about them being mixed up in this was utter bollocks. Also I was still furious about losing my best jacket. Now I came to think of it, my only jacket apart from my oilskins.

I realised that I was starving. I hadn't eaten since breakfast time. I got dried and dressed and headed down to the club. I hadn't had indigestion from Eric's pies for an age. The nice thing about the club was, even if it was quiet, you could always sit at the bar and have something to eat while listening to Eric's latest theories on a selection of subjects, ranging widely from Weapons of Mass Destruction to the Eurovision Song Contest. The fun thing with Eric was seeing how long it took you to figure out what he was talking about. His remarks always assumed that you knew what was going on in his head previously. The result was almost psychedelic.

"They got that sorted then."

"Er, they did?"

"Yer.....should never 'ave let it go so far in the first place."

"Er, Iraq?"

"Wembley. Bloody disgrace it was. You shoulda seen them bogs."

"Well, the new place should be a lot better. I gather it's got a roof."

He nodded in assent.

"Not as if we bloody need one."

"What a roof on Wembley?"

"Bloody separate English assembly. Bloody nonsense. I mean, I can see why the Welsh and the Scots might need something like that. Too remote they are. None of our business. No, we manage fine with Westminster I reckon."

I concentrated on my food. I had no intention of getting into a complicated political argument with Eric. There was no telling where that might lead.

"Boys did bloody well, though, eh?"

"Er, Arsenal?"

"No, bloody useless they were. Four nil at 'ome? You're having a laugh ain't ya? No the Paras. Bloody Basra. Bloody brilliant. Much better than them yanks up in Baghdad. Had the kiddies playing footer in no time. Amazing. Imagine being able to teach Arabs about footer so quick." He shook his head in wonder.

"Arsenal.....I don't know....mind you it could have been worse!"

"What five-nil at home?"

"Eh? No! The fire down the chippy. Last night. Di'n you see it? Bloody hell, I thought the whole place would go up! I were just about to go in to buy some fish and chips and the bloody fryer went up like a volcano. Poor Madge was trapped behind all them flames!"

"God, Eric, that was terrible! What did you do?"

"Went for a pizza instead, di'n I?"

"No, I mean about the fire you idiot! What happened with the fire?"

"Oh, Charlie took a big scoop of flour and swiped it out in one go. Bloody amazing. Said it's an old trick his dad taught him. Buggered up the fat, though, so no chips. I quite like pizza, though, so no worries, eh?"

"So no one was hurt?"

"Nah, Madge's eyebrows was a bit singed like, and the roof'll need painting, but nothing serious. Want a top-up?" He pointed an elbow at my nearly empty pint.

"Yes, go on then, one for the road."

"Where's yer mate, then? The fat bloke with the glasses. Haven't seen 'im in 'ere in an age."

"He's, er, out of town. On business......."

"Haven't seen that bird of yours, either for a while. You know, the one used to be wed to the soldier bloke."

"She was.....is....his sister....." I had to get a grip. I had her mentally dead.

"She away on 'business' too, then?" He winked lasciviously,

"You want to watch that pair, you do. Thick as thieves they are."

"What are you talking about?"

"I've seen them in here, talking like. Very chummy they are if you see wha......."

"They've been friends for years! Why shouldn't they have a drink together?"

"OK, squire, keep yer wig on. Only making polite conversation. No need to be so touchy." And he moved away to serve someone. Very chummy indeed! I knew what he meant by 'very chummy'. How wrong could he be? Or could I be even more wrong? Paranoia is a terrible thing, but as the man said, 'just because you're paranoid, doesn't mean they're *not* out to get you'.

I finished my pint in merciful peace. Where the fuck was Les? And where the double fuck was Frieda and Frazer? This was all getting out of hand.

CHAPTER 24

"I don't fucking believe this!" Frazer had been grabbed from behind by someone who clearly was in no mood to be gentle. "What the fuck's going on Les? Are you in on this?"

"Nice one Frazer. You almost had me believing you. That's one hell of a double act you two have been putting up all these years. Your mate Tom, poor sod, is completely convinced. Or maybe he's as good an actor as you two? Is he in on it too? Is it a treble, Frazer?"

"What.....? What the hell are you talking about? How did you find us here?"

"We got a nice juicy tip-off about a blue van coming and going here......"

"Yes, that's a point," Frieda had given up struggling, "*where* exactly is *here*?"

"Come off it Frieda..... the game's up....anyway, as I was saying, we got this tip-off and so we checked it out, and surprise, surprise we arrived to see the van buggering off. We waited a few minutes and then decided to have a look round, and who should step out as we open the door but my little friend here!"

"Les, you've got it completely wrong. Could you please put that silly gun away? I'm not going anywhere. We were locked up in there. We've just managed to escape!"

"And you think we're part of this stupid drug thing? Thanks a bundle, friend."

"You're welcome. Put them in the car, sergeant. We'll have a look round before we go. I can hardly wait to see this prison cell they've been locked up in! Probably got chintz curtains and a nice comfy four-poster."

Frazer sat seething in the back of the car. The fact that he was once again handcuffed didn't improve his mood as he waited for Les and his man to re-emerge. Frieda was too utterly miserable to care much. She had a tiny crumb of comfort from the fact that the future atmosphere of the car would not be improved by the fact that she was still damp with pee and was certainly transferring much of it to the cloth seat covers.

Les and the sergeant re-emerged from the building. They had a brief exchange and the sergeant went back into the building. Les strode over to the car.

"If I undo the cuffs, Frazer, do you promise not to try and kill me?"

"I think you'd better leave the fuckers on, Les. I assume an abject apology is forthcoming, or did you find that four-poster?"

"Look, Frazer, I'm really sorry, but I have to follow all my leads." He undid their handcuffs and handed Frieda a box of tissues. "Sorry Frieda, I hope I didn't scare you too much."

"Just get me home, Les. I don't think I can take much more tonight. I need a bath. I need a drink and I need something to eat. If you can provide any or all of these items right now, I'd be eternally grateful."

Les produced a bottle of vodka from the glove box.

"One thing you have to say for Customs men," Frazer observed, "they've always got a bottle or two handy. Funny that." He waited patiently as Frieda took a good hit and accepted it gratefully when she finished.

"Sorry I can't do a bath or even a spot of dinner, but I'm sure you're prepared to wait for that. To answer your previous question, by the way, you're in Gloucester. Not far from the docks. Look, it's quite a long journey home. Why don't I check you into......."

Frieda's scream brought the sergeant running from the shed, drawing his pistol as he ran. Through watering eyes, Les said, "I take it that's a 'no' then."

"I don't think I'll be able to enter an hotel for the rest of my life. Just get us home, Les, oh, sorry Frazer, I forgot you. What do you want to do?"

"Home, James, and don't spare the horses."

As the miles rolled by, Frazer and Frieda set about finishing the vodka. By Exeter they were both fast asleep in the back.

"Do you think they bought it?"

"Yeah, no sweat."

They dropped Frieda off at her place in the early hours and then drove round to Frazer's. Frazer had woken up when Frieda got out but was pretty woozy and still half drunk.

"OK, sleeping beauty, we're here."

Frazer struggled out of the back seat and dug out his keys.

"Listen Frazer, I know it's late, but could I just have a couple of minutes. We need to get a handle on your kidnapping."

"Christ, do you guys never sleep? Yes, sure, come in. I need a cup of coffee to clear my head anyway."

Les and the sergeant followed him into the lodge. Frazer set about boiling the kettle and getting coffee mugs out as the others settled into comfy chairs.

"Bloody hell, my back's killing me! I hate long drives. I think the shocks on that bloody Vectra are shot too."

Frazer handed coffee round and settled into a sofa.

"OK, what can I tell you?"

"Well, from the start, really. Just the bones of it for now, anyway. Have you any idea what they were after? I mean we haven't had any demands from them so far."

"I don't know, Les. They must have drugged us in the hotel.... we had these complimentary drinks.... and then next thing we knew we were tied up in that room. At one point they filmed us with a newspaper held up in front, but that's really all that happened until we managed to escape."

"Yes, how did you manage that? I'm curious."

"Sheer bloody luck, actually. Frieda found this old bit of hacksaw blade tucked down the side of the lino. If we hadn't found that we would still be there. These plastic ties are bloody hard to get out of!"

"But the door must have been locked too, surely?"

"Piece of piss that was. They obviously assumed we wouldn't get beyond the ties. Their biggest mistake was untying Frieda's hands so we could eat. No, between my weight and that door there was no contest."

"Hmm.... Can you describe them? Were they both white, for instance? What were they wearing?"

Frazer chuckled at the memory of Frieda's scare seeing Tony Blair.

"They were wearing these silly masks, one was Tony Blair and the other was George Bush. Frieda literally wet herself when she saw them."

"Yes, I noticed she was a bit uncomfortable."

"Apart from that, they were dressed in overalls and knitted hats, both white I think, both quite big blokes. They didn't say much, so I can't really give a clue about accent. How did you know there were two of them?"

"Eh?"

"You said, 'were they *both* white' or something. How did you know.....?"

"You told me earlier on. You must have said something about two blokes. I can't remember. Anyway you were half cut with that Vodka."

"Oh, yes. Listen, Les, if you don't mind....."

"Of course, sorry mate. 'Nuff said. OK sergeant, let's hit the trail. Christ knows when either of us is going to get any bloody sleep. All right for some, eh?" and he winked at Frazer.

"Yeah, cheers, lads. Take it easy. Don't want you having an accident driving up that road."

"No danger of that mate, we've got a room down at the Marine organised. See you tomorrow probably." And they let themselves out of the house.

Frazer headed groggily for the bedroom dumping clothes as he went. 'Fuck showering' he thought as he fell into bed. He would have fallen asleep instantly, but there was something about that last conversation which was bothering him. He tried to get his head round it but failed completely. 'Paranoia' he thought as he finally drifted off to merciful sleep.

As Frazer was drifting off, I was being roused by the sound of the telephone. I had no idea how long it had been ringing and I finally managed to find it in the dark and pick it up.

"Hello?"

"Tom, it's me, Andy! We need to talk!"

"Andy? I thought you were in the Gulf somewhere? What.....? What time is it? It's three thirty...Andy....."

"Shut up, Tom and listen. I *am* in the Gulf. I'm in Qatar. Listen Tom, something awful has come up. I got a parcel this morning with a video tape in it. As far as I could make out it showed Frazer and Frieda tied up somewhere with yesterday's newspaper. Then a guy in a Tony Blair mask came on......."

"Just a minute, Andy. I'm not getting this. What has Tony Blair got to do with.....? I know that Frieda and Frazer were kidnapped, but...."

"What? You knew they were taken? Why the fuck didn't you call me? What's going on?"

"Yes, well, sorry Andy, but we really didn't know how to reach you. Frieda and Frazer are the only ones with your contact details. We would...."

"OK, OK, I'm sorry. Of course you couldn't. Look, Tom, this is serious. These bastards are making some pretty heavy demands. They are holding Frieda and Frazer hostage to force me to help them in a big heist. Now, I can't talk over the phone. I'm coming back today. It's, what, seven thirty now. I can get on the morning flight. I'll be in Lyneham by four this afternoon. Meet me there."

"Yes, OK Andy, but listen. We're sure this has something to do with that drug business I got mixed up with. Les is still on the case. I think he should be in on this too. I'll try and contact him and bring him along...."

"No, Tom! No one else has to know! They've said that if I contact the police Frieda and Frazer get killed. I can't take the chance! Jesus, I don't even know if they're alive still. This is a bloody nightmare. Christ knows what the hell I'm going to tell the C in C."

"Andy, tell me, how did Frieda look? Did she seem hurt?"

"No, mate. They looked OK. Both were bound and gagged and, as you might imagine, Frieda looked absolutely bloody furious. But no blood, no black eyes. How were they taken?"

"From a hotel in Bristol. Les had taken us all there for questioning and..... listen Andy, can this wait? I'm still a bit confused.....?

"Yes, Tom, sorry. Anyway I have to go. The bloody plane's warming up as I speak. Thank fuck I've got something available faster than a Herc'. See you at four. When you get to the gate, give them my name and use the code word 'Golden Bollocks'."

"Golden Bollocks? That's not very military!"

"I've had to use worse, mate. Just be there." The line went dead.

I lay awake trying to get my head round this latest piece of news. What the hell had Andy to do with all this? What were the demands they were making? I really wanted to talk this through with Les, but I hadn't a clue where the man was. I decided the best thing to do right now was get some more sleep. But how the hell could I sleep now? I decided to get up and make a hot drink. Five minutes later the phone rang.

"Andy??"

"No, Tom, it's me, Les. I thought you'd want to know we've got Frieda and Frazer."

"Oh, God! Thank, fuck! Oh, shit Les, that's great news. Are they OK?"

"Yes, mate, fit and well, if a bit knackered and very pissed off. Listen, we need to talk and soon. The kidnappers are up to something. There seems to be some sort of ransom plan.... I don't know....."

"No, Les, listen! Andy said I hadn't to talk to you but now that I know Frieda and Frazer are safe......"

"Andy? Frieda's brother? What the hell has he got to do with all this?"

I told him about Andy's call and that he would be here later today. Yes, it was today. The sun was cutting a swathe across the room as it shone through a gap in the curtains. I was vaguely aware that any hope of sleep had completely evaporated. I was up for good. Oh well.

"OK, Tom, we'll both go and meet him. Let's find out what these people want."

"But surely when they discover that Frieda and Frazer are gone.....?"

"Listen, Tom. My experience with stuff like this is that once they took the pictures, I'm afraid your friends became expendable. No, I doubt if these guys will go anywhere near that shed now. However, if they do, we've got them. I've got a team of heavies planted there just waiting to collar them. No, no worries on that score. I've also got people watching Frazer and Frieda's places."

"Oh, thanks Les. I'll see them later, then. And you, of course."

"Yes, OK, Tom. And Tom?"

"What?"

"Do try and get more sleep. You sound terrible!"

We arrived at the airfield just on four and I somewhat self-consciously volunteered the password. The guard didn't even blink.

"Could I have your name sir? Some form of ID?"

I had figured that I might be asked for identification and had taken my passport with me. I handed it over. The guard studied it for a moment and returned it. He ducked down and checked Les.

"And you are? I'm expecting Mr Prentice on his own."

Les produced his R&C identification.

"Leslie Dawson, Her Majesty's Revenue and Customs," read the guard. "Les Dawson! Well, well, well. It's a while since the lads have had a laugh. Could you just step out of the car for a moment Mr Dawson?"

Les got out of the car with a lot more grace than I had anticipated in view of the guard's rather sarcastic tone. He walked round the front of the car and ignoring the guard completely entered the guard house. The guard, taken somewhat by surprise went to follow him. Then he remembered he was checking me and hesitated. He was fumbling with his gun, not quite sure whether to shoot Les or me first.

"Wait there! Don't fucking move, OK?"

I raised my hands in agreement. No way was I moving. I wanted to watch the show. I wasn't disappointed.

Les emerged from the guard house.

"Hey you!" he yelled at the guard, "Golden Bollocks! You're wanted on the phone."

The guard took a step towards the guard house and then looked back at me. Once more I signalled my compliance. He went inside. In a few moments Les emerged followed by a very flustered guard who succeeded in beating Les to the car door. He wrenched the door open and stood to attention at full salute.

"Thank you Corporal. You've been very helpful." Les settled into his seat as the guard gently closed the door.

"No problem Mr Dawson *Sir!!* Sorry to have kept you *Sir!!!*"

"Can we go now?" I asked tentatively.

"Yes sir, Mr Prentice sir! Drive on through and park up in front of the big hangar you see over there, sir! The aircraft is due to land in about twenty minutes, sir!"

"Thank you Corporal," Les oozed, "and take it easy. You might pull something standing like that."

"Yes, sir, thank you sir!"

"Drive on Tom, before he expires."

I followed my instructions and stuck the car on the end of a line of rather more imposing vehicles. I shut down the engine and loosened my seat belt. Les had a cheesy grin all over his face.

"What was that all about?"

"The nice corporal has just had his balls chewed by his CO for giving cheek to a senior member of HMR&C. It was pointed out to him that as I have the equivalent rank of Brigadier in the service he could be court-martialled if I so desired. I think he got the message."

"Oh dear. You enjoyed that, didn't you?"

"It's called Dawson's revenge on the world. Or at least on Britain. I don't have any trouble abroad."

"No, old Les didn't travel well I suppose. I don't imagine there were many of his shows dubbed into German. Although, I could be wrong. I once saw Yogi Bear dubbed into Arabic, and I think The Benny Hill Show went to half the world."

"Albania."

"What?"

"Albania. They loved Les Dawson in Albania I understand."

"You're kidding."

"No, him and Norman Wisdom. Icons they were."

"Bugger me."

We sat pondering these wonders for a few moments.

"Listen, Les. I think it would be a good idea if I went and met Andy off the plane on my own, you know, just to warn him that you are here. He doesn't know about Frazer and Frieda yet."

"Yes, good idea Tom. No problem. I'll wait here. This looks like the plane now." He nodded in the direction of the runway. A small twin engined jet touched down and taxied towards us. I got out of the car and waited until the engines stopped and the door folded down. Five or six uniformed men and women emerged and then I spotted Andy. I gave him a wave and he waved back. We met half way.

"Hi Tom. Am I glad to see you! Any news of....."

"It's OK Andy. Frazer and Frieda are OK. They got away."

"Oh thank Christ! I've been at my wits end on that flight."

"Listen, Andy, I've brought Dawson from Customs along. He's leading the investigation into this mess. He wants you to brief him as soon as possible."

"Yes, OK, but it's not a problem any more if Frazer and Frieda got away. Surely...."

"I think you should talk to him. I think he has some plan to catch these people."

"OK, fair enough. I wouldn't mind getting my hands on them myself. I could have done without all this right now."

As we walked back to the car I gave the thumbs up sign and Les got out to meet us.

"Andy, this is Les. Les, Andy. I don't think you two have met."

"No, but I've heard a lot about you. How are you sir?" They shook hands. Les was being singularly deferential. This rank thing was beyond me, but it was clearly important in these circles.

"I'm fine, er, Les. Let's get out of here. I gather we need to talk."

We climbed, somewhat self-consciously it should be said, into my humble transport. All around us Jaguars and Rovers were purring off, topped up with uniformed brass. Andy was in civvies and we looked like we had lost our way going to the pub. As we passed the gate, however, we were honoured with an outrageously ostentatious salute from our friend the corporal. Andy gazed at the guard in amazement.

"What the hell brought that on? Is that guard on something?"

"Just showing you the respect you deserve, Andy." Les was still smiling as we hit the M5 heading south.

We drove south in silence for a while. The radio was tuned quietly to some anonymous music station and I was wondering who would break the silence. In the event it was Les who cracked.

"Er, Andy, can we maybe talk about this package you got? What's the story?"

Andy was in the back, and I honestly thought he had drifted off to sleep.

"Oh bloody hell! I've been sitting here wondering how much I can say about all this. It's so bloody secret you wouldn't believe. Listen, I want you both to swear that what I am about to tell you stays totally 'entre nous'. Is that clear? I could be in serious shit for this, I can tell you. Having said that, there must be a serious leak in the system somewhere as you will soon realise. I do really want to get these bastards and if you can help, Les, then I suppose I have to fill you in."

"Look Andy. I've been chasing these bastards for months. I need a result here. I'll do all I can and of course it won't get out. I can promise you that."

"Tom?"

"Eh? Oh sure. Mum's the word. Who would I tell?"

"OK. As I told Tom, the tape showed Frieda and Frazer tied and gagged. A guy in a party mask looking like Tony Blair said they would be killed if I didn't do exactly as he demanded. Now, I need to give you a bit of background here. This is the sensitive stuff. As you know I'm heading up an operation in Iraq. It's a bit dodgy actually, but I do what I'm told by the politicos. You may have heard rumours of vast hoards of gold bullion lying around Baghdad and the like. In fact there is more than anyone realised. Some of it can be fed back into the Iraqi system, but not all. Apparently it would throw the entire Middle Eastern economy into turmoil. A decision was taken to, shall we say, put some of it on ice, until the situation out there stabilised. My job is to coordinate the move."

"Ah!" I had made a connection. I'm quick that way.

"What?"

"The password. Golden Bollocks. I get it now."

"Yes, anyway, at the moment the bullion is stored under heavy guard at Baghdad airport....."

"How much, exactly, are we talking about here?" I knew little about the value of gold. What did 'a lot of gold' look like?

"A ton of gold is worth about $14million. I'm looking at forty tons of the stuff."

A quick calculation had me gasping.

"That's more that half a billion dollars! Bloody hell!"

"Quite. Unfortunately word of the move has got out somehow. What these guys want me to do is help them to steal the gold."

"And they're using Frieda and Frazer as hostages to persuade you." Les was in full planning mode. I recognised the expression on his face. "What's the angle? I mean how do they want you to help?"

"Apparently they have got a hold of some sort of drug and....."

"Bingo! The connection! I wondered what it would be. Go on."

"Well, they somehow found out that once the stuff is brought out....oh, did I say we're flying it here? Anyway, it'll be stored in a sealed government depot not far from here until it can be moved to vaults which are being prepared somewhere in Wiltshire. I think it'll be in the old underground workings near Bath. Anyway, they want me to get this stuff into the sealed water system at the depot. This'll knock out the guards long enough for them to load the stuff on trucks and head off to a happy retirement."

"How do they know that all the guards'll have a drink of water though? I mean what if someone only likes Lucozade for instance?" It all sounded a bit 'iffy' to me.

"They don't have to drink the water. It's a sealed depot remember. It has sealed aircon with humidifiers. Apparently this stuff can be inhaled as vapour."

"Cunning bastards. What do you think, Les?"

"Cunning bastards indeed. It might just work."

"Just as well Frazer and Frieda got away. I would really be in the shit if that ever went down."

"Yes, but we want to catch these guys, remember."

"No problem. I'll carry on with the plan but I'll get the guards to fake being drugged. When the bad guys turn up we nab them!"

"Except that they won't turn up."

"Sorry? Surely if...."

"Remember, Andy. Your system already has a leak somewhere. If you set up a trap in the depot you will have to tell everyone about it. Your mole could easily tip off the gang that there was a sting set up."

"Hmmm. Yes, you could be right. What do we do?"

"We go along with the plan and drug the guards. I'll have a bunch of guys waiting for the gang when they appear and we'll bottle them up inside the depot compound."

"No way! Absolutely not! I can't go drugging soldiers. Anyway it might be harmful....."

"Listen Andy. That stuff is pretty harmless. All they'll get is a good few hours sleep."

"Not sure. Let me think about it. I can't make a decision like that right now. I've got to contact the group tomorrow. Let's meet tomorrow morning and finalise."

"OK, no problem Andy, but remember, these bastards were going to kill Frieda and Frazer."

"I haven't forgotten that. Don't worry."

This time Andy really did go to sleep in the back seat. Les sat quietly beside me deep in thought. I turned up the radio. Eva Cassidy was on.

When we got back home, I dropped Andy off at my place where he was greeted by Frieda and Frazer. After prolonged kisses and cuddles all round they went inside. Frieda was trying to tell Andy all about the kidnap without actually taking a breath and Frazer was trying not to cry.

I left them to it and drove Les to the Marine.

"A cosy little trio there. Quite touching really."

"Fuck off Les. Sometimes your cynicism gets up my nose."

"Sorry mate. Just drop me off here. I think I need some fresh air."

CHAPTER 25

"Do you think Andy will go along with Dawson's plan? Ow!!"

I was in no mood to talk about any of the stuff that had been going on recently. I was naked in bed with my favourite lady, who happily, was also completely naked. We had retired to bed with a couple of stiff whiskies once Frazer and Andy had gone home and had made a pretty good effort of re-establishing our credentials as a serious item. A short post-coital snooze had re-charged the old dick battery and I was busy exploring the erectile properties of a particularly tasty nipple. A judicious nip was sufficient to interrupt the question in question.

"That hurt! How would you like it if I did that to you?"

"I'm wiwwin to giw it w twy."

"Don't talk with your mouth full.... it's rude."

I moved to the other nipple. Always one for equality, me.

"Mmmm. I do like that. I get all hot and wet. How's.... you know who....?"

"I think he's getting bored....bored stiff in fact."

"Poor thing, let me see if I can cheer him up a bit......."

"Gosh, that was good.....No, but really. Do you think.....?"

"OK, I give in. Let's talk. I'll get a couple of refills. Same again?"

I padded through to the dining room with the glasses. Pouring whisky naked must come pretty high on my list of seriously decadent activities. Second only, maybe, to using ice-cold Veuve to.....anyway, I digress.

"Frazer was really angry that Les should think we were on the wrong side of this."

I only caught the end of that shouted remark and was somewhat taken aback.

"What? You're what?!"

"We're nothing. Les thought we were somehow involved with the bad guys and Frazer was really angry. I think that's why he was trying to put Andy off the idea Les had to catch these guys. I got bored with them arguing and went for a long bath. Andy's pretty wound up about the whole thing, though. I wish he would drop it."

"Yes, I don't think he will, though.....water?"

"Just a splash......thanks." She sipped her drink thoughtfully. "You know, there's something very odd about this whole business. I've never really been involved in criminal activities. My only experience is reading crime novels where everything is carefully plotted and clever. This is just a mess if you ask me."

"Well, maybe that's because it's the real thing. Maybe real criminals are much thicker than the ones in novels."

"I suppose so. You have to be pretty thick I suppose to think you'll get away with it."

"Not that the average plod is much better, mind you. Remember, a lot of the mess here is down to Les. He hasn't exactly set himself up for a Mensa award, has he?"

"No.... all the more reason for Andy to think more than twice about Les's scheme...... Tom?"

"Hmmm?"

"Andy was pretty sure that the gang would have just abandoned us in that shed. What if they find out we're not there and come after us again?"

"Les said that he had guys staking the place out, didn't he? If they come back he's got them. In fact that would be ideal as it would be an end to it."

"Yes, I suppose so. But what if they found out we had escaped without going back?"

"How, exactly?"

"Well, they're supposed to be in contact with Andy. What if they've been shadowing him? They might have seen us outside your house."

I chewed this one over. She had a point, but I was pretty sure the place was deserted when we got back. No strange vehicles, no shadowy figures. But then....

"Well, either way, the game's a bogie. If they know you're free and they know Andy knows, the leverage is gone. There'll be no contact with Andy, the gold will be tucked away safely and that will be that."

"So why doesn't Andy tell them we're free when he makes contact?"

"He wants a shot at catching them remember."

"Oh, yes, I forgot..... Tom, I'm still scared."

"Yes, I don't blame you...... I've been thinking. I think that you and Frazer need to be out of the picture for a while..... at least until this lot blows over. I have a cunning plan, as Baldrick would say."

"It'd better be better than one of Baldrick's cunning plans. Let's hear it."

"It's cunninger than a cunning thing from the planet cunn....."

"TOM!"

"Sorry. This is it. Sligo Bay is sitting doing nothing just now and I thought that since we are having a lovely spell of weather, a little trip to the Channel Islands and hence to La Belle France might just take long enough to allow the big boys to sort out the baddies. I would, of course, be happy to skipper the enterprise. Let's see... a day over to Guernsey, a couple of days tucked up in St Peter Port sampling the local ales, then a short hop to Jersey.... see if we can find Bergerac for you....then off over to Lesadrieaux or maybe Paimpol for a few days of oysters and Gros Plant. If it stays good we could coast hop south."

"Oh, Tom, I don't know. You know how I am with boats."

"You were OK going up to Bristol that time."

"Yes, well that was a river. It was flat. The Channel is bumpy I am told. God, I feel queasy just talking about it."

"Listen Frieda, there's a huge 'high' coming in off the Atlantic. The Channel will be like a mill-pond for days. I doubt if we'll even get to sail much. We'll be motoring most of the time. Once we get to the French coast it's all pretty sheltered. And anyway, Sligo sails like a brick bungalow."

I knew I was lying through my teeth.... not about the 'high'.... it really was forecast, but about the picture I was painting of calm seas and sheltered harbours. The Channel is not a nice bit of water. It's unpredictable and dangerous unless you know what you're doing. Particularly around the Channel Islands, oh, and the French coast. Fortunately I know what I'm doing, but I certainly couldn't guarantee the sort of seas that would allow Frieda to retain even one of her meals. Having said all that, I really have been on the Channel when it was calm for days. Once. Years ago.

"I haven't got anything to wear, though. What about oilskins and stuff? Will I be able to take a bikini?"

"I'd be furious if you didn't take your bikini. Oilskins we can get."

"I want nice ones though. Not these horrible red and blue jobs that make you look like a postman."

"As a matter of fact, I saw a nice, sort of pinkish mauve set in the chandler's just the other day. They were good too. Henri Lloyd. Very expensive."

"Oooh I like the sound of these. Can we go and see them tomorrow?"

"Sure, and we can get you matching wellies and docksiders while we're there."

I had forgotten that the prospect of buying expensive clothes wiped all other thoughts from the average female mind and Frieda was no exception. I reckoned I could dose her up with enough Stugeron to keep her reasonably happy until we got to Guernsey. There are lots of nice shops there, and if she was utterly miserable on the crossing we could stay there indefinitely, and if necessary she could fly home. I'd cracked it.

"OK, so what's today... Tuesday. Let's plan to leave some time Thursday. I'll do my tide calcs tomorrow and check the long term forecast and.....Frieda?"

"Zzzzzzzzzz...."

"'Night love. Sleep tight."

The utter normality of my office felt strange after all that had happened in the last few days. But bills and wages still had to be paid, invoices sent, orders placed. I had been at my desk for at least an hour, Cath tapping away in the background on her computer, a lukewarm coffee at my elbow, before I noticed that my faithful old leather jacket was hanging behind the office door. I got up to inspect it. Yes, it was mine all right. I checked the pockets. A letter and a couple of invoices were still in the inside pocket. A packet of mints was still there in an outside pocket. I was confused.

"Er, Cath?"

"Yes, Tom?"

"I seem to have found my jacket. You may remember the one you left in the pub in Clifton? Can you perhaps cast any light on its reappearance?"

"Oh, yes. I meant to tell you. Ben brought it back."

"Ben. You mean Ben who tied you up. Ben who fell off his bike. Ben who called me a c......."

"Yes!......Yes, that Ben. He, er, thought you, that is, I would want it back, so he, sort of, dropped it round my place yesterday."

"This Ben, Cath. He wouldn't be a detective of some kind, or a clairvoyant maybe? I mean, I know I'm going to regret asking this question, but how did he know where you lived?"

"Well, you see, when we were talking, you know, in the shed place, it just sort of came up in the conversation."

"Just sort of came up. Oh, of course, you were saying, 'untie me you bastard, and by the way I live at number three Sandford Way........"

"Don't be silly Tom. That's not how it was at all. And anyway I phoned the hospital to find out how he was getting on and I, well, left my phone number. He called back and offered to bring back the jacket. I thought it was rather sweet of him actually."

"Sweet."

"Yes."

"Ben."

"Yes. Tom, he's really a nice person. I think he's just had an unfortunate start. He told me about his childhood in St Pauls and how......." My raised hand stopped the flow.

"Cath, he is a criminal. He consorts with drug dealers. He is not, as you put it, a 'nice person'."

"No really, Tom. He says he's a reformed character. He says meeting me and then falling off his bike has changed him. He....."

"Please, for f.... goodness sake Cath, don't tell me he's been 'born again' or I shall vomit."

"No, I don't think it's religious. I just think he's not mixed with very nice people and now that he's met some decent kind people, he realises where he's been going wrong...... What? Why are you looking at me like that?"

"You fancy him! Of course! You bloody fancy the guy! Well, bugger me!"

"No! That's not.... well not really. I do like him Tom. I hardly know him. But he's got problems. His girl has chucked him out.

He's broke. He can't afford to fix his bike, so he can't work......."

The distinct aroma of rodent was beginning to fill the air between us.

"Er, Cath. I hardly dare ask, but where exactly is Ben right now?"

"..........'samyouse....."

"Sorry, I didn't quite catch that. Where did you say he was?"

"It was mum's idea. She felt sorry for him. She...... Tom? What are you doing?"

"We're going to your house now. God knows what we'll find when we get there. Nothing probably, and I mean absolutely nothing. No furniture, no TV, no hi-fi, no mum...."

Outside Cath's house I yanked on the handbrake, flung open the car door and hit the pavement in one fluid motion. Well, it would have been fluid but for the unfortunate intervention of the seat belt which I forgot to undo. I nearly strangled myself. Once clear of the car I ran up the path with Cath behind me protesting Ben's incipient sainthood.

The front door was ajar. I crashed into the hallway and flattened a very startled Ben against the wall.

"What the fuck?! Well, fuck me! It's my dear old friend Tom. What's the matter with you? Do you like seeing me in hospital clothes or sumfin?"

I grabbed him by the collar of his overalls.

"You! Out! Cath find your mum. Make sure she's OK."

"What the fuck? Course she's OK. She's in the kitchen making a brew. She promised me a cuppa when I'd finished fixing her door bell. What's the matter wiv you anyway? You're fuckin' mental you are."

Cath's mum appeared from the kitchen carrying a tray of tea things.

"Oh, hello Tom dear. Cath, you should have said Tom was coming, I'd have made more scones. Just you boys relax and I'll get more cups." She toddled back to the kitchen.

"OK, now let me get this straight. Cath's mum is letting you use the spare room in return for doing some much needed repairs around the house?"

"Until he gets a job of course," Cath explained.

"Correct squire. Quid pro quo and all that. D'you know how much a good handyman costs these days?"

"You'll forgive me for being just a teensy bit sceptical here, Ben. Are you saying that you are giving up the criminal way of life for a life of good deeds and philanthropy? The old Damascus road bit?"

"Damascus Road? Don't know it mate. Actually I've never been a criminal. That business with Lacey was my first dodgy job. I thought it was a joke. Now my bird's left me because of it."

"A joke?! Are you serious?"

"Yeah, well, bloody Lacey talked me into it, didn't he? Said he was just trying to take the piss. I realised it wasn't kosher when I talked to Caff 'ere. She didn't seem like one of Lacey's mates bints some'ow. An' when you turned up I knew for sure I was dealin' wiv wallies.....no offence."

"None taken I'm sure."

"I've never been inside or anything. I've done all me probation an' community service too!"

"Well, that's all right then." I was becoming painfully aware of the sheltered life I had been leading up until now. Here was someone who thought that not actually going to jail was a positive character trait. I was going to have to alter my perception somewhat. Or could there be a fault in my reality?

"So are you serious about finding a job?"

"Dead serious. I need some dosh to get me bike fixed. That ambulance bloke..... a real gent, by the way.... got it collected and he's stripped it down at 'is place, but I need a new front wheel and forks."

"Can't you claim from the other bloke's insurance?"

"Arseole didn't 'ave any, did he? Bloody disgrace."

"Well, what about yours?"

"Yeah, well......."

"Well, if you're interested I could use another body down at the boatyard. It'll be messy, though. Stripping back, anti-fouling, general preparation work, but I pay well. £250 a week plus overtime. Interested?"

"Yeah! I'm your man for sure! I don't mind a bit of hard work. Thanks Tom, you're a diamond, straight up!"

"Yes, well, it has to be above board. I want a P45 from you. No fiddling the social. When do you want to start?"

"Well, I've got this bell to finish and I said I'd clean the gutters, then there's........."

"Tomorrow?"

"No sweat. Tomorrow it is squire. I'll be there.....what time do you clock on?"

"We start at eight. An hour for lunch and knock off at five, unless there's a big job on then you're in for overtime."

"Brilliant! I'll have me bike back in no time!"

Over tea we chatted about this and that. I asked after Ben's injuries and it turned out he had only dislocated his thumb and suffered a few scrapes and bruises. His hand was still strapped up but it didn't seem to slow him down much. Soon he was off doing his odd jobs with an enthusiasm I had to confess I found most surprising.

"He's a good worker, isn't he Tom?"

"Well, he certainly seems to be, Cath. I must say I'm impressed."

"Listen, Tom, you couldn't maybe advance him the money for his bike. He hasn't got any transport and he likes to see his mum in Bristol at weekends."

"Now hold on Cath. One step at a time. I've stuck my neck out offering him a job. Let's get the first week over at least and then I'll think about it."

"Oh, all right. Maybe...."

"No! Forget it Cath!"

"What? You don't know what I was going to say!"

"Now, let me guess. You've got a few quid tucked away for a rainy day, and you thought....."

"Well, I don't need it just now....."

"No, Cath. If he's as decent as you say he is he won't accept it anyway. If he isn't......."

There was a crash from outside. We could hear Ben talking to Cath's mum.

".....really sorry missus, I didn't see it there......"

"......never mind, I didn't much like that gnome anyway...."

"I gave her that gnome. Last year," Cath sniffed.

"Yes, well, I hate to leave this cosy scene, but I've still got work to do.... and so have you miss! Come on, let's get out of here before he breaks anything else."

When we got back to the office Frazer was ensconced behind my desk with his feet up on my accounts.

"All right for some, eh? Skiving off half the bloody morning when there's people waiting at your place of business. I could have been a serious customer for all you knew. I could have been wanting an entire fleet of trawlers re-fitted as luxury....."

"Fuck off out of my chair Frazer and get your mucky boots off my paperwork. To what do we owe the dubious pleasure?"

Frazer heaved himself to his feet and parked himself on the other side of the desk.

"I hear we're going sailing. Is that your old jacket? I thought you'd lost it?"

"Yes, yes, and it's a long story."

"I'm in no rush. I suppose a cup of coffee is completely out of the question?"

Cath appeared with two steaming mugs and plonked them down on the desk.

"You're a mind reader, girl. Did I ever tell you that, Tom? She's a mind reader."

"Oh, Frazer. You know you always want coffee when you come here. You always ask if it's out of the question too."

"Oh God, I hate it when people expose my repartee as predictable rubbish. I suppose....."

"The rum's over there where it always is. Now, what do you think? I think I've talked Frieda round. We're going shopping for oilskins later."

"Yes, I must say I was slightly taken aback when she told me. I've known Frieda longer than you and I just can't imagine her agreeing to a sail. You've changed her, Tom."

"Is that a compliment?"

"No, not particularly, why should it be?"

"No reason.....any way, are you up for it?"

"Yes, sure. Apart from the burning desire to be out of reach of certain loonies around here, I could do with a dose of the Channel. Not to mention some French gastronomy."

"Right.... listen Frazer, do me a favour. Shop around for some booze and basics and stow them for me. Could you check out Sligo too and top up the diesel and water. I'm up to my bloody neck here. I've got a heap to do before we go."

"Aye, aye skipper. No sweat. God, I love it! A couple of weeks afloat. PFM!!"

He almost skipped out of the office. Cath watched his retreating bulk.

"What's PFM Tom? Is it a nautical term?"

"Cath, it means 'Pure Fucking Magic', but I know he wouldn't want you to hear him say such a thing!"

CHAPTER 26

"Hello?"

"OK, Prentice. Do you have a date for us?"

"Who is this?" Andy was disinclined to be polite when addressed so rudely. He knew perfectly well who it was.

"Don't piss about Prentice. You know who this is, now do you have a date for us?"

"Look, how do I know my friends are OK? I need to know you haven't harmed them."

"They're OK. But I can promise you one thing. If you don't stop pissing around, they won't be. Now the date."

"The, er, stuff comes in Thursday. That's the 20th."

"OK, here's what happens. You dump the drug in the aircon at midnight on the 20th. It'll take about an hour to work. You hang about outside where you can see the security people inside. As soon as they are knocked out you SMS us on this number. Oh, and don't try tracing it, it's a pirate. Have you got that?"

"Yes, send an SMS to this number."

"Right. Now the drug. You'll find it in a medical saline bag inside the cistern of the gents toilet in the bookies in the High Street at five tomorrow evening."

"What here? In town here?"

"Yes. I'd hate to have you go out of your way."

"Thanks a bunch. Listen, this drug. How do I know it's safe? Are you sure it won't kill all these guys?"

"It's safe. We tested it. On your friends, as a matter of fact. Slept like babies they did. You saw them in the video after it wore off. Now listen. We'll wait for your SMS and then arrive in two vans. You open the gates and doors for us and then bugger off. And I mean bugger off. No hanging around, spying. We'll load as much as we can in half an hour."

"And my friends......?"

"As soon as we're clear and safe, I'll call you with the information that'll let you find them."

"How do I know you'll call?"

"You don't. You'll just have to trust me won't you? Just remember, you fuck up in any way, or have us followed and I most certainly won't call."

"Look, I think you could at least let me talk......hello? Hello?"

"......................click!"

"OK, it's on for the 20th. I'm going along with this, Les. I'm not happy, but I can't say I can think of a better way of catching them."

"Don't worry Andy. I've organised a serious team. I've got the police involved, against my better judgement I should add, but the chief insisted. We'll be well dug in at the side of the approach road when they turn up. There's no way they are going to get away again. Not under their own steam anyway. You haven't said anything to your lot, I hope?"

"No, nothing."

"Good. I've a feeling that when we blow this job apart there will be a few big names looking at serious trouble. This had to have had some very high up involvement."

"How do you know *I'm* not involved?"

Les put down his beer.

"I don't. Not for sure. You've always been in my mind as a possible. But I have a pretty good idea that you wouldn't have put your friends at risk like that. And you'd hardly have told me about it, now would you?"

"I might be lying, you know, about the dates etc."

"Are you? Listen Andy, to put it bluntly, if it turns out that you and your friends are planning to bugger off to Brazil with a couple of tons of gold in your rucksack, I'd be interested to find out how you are going to do it, but oddly, I'd probably say 'good luck'. No, the gold's your problem. All I'm interested in is busting a drug ring and you want to get the people who kidnapped your friends, so I'm putting my money on your cooperation for now."

"Don't worry Les. I'm with you. One more for the road?"

"Les? It's me........Yeah, now listen. That boat, Sligo Bay........yes Morton's boat. How much do you reckon it could carry in that hold?......what? About five? Five ton?........well, maybe nothing, but I've been watching that guy Frazer and he seems to be getting it ready for a pretty long passage by the look of the stuff he's stowing on board......yes, fuel, water, food, beer, that kind of stuff. He also heaved a lot of junk out of the hold........yes, that had crossed my mind too. Bit of private enterprise........OK, I'll keep you posted, cheers."

Andy got to the bookie's about 4.45. The place was pretty quiet and it was clear that they were getting ready to close up shop. He had never been in a bookmakers establishment in his life before and hadn't a clue what was expected of him, however he decided to try and blend in. He noticed a bloke taking a piece of paper from a box and he was writing on it with reference to one of the many TV screens dotted about the place. He did the same and pretended to concentrate on the screen nearest to him. The minutes passed and the shop emptied. He had clocked the gents earlier and was just about to head in that direction when a woman behind the glass screen called him over.

"In here from the cold love?"

"Pardon?"

"I asked if you were in here from the cold? We're closing and if you want to place a bet, you'll have to be quick. Oh, and if you're thinking of going for a pee, forget it. The bog's out of action."

"What? Er, but I really need to go......" and he made a dash for the door. It was locked.

"Forget it love. Use the one in the square. Some nutter put a bag of stuff in the cistern earlier and flooded the place. You can never get a plumber when you need one, eh?"

Andy goggled at her as she busied herself tidying pens and paper.

"Er, this bag of stuff. You still have it?"

"Why, was it you put it there? Cos if it was......"

Andy thought fast. This was not in the script at all.

"No, no, not me, er, actually I'm an, er, public health expert. I would be interested to see what caused the problem, that's all. Can I see it?"

221

"OK, I think it's through the back somewhere," and she disappeared. Andy heaved a sigh of relief.

The woman reappeared with the bag. It was clearly empty.

"It's empty."

"Yes, well, there was water in it, but I flushed that down the bog. Didn't seem to be much point in keeping that. It would have leaked all over the place."

Andy took the bag lamely.

"Thanks. I'll, er, get this checked. I'll just go and......"

"Oh yes. Bogs in the square love. You can't miss them. See you tomorrow maybe. We open at nine. 'Night!"

Andy stuffed the bag into his pocket and left the shop. Les was waiting in the car.

"You get the bag?"

"Yes, I got the bag." He handed it to Les.

"It's empty. Why's it empty for fuck sake?"

"She flushed it down the bog. The idiot who put it there jammed something in the cistern and flooded the place. Sorry."

"Christ almighty. You can't even trust bloody criminals these days not to cock things up."

"What do we do now?"

"I dunno. Let me think......."

"We could stick to my original plan."

"Which was......?"

"Get the guards to pretend to be asleep. If I brief them and only them, and do it as late as possible, the inside man might not find out."

"Yes, well, I reckon that it's our only chance now. If it works it works, if it doesn't, well they just won't show. Is anything ever going to go right with this bloody job?"

"Look, I think I can keep it tight. The advantage is that we'll have more bodies to round them up. Your lot can follow the gang into the warehouse and my boys will already be inside fully awake and armed."

"Hmm. It could work. But your men would have to make it look convincing. They'd have to let the gang get well and truly inside and virtually at the loading stage before they 'woke up'."

"Oh, I think my guys could manage that OK. I've seen them on guard duty!"

"I hope you're joking."

"Yes, of course I'm joking. It'll work. Don't worry. Er, do you think that flushing that stuff down the loo will do any harm? I mean I suppose the sewers will deal with it OK?"

"I haven't a bloody clue mate. I don't know how sewers work. Mind you, I wouldn't go for a swim in the sea in the next couple of days. You don't want to get attacked by a pissed haddock, do you?"

"No danger of that. I think I might be a bit too busy for the next few days to think about swimming. It's a point though. We can't really warn the life guards though, can we?"

"Er, no. I think we'd sound a bit silly, don't you? I know they warn people about swimming while drunk, but getting drunk while swimming might stretch their credibility a bit."

Les started the car and moved out into the traffic.

"Right, game on. You do your bit of organising and I'll finalise with my team. We shouldn't need to meet before the operation, so good luck. Oh, and Andy. I suggest you don't say anything about the details to your friends."

"It's OK, Les. They'll be well away by then. They're taking a sailing holiday in the Channel for the next few days. I think that's actually a pretty wise idea, don't you?"

"Yes. Brilliant. Keeps them out of harm's way. I hope the weather holds for them."

"You don't know how relevant that wish might be, mate."

"Oh, just a small point. How big's your team inside the warehouse? You know, just so's I can be sure I've got enough cover."

"Two at the entrance and four inside. They're a tight team. Good lads."

"Hmm, sounds a bit light to me, but I'm sure you know what you're doing."

"Indeed I do, Les. Indeed I do."

"Now that's what I call a set of oilskins!" Frazer was clearly impressed.

We were just clearing the bar at the mouth of the estuary and already Frieda's smile was beginning to look a bit thin. It was a glorious day. Rumour had it that it was going to be the hottest for years, and the wind was almost non-existent. Frazer was dressed in a fetching combination of baseball cap sporting the logo of a well-known pharmaceutical company, a pair of rather inadequate rugby shorts and the oldest known existing pair of Sebagos in the world.

"...but with respect, I think you might be a bit hot, don't you?"

Frieda had insisted on donning the full outfit before we cast off on the grounds that if she had to put them on later, she might not have the stomach to go below. Certainly beads of sweat were clearly visible on her top lip, and the combination of too hot and slightly sea-sick produced a very strange hue to her complexion.

"I think you could at least take off the jacket, Frieda. I can hang it here in the wheel-house so you can get it if you need it. I really don't think we'll see much bad weather today."

I was setting the auto-pilot more or less due south for a long boring motor down to the islands. The main was up, but sheeted tight purely for stability's sake and I had rigged an awning from the mizzen for a bit of shade on deck. The Channel was as mill-pond like as I had ever seen it. We felt like we were on rails. The tides had been perfect and I figured that setting off as we did around ten, we would be through the shipping lanes before nightfall and sight the Guernsey light before dawn next morning. We would be nicely berthed in time for breakfast.

Frieda grudgingly removed her jacket revealing a top of the range fleece tucked into her trousers. She wedged herself into a corner of the cockpit and studiously studied the horizon.

"Er, how do you feel? It's pretty flat, Frieda. Are you sure you're not too hot?"

There was, admittedly, a long swell, but nothing that could be described as a sea.

"I'll be fine Tom, if you don't keep asking me how I am. Just you get on with the stuff you need to do...." and she waved her hand vaguely in my direction and resumed her scrutiny of the horizon.

Frazer was well ensconced on the hatch cover with a book, a beer and a pillow from his bunk.

"PFM! What more could a chap ask for.... don't answer that. By the way, who's on watch?"

"Sod off Frazer. We won't need formal watches. I do know who's on lunch duty, though."

"I was hoping that since Frieda wasn't doing any sailing duties, she could do the catering."

Frieda looked stricken.

"What? No way, Frazer. I couldn't possibly......"

"He's teasing, Frieda. Don't panic. I'll cook."

"I don't think I'll be terribly hungry actually, Tom. I'll just sit here. Maybe something later...."

My cell phone rang. Frazer sat up and glared round.

"Is that your bloody phone Tom? Why did you bring that?"

"Sorry Frazer, I just thought it might be a good idea.....Hello? Andy?"

"Hi Tom. Where are you?"

"Just a couple of miles out. What's up?"

"Maybe nothing. Listen, did you tell the coastguard where you were going?"

"Yes, we filed the usual......"

"Did you use the VHF?"

"No, we just dropped the papers as usual, what's the problem."

"No problem Tom. That's fine. Now don't use the VHF unless you really need to. Use your phone if you want to talk to me, OK?"

"Yes, OK. But why.....?"

"Don't worry. I just want to know you are all safely away. I think the shit's going to hit the fan with this operation and I don't want anyone anywhere near you until it's over. OK?"

"OK, we'll be fine.....Andy?"

"What?"

"Be careful, mate."

"Careful is my middle name, Tom. Don't worry. Have a good trip. See if you can get Frieda a decent tan!"

"Will do. See you when we get back."

"The champagne will be on ice. Cheers."

Frazer and Frieda had been watching me during this exchange. They were clearly both puzzled and worried.

"What's up Tom?"

"I don't know. Andy wanted to make sure we hadn't said where we were going over the radio. I think he's worried that we are being followed or at least monitored."

"Well, if we're being followed it won't be too difficult for whoever is following us to catch us. It would be the slowest high-speed chase in history."

"Well, let's just keep a weather eye out."

"What about the radar? That might show someone behind us?"

"No, it's no use astern. No we'll just have to keep a look out. I don't think it's a problem though. Just Andy being over cautious."

"Fair enough. Right, who needs a beer?"

"Hello, Les?......yes, they've sailed........ I dunno, last seen heading out of the estuary. They told the harbourmaster they were going to Guernsey......OK, I'll monitor the VHF traffic and keep you posted......sure, cheers."

CHAPTER 27

"Ben?"

"What?"

"You're hurting my hand"

"Oh, sorry princess. I was engrossed..... sorry."

"Do you like this film?"

"Yeah, sure. I seen it before, but I don't mind watchin' it again. I never watched a movie in a church 'all before, though."

"Really? Well, I like it. And it's not as dear as the cinema."

"Yeah, sure. No popcorn though. Or choc ices. I like choc ices."

"I always used to drop a bit of chocolate and not notice until I came out and there it was all over my skirt!"

They giggled like school kids. The woman behind shushed them impatiently.

"Sorry missus......."

Ben dropped his voice to a whisper.

"I'm a bit surprised though. You, know, showin' 'The Full Monty' in a church 'all."

"The minister is very progressive."

"He's not bloody gay, is he?" Ben forgot himself and got shushed again.

"No, *she's* not gay."

"She?!"

"Listen young man. If you don't be quiet I shall ask the verger to ask you to leave!"

"Oh, yeah, sorry missus......silly old bat....she?"

Cath patted his hand and gazed fixedly at the screen. Ben got the message and settled down to watch the movie. He tried to put his consternation at developments such as female ministers and blue movies in churches to the back of his mind. His mum would have been shocked. Truly she would.

"Da,da,daaah,....dada, da daaahhh!"

Frazer was giving a rather tuneless rendition of 'The Stripper' as Frieda finally realised she was not on the verge of succumbing to hyperthermia and started to struggle out of her oilskin trousers. She had joined Frazer (after considerable cajoling and the dawning realisation that she was, in fact, not even slightly seasick) on the hatch cover, and even risked sipping at a cold Coke. She was soon down to jeans and a tee-shirt and were it not for the fact that there was clearly nothing under that, would have gone further.

"This isn't half bad. I could get used to this type of sailing!"

"Well, maybe some time in the future we'll get as far as the Med. I'll show you serious bikini sailing."

"Yes, and even some serious non-bikini sailing!" Frazer had still not quite recovered from a holiday he once took in what is now known as Croatia. Clothing was seldom to be seen anywhere among the Dalmatian Islands and he hankered to return.

"Go and put your cossie on for goodness sake. You look overdressed for this weather."

"Let me get used to this first, Tom. I'm still not sure about going below for too long. It's that diesel smell that gets me I think."

I tended to agree with her on that one. It hadn't helped that Frazer had been a tad over enthusiastic in filling the tanks and slopped a load of fuel into the bilges. It's a horrible smell and almost impossible to get rid of. I'd pumped out as much as I could but it still lingered.

We were well into the shipping lanes and some pretty impressive vessels were passing ahead and astern of us. We were dodging them without too much in the way of course changes, but it meant that someone had to helm continuously. I was getting bored.

"Do you want to try steering for a bit, Frieda? It's quite easy."

"Am I allowed? I don't have a license or anything."

"It's OK, Frieda," Frazer piped, "you can use your car license. If the cops stop you just show them that. You'll be OK, honest."

Frieda looked doubtful.

"Is that right, Tom? I never know when Frazer is joking. I don't want to get into bother."

"Yes, absolutely correct, Frieda. It's an international law. Any driving license is fine at sea."

"Particularly a British one!"

"Well of course! Rule Britannia and all that!"

"Yup, next time a police boat pulls alongside all you need to do is flash a British license and they won't even board you. Even French Police boats."

"You have to watch these Chinese ones, though. Very iffy they are. Always wanting to check your scuppers. Damned inconvenient."

Frieda was looking even more confused.

"Chinese? Here??"

"These bloody Chinese get everywhere. Think they own the bloody sea."

I found the need to go below. I was in danger of wetting my pants. Frazer was the first to crack.

"........You bastards! You're taking the piss! Right, you can drive the bloody boat yourselves! Chinese police indeed. That's it! If the police boat comes, you'd just better have *your* driving license with you, that's all!"

Frazer exploded. Frieda made her way to the bow and sat with her legs dangling over the side. Silence reigned.

A deeper silence reigned that evening in a military warehouse on the edge of Salisbury Plain. Shortly before midnight, if anyone had been watching, a shadowy figure could be seen opening the steel gates to the fenced yard and shortly thereafter the rising roller door to the warehouse itself revealed a strange sight. The brightly lit interior of the warehouse was relatively empty, however in the middle of the floor stood several pallets loaded with a solid, heavily wrapped cargo. This was, admittedly, not very strange. What would have been extremely strange to a casual observer would have been the somnolent aspect of the guards protecting the cargo. All lay or slumped in a variety of positions indicating a rapid onset of unconsciousness. To a close observer these positions may have been construed as somewhat theatrical, but there were no close observers.

One observer had positioned himself at a safe distance, however. Andy was tucked up in the back of a dilapidated Land Rover parked up near the perimeter fence, but with a clear view of the gate. To say he was nervous was an understatement. He was pumped to the maximum. But Andy was a soldier. An old soldier admittedly. The Falklands was the last real action he had seen. He was, however fully aware that he was almost euphoric with anticipation. This was going to be......fun! Yes!

The silence and his thoughts were interrupted by the sound of approaching vehicles. He ducked down deeper into the Land Rover. He could just make out the silhouette of two large vans approaching with all lights out. They were taking no chances.

The 'sleeping' guards had been briefed to remain somnolent until the gang started in on the cargo. By then Les's team would be in place. The agreed signal for action would be a loud whistle blast.

What they had not been briefed to expect was the sensation of a machine pistol pressed to their necks and the order to stay down while they were trussed like turkeys for the pot.

Some decided to continue with the sham of being unconscious, however one or two realised that things weren't working out quite as planned and began to make rather a fuss. This merely earned them a good kicking.

The continued absence of any form of whistle signal as the heavily masked gang now began loading gold bars into trucks brought home to Andy the total realisation that somehow the plan had backfired and questions could well be asked in high places come the morning.

Andy watched and waited. He had also come to the conclusion that plan 'A', as he had anticipated, had been bypassed and quite possibly plan 'B' should now be considered as a matter of some urgency.

The heavily laden vans were now passing unchallenged through the warehouse gates and gathering speed in the direction of the main road.

This clearly was not going at all according to plan. Andy reached for his radio.

The vans would have got away if it hadn't been for the line of armoured vehicles which now seemed to be blocking the road. The gang could be seen trying to back up the convoy and escape into the countryside, but a few warning shots from a heavy machine gun into the engine of the lead vehicle, followed by the eruption of the road behind the last vehicle soon put a stop to that plan. A group of Paras raced toward the vehicles and soon had all of the gang on the floor trussed up tighter than the warehouse guards. A Land Rover pulled up and Andy stepped out. He surveyed the sorry looking bunch and strode over to a guy in a combat jacket. He flipped him onto his back and, grabbing him by the lapels, whipped off his balaclava.

"Hi Les. Fancy meeting you here. I thought for a moment you weren't going to turn up."

"Where the fuck did that lot come from?" Les spat nodding towards the Paras.

"Let's just say they're mates of mine. You see, Les, you were a bit careless earlier on. It was something you said to Frazer which caught you out. You remember when you were quizzing him after you brought him home? You let slip you knew there were two kidnappers. Now, Frazer was pretty sure he hadn't mentioned the numbers, but he bought your explanation. However when you said you had a room booked at the Marine, the penny dropped. I mean, if you were on a stake out in Gloucester, you were hardly going to book accommodation deep in the West Country, now were you? You obviously knew that you were going to be back there that night. So, putting two and two together, he at least had grounds for a bit of a nagging suspicion that all was not as it seemed. He, being a good mate, of course passed this titbit on to me. Then the other night you said that 'all you were interested in was busting a drug ring' when we all knew that the original drug runners were already out of the picture. Very careless Les. So I decided to take out, let us call it some personal insurance. The chaps you see before you are all hand picked from my old regiment. Very faithful and very discreet. Happy now?"

Les collapsed like a punctured balloon as Andy released his collar.

"OK, lads, lets get this lot to the brig. Leave the vans here. We'll empty them tomorrow."

Les half sat up. The rest of the gang were not looking any too pleased.

"Oh, yes, Les. Sorry, I nearly forgot to tell you that. What you stole was some very nicely painted lead bricks. You weren't to know that, of course. Oh, and I'm sorry I let the cat out of the bag about your little slips of the tongue in front of all your pals. I'm sure they'll forgive you.....in time."

231

CHAPTER 28

There is something mystical about a yacht haven early on a summer morning. Just before sunrise the water is like....well, the temptation is to say 'like a millpond', but this does it no justice whatever. Most millponds I have seen are pretty boring. No, it's like silver, gold and platinum all merged together and rolled out flat. Often a light mist hangs in the air. The decks of the yachts are slightly damp with dew. Here and there the faint sound of water falling can be heard as a sleepy crew member thoughtfully takes a pee over the side to avoid wakening his companions with the unpleasant mechanics of the sea-toilet. Could this be where female sailors lose the edge as fellow crew-members? Perish the thought.

Such thoughts were barely troubling my mind as, coffee in hand, morning bladder empty, I took in the scene around me. Sligo had made much better time than anticipated, helped by a following breeze and a well-timed roller-coaster ride down the Guernsey Race. We were snugly moored alongside a very sleek ocean racer by 3.00 am. Everyone turned in for a few hours sleep with the happy prospect of an early shower in the excellent ablutions on St Peter Port Harbour. At this precise moment in time, life was as perfect as any mortal could wish.

The companionway hatch slid back.

"May I suggest an orifice up which you can shove this bloody phone? It's been tinkling away for at least a minute down here. Are you bloody deaf or what?!"

"And a good morning to you too, Frazer. And who, may I ask is calling at this time of the morning?"

"Fucked if I know. Bloody thing stopped. Here, take it. They might call back, and if they do, I don't want to be in a position to throw it overboard."

The hatch slid shut.

I checked the 'missed call' message. It was Andy. I hit the 'call' button.

"Tom? Thanks for calling back mate. Oh, I didn't wake you? No, anyway, listen. Not much time. It's all over this end. I'll tell you about it when we get there. We're catching the early flight from Exeter to Jersey then we'll get the foil over to you guys. Should be there about lunch time. We'll meet you in the Yacht Club bar. See you later, I have to go...."

"Andy? Andy?!"

All over? We're catching the early flight? I called the number back.

"...The number you have called cannot be reached at the moment, please try later...."

Bugger! He's switched off! How could he do this? Who's coming? Andy obviously, but who else? Cath? Les? I banged on the hatch.

"Frazer!!"

He appeared quicker than I expected, a coffee mug in hand.

"Well? I take it we have news?"

"Well, yes and no. They're coming over to meet us. They'll be here around lunch time apparently."

"Oh good. Company. Why not. Let's have a party. Who?"

"Well, that's the thing. He didn't say."

"Just have to wait then, won't we......nature calls!" and he disappeared below.

I had a feeling he had a better idea about who would be arriving than I had.

The Yacht Club was pretty quiet at lunch time and we managed to get a table overlooking the harbour. Andy had arrived as promised and the 'we' to my amusement was made up of Cath and a very subdued Ben.

"No Les?"

"No, Tom. No Les. He is otherwise engaged just at the moment."

Andy and Frazer exchanged knowing looks.

Over assorted drinks, Andy filled us in on the proceedings of the previous evening. I listened with amazement. I couldn't believe that Les had been the bad guy all along.

"Well, no Tom. Quite clearly he couldn't have been the baddy all along. The sting for the drugs people was quite genuine. It wasn't until he got wind of the 'Golden Bollocks' operation from a mate in the service.....who is, incidentally, at this moment under the care of Her Majesty's Military Police....that he put the plan together to kidnap Frieda and Frazer, hide the fact that Revenue and Customs had recovered the drugs, drug the guards and steal the gold!"

"So the people who unloaded the beer from Sligo in Bristol......?"

".....actually were Les's people. They used fake number plates on the van when they dumped the pulped cardboard, sneaky buggers!"

"So I got a bollocking for nothing! Bloody hell......but wait a minute. The pictures that we gave to Lacey's mob. You know, the ones of the van and the guys loading the beer. Surely they wouldn't want Lacey....?"

"Doctored. Actually, I liked that little bit of the story. Les has been chasing one or two gangs around Bristol and has a fair old collection of photos of people he wanted to collar, so he had a nice little collage made up. Apparently Lacey did a pretty good job of sorting out a bunch from Hartlepool that had been a bit of an irritant. Quite a schemer is our Les."

"Bloody hell! But how did you know about Les going after the gold?"

"Well, apart from Frazer's suspicions...."

".....yes, and we all know how seriously we usually take these!"

"Oh, cheers, Tom. Good to know how much your pals trust you."

"Yes, anyway, and apart from Les's little slip of the tongue, which really confirmed it for me, the whole thing stank from the beginning.....I mean, would a real gang really not know that Frazer and Frieda had escaped? Once in the warehouse, would they be prepared to take the risk of simply letting the guards sleep on? With that amount of gold at stake they wouldn't think twice about killing the sleeping guards. No, I'm afraid Les just didn't have the evil in him to make a real master criminal. Not that I'm excusing him. I'm still pissed off at him drugging and capturing you guys."

"Ruined my nails, apart from anything else," Frieda had been silent up to now, "but what I want to know is, how early on did Frazer know about Les? Had you two worked this out between you?"

"Yes, actually it was Frazer who really helped me to fit it all together. He should be a detective."

"Andy, you say the nicest things!"

"Yuck! Sorry!"

We had forgotten about Cath and Ben. They were sitting quietly listening to all this, but clearly Cath was anxious to say something.

"Sorry, Cath, Ben, really glad you could come. How'd you like Guernsey, Ben?"

"Yeah, cool. Never been on a plane before....or one 'a them foil things. Is it an actual boat? I like your boat though, can we go out in it some time maybe?"

"Sure, no problem, we could go out this afternoon....round the island maybe?"

Cath was rummaging in her bag for something.

"Tom, I want to say something important." She was waving an envelope at me. I took it and opened it. It contained a letter carefully typed and signed by Cath. I read it with mounting incredulity.

"Er, Cath, this is a letter of resignation. Why are you resigning? Is there a problem?"

"No, Tom. I've, er, had an offer, that is, an opportunity has come up....."

Frazer and Andy exchanged glances.

"I think we'll go for a walk now. See you later...." and they made for the door dragging Frieda with them. The buggers were smirking!

"What...? What's going on? Come on Cath, out with it. What's this offer you couldn't refuse?"

"Right, OK. Now listen Tom. Don't think it's anything you've done. You've been a great boss and very good to me. I've loved working in the boat yard. I just feel it's time for me to, well, branch out a bit...."

"Branch out a bit?" I looked at Ben who was carefully studying his hands. No help there then.

"Yes, a change of direction, so to speak."

"OK, I'll buy that. Do you want to tell me about it?"

"Listen Tom, I don't want you to feel......"

"Cath! Please! Put me out of my misery!"

"Oh, dear. Where to start. Right, remember when you and Frazer and Les were away in Ireland? Well one night me and Carol and Frieda went to this, sort of, show in the Marine Hotel. Maybe Frieda told you about it?"

Frieda had most certainly told me about it....in lurid detail too. My mind was boggling at the possible direction this story might take. Ben was now scanning the horizon.

"Yeeeeess....go on."

"I have to say, I was a bit shocked by it at the time. I mean, I had no idea people did that sort of thing...."

"What, stripping?"

"No, no, I knew people stripped. It was the women in the audience I was shocked at. I mean, they were....."

"Yes, spare me the details for a second time please."

"Oh, OK. Anyway, by a strange coincidence, I was in the launderette the next day, and the three men from the show were in there doing their washing, and, I, er, got talking to them, you know, about this and that."

"This and that?"

"Yes, they were really nice people....."

"Oh no, not again....."

"No, really, Tom. Just ordinary blokes, just like in 'The Full Monty'."

"Good film that!" Ben offered.

"You went to see 'The Full Monty'?"

"Yeah, Cath took me to see it in the Church Hall!"

I was sinking fast.

"Tom? Are you listening? Well it turned out that the young one, the, er, fireman actually, is a student but his mum was giving him a hard time about the stripping and he wasn't getting enough time to study as he was doing the business side of the, er, business, and he wanted to leave. They thought they would have to break up probably. Anyway after we left the launderette, we went for a walk along the front....."

"Just a minute, Cath. You didn't happen to take a snap......"

"Oh, yes, sorry I lied to you about that. Yes, that was them in the picture. Anyway, we swapped phone numbers....."

"As you do."

"Yes, and they said 'bye-bye' and I thought 'that's the end of that'."

"But......?"

"Well, that night we went to see the film gave me an idea. You know how Ben's, well, quite well built?.....What?!"

"Nothing. Go on." I know I shouldn't have taken a sip of my drink at that point. I dried my shirt with a tissue.

"Yes, and he needs a job, and the troupe needed a new man, so...."

I looked over to Ben. He smiled and shrugged.

"Er, and where do you come into this, Cath?"

"Well, when I contacted them they were really pleased and, well, to cut a long story short....."

"Please do. I can't wait any longer."

".....they asked me to be their manager."

"And you said yes."

"Yes."

"Bloody hell. I've created a monster."

"Hardly, Tom. But, I have found you a new secretary. Carol said she would be happy to step in!"

Deja vu all over again.

Printed in the United Kingdom
by Lightning Source UK Ltd.
132660UK00001B/121-138/P